A PROMISE OF TOMORROW

Medieval Runaway Wives
Book 2

Alexa Aston

Dragonblade Publishing, Inc. is an imprint of Kathryn Le Veque Novels, Inc.
P.O. Box 7968
La Verne CA 91750
ceo@dragonbladepublishing.com

Produced in the United States of America

First Edition August 2020
Mass Market Paperback Edition

ARE YOU SIGNED UP FOR DRAGONBLADE'S BLOG?

You'll get the latest news and information on exclusive giveaways, exclusive excerpts, coming releases, sales, free books, cover reveals and more.

Check out our complete list of authors, too!

No spam, no junk. That's a promise!

Sign Up Here

www.dragonbladepublishing.com

Dearest Reader;

Thank you for your support of a small press. At Dragonblade Publishing, we strive to bring you the highest quality Historical Romance from the some of the best authors in the business. Without your support, there is no 'us', so we sincerely hope you adore these stories and find some new favorite authors along the way.

Happy Reading!

CEO, Dragonblade Publishing

Additional Dragonblade books by Author Alexa Aston

Medieval Runaway Wives
Song of the Heart
A Promise of Tomorrow

King's Cousins Series
The Pawn
The Heir
The Bastard

Knights of Honor Series
Word of Honor
Marked by Honor
Code of Honor
Journey to Honor
Heart of Honor
Bold in Honor
Love and Honor
Gift of Honor
Path to Honor
Return to Honor

The St. Clairs Series
Devoted to the Duke
Midnight with the Marquess
Embracing the Earl

Defending the Duke
Suddenly a St. Clair
Starlight Night

Soldiers & Soulmates Series
To Heal an Earl
To Tame a Rogue
To Trust a Duke
To Save a Love
To Win a Widow

The Lyon's Den Connected World
The Lyon's Lady Love

PROLOGUE

Libourne, France—1328

S*HE HAD TRADED one prison for another.*
Marielle Matesse gazed across the cramped shop crowded with rugs of varying sizes and shapes and actually wished she were back at Sisters of Merciful Heart. The convent might be gloomy but at least its spacious, high ceilings and minimal furniture gave her room to breathe. The long masses also provided time for her to daydream of places beyond Libourne. Paris. London. Even the Far East.

In their infrequent chats, Father Julien had woven fascinating tales of life outside the imposing stone walls of the nunnery. The priest had traveled extensively and the pictures he painted of people and places whetted her appetite. That, coupled with her eavesdropping on travelers who sought shelter within the convent, gave Marielle plenty of ideas to conjure visions of a life unlike her own. The narrow confines and religious rules did not bind her spirit from soaring to new places. What she wouldn't give to see the ancient ruins in Greece or stroll along the crowded streets of Rome. Even if she could only journey to Paris and see the cathedral of Notre Dame or stroll along the Seine, her sense of adventure might be satisfied.

Unfortunately, that brought her thoughts back to the carpets that filled her father's place of business. Yes, they came from worlds away. As a small child, she had enjoyed tracing their intricate designs. Now, they simply represented wares that must be sold, if not today, then the next or the day after that. Her life was one of staring at carpets and waiting for someone to enter the shop and break up the monotony of every day. A buyer was preferred but she longed to talk to anyone who might venture inside. Instead, hours crawled by as she sat, bored and frustrated.

Would she be trapped here forever?

Marielle smiled inwardly, not daring to allow her father to catch a glimpse of upturned lips. He was a man for whom mirth did not exist and he refused to condone merriment in those around him. She couldn't recall ever having seen him smile. Certainly not on that last day, the day he cast her from his life and into the hands of the good sisters. She shuddered, wishing to pull a curtain on the past. It was better to push it from her mind before the clammy palms returned with the tightness in her chest.

That day ended her freedom as a carefree child.

In her heart, Marielle would never forget the events, though she'd been but five years of age. It seemed a lifetime ago. Ten long years with her in exile had passed, with Sisters of Merciful Heart being her place of residence. The nuns allowed her to visit with her family in Libourne once a year since the convent rested on the town's outskirts.

It might have been a world away, however. Her father greeted her presence with stony silence. Her mother, frightened of her domineering husband, followed his example and ignored her. Marielle was left to sit alone for those few hours in the rooms above the shop, where she would gaze out the window and watch passersby bargaining at the market. Each year when she returned, another of her brothers and sisters had fled the Matesse household, off to seek their fortune or having wed.

Until only she was left.

Marielle's eyes burned. She bit her tongue until she tasted blood. The pain took attention from the tears that she would not allow to fall. She refused to show any weakness in her father's sight. Her sins—in his eyes—were abundant enough. She would not give him cause to berate her further.

She walked to the portal and looked out upon the square. The midday heat poured onto those scurrying to and fro, women with tall loaves of bread, men carrying jugs of wine, carts rumbling by filled with hay and apples and wood. Everyone rushed somewhere.

Except for her.

She'd run away once before at age four. Even at a young age, she had sensed the unhappiness around her and was driven by a need to escape it. She didn't get very far. Arielle had tripped and scraped her knee badly. The sight of blood terrified her sister and Marielle distracted her twin as best she could. When the tears subsided, Arielle refused to go any further. Marielle couldn't very well leave her so she sat by her twin's side until Gustave came looking for them. She still remembered her brother's words.

"Are you addlebrained dolts? Or are you just stubborn fools? Papa will have your hides and mine made into rugs."

He swept one girl under each arm and marched back home. She wondered how many scrapes Gustave had rescued them from, all ones of Marielle's making. Or so her father would point out. He had a great love for Arielle, which she understood. Everyone loved Arielle. Her sister was all sunshine and sweetness.

But Marielle hadn't understood why not even a smidgen of that love extended her way. From her earliest memories, Gautier Matesse criticized her, scolded her, berated her, or worse—ignored her.

Even at four, Marielle was not one willing to be ignored.

She sighed and watched a flock of birds fly overhead, their shadows thick upon the ground below.

"Pardonez-moi, Mademoiselle."

Marielle glanced up to see she was blocking the entrance to the shop. She quickly curtsied to the well-dressed customer and stepped aside to allow him to enter. He smiled at her kindly.

She couldn't remember the last time anyone smiled at her.

Marielle followed him inside, keeping a guarded distance. She would not want her father to accuse her of pestering a patron. From the looks and opulent dress of this man, he was wealthy, indeed. She returned to her place behind the counter, watching him surreptitiously as he perused the multitude of carpets.

Gautier Matesse took stock of the situation. Marielle watched his own furtive glances at the gentleman as he approached him cautiously. She had to admit that her father had perfected the fragile balance between providing just the right amount of assistance to a buyer and giving him room to look in peace.

"*Bienvenue.* May I assist you in any way, my lord?"

The man looked at several rugs with a discerning eye before asking Gautier to unroll two of the most expensive carpets. The stranger studied the patterns carefully, stooping to the floor in order to have a better look, even smoothing them with a careful hand.

"This is not a decision to be made lightly," the man muttered.

"Oh, yes, my lord. You are most correct. And quite perceptive. You have chosen two of the finest carpets in my humble establishment."

The man rose to his feet. "I will wait a day before I make a decision," he announced.

He strode toward the front of the store and then paused in the doorway and turned to face her.

"Good day," the nobleman said and nodded in her direction.

Marielle's cheeks heated with the sudden attention. She lowered her eyes, half-hoping he would still be there when she raised them. He was gone, however. She wondered at drawing his eye. Would her father be pleased or not? He was a hard man to understand, his moods mercurial.

Gautier studied her. He rubbed his chin in thought. "Mayhap he shall return. He was certainly wealthy enough to buy both rugs. Did you see his rich dress? And that ring upon his hand? It would buy everything in this store and then some."

Marielle nodded slightly in agreement. She did not want her father upset in any way. Now that Mother Superior had returned her to her parents' care, she would have nowhere to go if they turned her out again. She shivered as she thought of the street beggars that lined the walls just inside the city, dependent upon the kindness of strangers for even a hard crust of bread.

Even worse were the women who sold their bodies for a man's pleasure. Marielle hadn't dreamed such a practice existed until she'd seen it herself only last year in her final visit from the convent. Sister Clotilde had tried to hurry them along as Marielle stopped in utter horror of what she saw taking place in an alleyway.

She pushed such frightening thoughts from her mind. No, she must do nothing to anger her father. She watched as Gautier glanced out the door again and then brusquely said, "I must go tend to your mother. You are far too clumsy to do so. Watch things carefully. I will be a quarter of an hour at most."

He wove his way through the narrow aisles and up the back staircase that led to their rooms above. The minute he was gone, Marielle boosted herself upon the counter to give her aching feet a rest. She knew he would be gone far longer. Blanche Matesse's demands grew longer and more tiresome as the years passed. She blamed Marielle's birth for her being indisposed—and why not? Wasn't everything else blamed upon her? Left unsaid was that Arielle, too, had appeared at the same time. She had been the last babe pulled from her mother's womb.

Suddenly, a shadow darkened the doorway. Marielle quickly slipped down from the counter in order to greet the new customer.

Surprised filled her when she saw it was the customer who had recently left. He had a sad air about him, as if he'd experienced too many tragedies in his lifetime. She judged him to be a good score and then some, probably just a few years shy of two score, now that he moved toward her and she looked into his lined face. He paused in front of her, a man of average height. His weight had begun to settle around his middle, as it often did on men as they aged.

"Did you forget something, my lord?" she asked nervously.

He looked about, hesitating for a moment. Marielle realized what he wanted.

"I can fetch my father. He has only gone upstairs for a moment to check on my mother, who is ill. He'll be happy to answer any questions you might have regarding either of the rugs you looked at before."

She quickly walked toward the back of the shop, not wanting her father to lose this sale. Even if the man only purchased one of the rugs, it would pay for several months of food. If this stranger chose not to buy anything, somehow Marielle knew she would be blamed.

"No. Wait." He looked at her a long moment. "Come here," he added.

Returning to where the nobleman stood, she asked, "Might I show you either rug again?"

"How old are you?"

She was taken aback by such a personal question. "I . . . I will be ten and six within the month."

He pursed his lips. He seemed far away in thought. She wondered if she should call her father after all.

"Do you like your life here? In Libourne. With your parents."

How was she to answer such a question? She'd only returned to their house two months ago and, yet, already a lifetime had passed. Would it be improper to tell a stranger just how much she hated her existence? How she dreamed of exciting and distant places where she would find happiness and people who valued her?

Marielle opened her mouth to speak but he held up a hand to silence her.

"No. You need not tell me a thing. I can read it all in your face."

She flushed, remembering how Father Julien often told her the same thing.

"I can offer you something different."

Marielle's heart began to beat wildly. Escape from this jail? Was it possible? She found her voice. "Mayhap you need a new maid, my lord? Or a cook? I have recently left Sisters of Merciful Heart, where I learned to cook and sew and weave tapestries."

He cocked his head to one side. "Tapestries?" He chuckled. "I suppose Monteville could use more of those." He must have read her confused expression and said, "Monteville is my home, a great castle in Bordeaux. I grow the finest grapes in all France and they become the best of French wines."

He took a step closer to her and bowed stiffly. "My name is Jean-Paul, Comte de la Tresse."

She curtsied. "I am Marielle Matesse, daughter of Gautier and Blanche. How may I be of service to you, *Monsieur Comte?*" Already, thoughts of becoming a servant in a grand chateau held more interest for her than sitting day after day in this small shop and boring town.

"You are young." He frowned a moment then brightened. "But that can be a good thing." The comte looked her up and down. "Your hips are a trifle slender but I suppose they'll do."

Marielle felt the heated flush crawl up her neck, thanks to her embarrassment at his comment. She took several steps back, ready to flee.

"No, wait," he said softly, holding out a hand, palm down. "I seek a wife. I have no children from my first marriage. My wife died last Easter time. She was a good woman, but she was my parents' choice."

He stared into her eyes. "This time, I make my own choice."

Realization dawned quickly. "You . . . you would marry me?" She licked her lips nervously. "I don't understand, *Monsieur le Comte*. You must know a dozen women of your class. You could not possibly want me. I am but a common merchant's daughter."

The comte's eyes gleamed. "Oh, but I do. He was right. You are lovely to behold. Summon your father."

Marielle shuffled away as if in a dream. From the bottom of the staircase, she called for her father to come down. When he appeared, his anger melted instantly when he saw that his previous customer had returned.

"I see you made a quick decision, my lord. Which one will it be?"

He bowed low. "I am Comte Jean-Paul de la Tresse. I choose that one." He pointed at Marielle.

She fainted.

CHAPTER ONE

Stanbury, Sussex—1335

"GO TO BLOODY hell, Garrett."

Ashby fitz Waryn ground out the words with clenched teeth. "I refuse your pity. And I will not rely upon charity from my thick-headed best friend."

Garrett Stanbridge, the Earl of Montayne, glared at him as if he were a serf caught poaching on Stanbury lands. Let him glare all he wanted. Ashby's mind was made up. It was his life. His decision. Garrett could pester him until the Second Coming and Ashby wouldn't budge. He refused to take charity.

"You are an insufferable oaf, Ash. Full of foolish pride. Why do insist upon refusing my offer?"

He moved closer to Garrett, his words just

above a whisper. "Why do you continue to ram it down my throat?" He took a step back. "Besides, I have done nothing to deserve it. I do for you as I would for anyone."

His friend shook his head. "No. You have been as much of a brother to me as Luke was, lo those many years ago." Garrett's eyes searched his. "You are my chosen brother and friend of my heart, Ash. My cherished comrade and companion in battle. You have been at the birth of my children and are much beloved by my family."

Garrett's eyes pled with Ashby as much as his words. "Do not reject it outright. At least give it some thought."

Ashby tamped down the anger that surged through his veins and inclined his head. "As you wish." His words would placate Garrett.

For now.

He turned and strode across the great hall. He was reluctant to leave the warmth of the fire but he needed a surge of cool air outside to calm his temper. Usually the most easygoing of men, Garrett had hit upon the one thing that most bothered Ashby.

Land.

He wove his way through the crowded room. The remains of the evening meal had been cleared. The trestle tables had been placed against the walls in order to afford the occupants of Stanbury more room to relax and enjoy what was left of their evening. Music and chattering children now dominated the atmosphere.

"Ashby!"

He turned to Lyssa's call. All anger stirred by Garrett melted when he spied the nine-year-old girl.

"Come dance with me. Please," she entreated.

Although dancing was the last thing on his mind, he mustered a smile and took her hand. "Only one, my little love. I have business to attend."

Lyssa pouted prettily, giving him a glimpse of the woman she would become. "Papa keeps you much too busy. If I were you, I would tell him so to his face."

"You're a brave—and opinionated—child, Lyssa, and one dear to his heart. I am but your father's lowly man of business." Before she could protest his words, Ashby swept her up and into the dance.

As they moved around the room, he spied Garrett and Madeleine speaking by the fire in hushed tones. Madeleine held two-year-old Cynric in her arms, balanced upon one hip. She glanced up as he and Lyssa passed by, her lips pursed in displeasure.

If only things had been different. If he could have been the one to rescue Madeleine. He would now be Cynric's father—and Madeleine's husband.

He shrugged off such wistful thoughts. Regret didn't become him. He never would have made Madeleine a good husband. Nor any woman. No, he was pleased that she came into Garrett's life when she did. She saved his friend from the depths of despair. Madeleine had turned Stanbury into a place of happiness once again, through her gifts of storytelling and love. In truth, he felt honored to claim the countess as his friend. He treasured her wit and intelligence. She was a unique woman and he doubted he would ever be lucky enough to find one with her rare qualities and abilities.

Besides, what woman would want him? A third son, cast off, noble nonetheless, but with nothing to offer a woman other than a pleasing demeanor. No title, no lands, no home he could call his own. He would never ask any woman to follow him into marriage with so little future ahead of them.

The music ended. He swept a gallant bow to Lyssa.

"Time to depart, my fair maiden." He took her hand and brushed a swift kiss across her knuckles before leaving.

He chuckled to himself at the blush his gesture brought. Lyssa was caught up in a quandary. Part of her still loved to run with the boys of Stanbury in all their games, while a softer part longed to begin her journey toward womanhood. He'd been there the night Garrett's first wife gave birth to Lyssa. He looked forward to dancing at the girl's wedding someday, enjoying each phase of the transition she now discovered.

Ashby stepped through the massive oak doors and out into the crisp night air. Though only mid-September, the cool pierced his woolen shirt with a sharp bite. He sat upon the steps that led down into the bailey and leaned back, propping his elbows on the step above him as he studied the stars in the velvet sky.

He remained lost in thought some minutes when he heard the door open. It would either be Garrett come to argue with him again or Madeleine come to scold him. The voice that spoke took him by surprise.

"Ashby," Edith said, "you are behaving like a spoiled child."

He turned and looked up at the only mother he'd ever known. His own died in childbirth when Ashby was three so he only had a few dim recollections of Beatrice. They were more shadows of impressions than any real memories.

Yet the woman before him had seen him through childhood illness and washed and tended his scabbed knees. She'd taught him good manners and the proper way to treat a lady. Lady Edith was everything he wanted in a mother. He thanked the decision that brought him to foster at

Stanbury when he was but seven. Edith, more than anyone, had shaped him into the man he was today.

"Spoiled, you say?" he teased lightly. "And a child? Simply because I like dancing with Lyssa and getting down in the mud with Cynric? I should not think me a child, my lady."

She shook her head sadly. "What am I to do with you, my son? For that is what you are to me, as much as Garrett is. You both have been the joys of my life."

Edith knelt beside him and took his hand. "What has ruffled your feathers this time? Do not give me that innocent, charming look," she warned. "I saw you and Garrett together. Your conversation was tense. I know you argued, Ashby, before you stomped across the room."

Ashby took her hand and squeezed it. "Stomped is a harsh word, my lady. More like I stalked across the hall. But I think I recovered nicely when I took time to dance with Lyssa. She does have a soothing effect upon me."

"Children always calm you, my dear. It's the very reason I think you should have a few of your own."

He saw the glint in her eyes. "My dear Lady Edith, you know I have no plans to settle down with one woman when so many charming and delightful beauties are in my corner of the world. It wouldn't be fair to any child to have an absent father with a roving eye."

Standing, he took her hands and brought her to her feet. "My lot in life is to simply enjoy Lyssa and Cynric. After all, I have no soiled cloths to change nor whining to listen to. I have the freedom to enjoy them when they are pleasant to be around—and walk away when they're cross. I've had the best of both worlds."

"With none of the responsibility," she added sharply.

Ashby grinned at her. "You are in fine fighting form tonight, my lady. Mayhap Garrett should put you in the bailey to spar with his knights. You could teach them a thing or two."

"Making light of things will not always be the answer, Ashby. You would do well to remember that." She gazed at him with love in her eyes. "Please. Accept Garrett's offer of a manor house. Do it for me. Keep the peace between my two sons."

He bristled, dropping her hands. "I will not take from Garrett what is his. Ever. No matter how many times he offers—and tonight made the count at seven and twenty. It's his land and his manor. *Not mine.*"

Ashby tamped down the anger that sprang up so quickly again, knowing talk of the incredibly generous gift made him irritable. More than anything, he would love to possess his own manor. His ancestral home, Ashland, naturally passed to his eldest brother, also called Ashland. If anything ever happened to him, then his brother, Ashcroft, would take ownership, or one of their children. The only way Ashby would ever gain his own land was to join the king's army and do something so spectacular on the battlefield, the king would immediately bestow a title and castle upon him.

Since that was a far-fetched scheme which would never come to pass, he knew he must learn to be happy with his lot in life.

Part of him thought he was a coward, in some respects. Oh, he'd proved himself valiant in battle. Both he and Garrett owned more than a few scars between them to prove their prowess. Yet a secret part of him never wanted to leave Stanbury. It had been home to him these last two and twenty years since he'd come to foster as a boy. How could he leave it, much less Garrett and Madeleine, Edith and Lyssa, Cynric and all the friends he'd made?

No, his stubbornness and pride dug in their heels. This was where he'd grown up, where he'd reached his maturity. This was where he would stay.

"Shall we go in?" he asked Edith politely. She cast a look at him that would chill any knight in training but he knew how soft she was underneath the brittle glare. He took her arm and led her back inside, hoping he could avoid Garrett.

Ashby took to the shadows, sitting far from the fire and gaiety of the great hall, the better to become lost in his thoughts. In truth, he admitted it might be for the best if he did leave Stanbury, despite the great estate's pull on him. Things had been different before Madeleine came. He and Garrett lived their lives much as they pleased.

Madeleine Bouchard changed everything. She brought light and grace and charm to Stanbury. For all his fierce ways before, Garrett was now tamed from his wild days. He was utterly, madly in love with his wife and two children.

Watching the happy family together ate away at Ashby's core. Though he knew he would never have greater friends than Garrett and Madeleine, his jealousy of their closeness and joy might well destroy him. How could he love the two of them as much as he did and yet despise everything about them? He wanted what they had, something he could never attain.

Because the intensity of his feelings had grown stronger over the past few months, he realized the time had come. He must move beyond Stanbury, else his unreasonable envy would cost him everything he held dear.

Yet he hesitated. How would he explain to them where he went or why he must leave? Garrett offered him a way out but Ashby did not feel right in taking it. His frustration with abandoning all that was dear to him warred with his strong sense of pride. He refused to be treated as a charity case. He must make his own way. The time had come to cut his ties with Stanbury. Ashby pushed aside the heaviness in his heart. Leaving would be best for all. He would speak to Garrett immediately. Before he changed his mind.

He rose and made his way around the great hall, scanning the crowd in search of Garrett. He spied him and felt the knife twist in his heart at the warm smile his friend gave him.

Garrett motioned him over into a corner. Madeleine was no longer there, probably having gone to put Cynric to bed. Ashby took a seat.

"I don't want us to quarrel, Ash. I will respect your wishes and swear I shall not bring it up again."

"Not at least for a sennight," he piped in, reverting to his usual quick wit. How could he broach the subject? Already his resolve wavered.

Garrett's mouth tightened and he shook his head. He laid a hand on Ashby's shoulder. "Why do I put up with you?" he asked softly.

"Because no one else besides Madeleine, of course, will put up with you. You should be grateful that I am your staunch supporter and truest friend."

Garrett laughed. "You will be the death of me, Ash. That or Cynric, now that he is walking and into everything not nailed shut." His friend grew more serious. "I think the time is right for you to go to France. It's something I have pondered upon for many months now."

Ashby sat up expectantly. No one had visited the French vineyards in close to five years. Garrett himself went then, staying for a few months and learning all he could about the grape. Then he'd met Madeleine. That had kept the earl close to Stanbury.

Maybe Garrett's request would lead to new opportunities. At any rate, it would give Ashby more time to think his plans through.

"I would need you to go to the Bouchards first," Garrett said. "Pierre is in total charge since Madeleine's father fell ill last spring. I would also like you to go to a neighboring vineyard, that of a Comte de la Tresse. I would go myself but I have no wish to be gone for too long a time."

Ashby smiled. "Unless you took Madeleine with you. I am sure she has said no for the time being, wishing Cynric to be a bit older and less troublesome."

Garrett broke out in a grin. "Do you skulk about under our bed while we have our private conversations, Ash? You know far too much about us."

He shrugged. "I do know you, my friend. You both are miserably predictable. It's what happens to old married folk. Now I, on the other hand, as a man with no ties, beholden to no other—I move as the wind blows me."

Garrett snorted. "Yes, from one young maiden to the next."

He chuckled. "Shouldn't I have the freedom to sample the wares of all the flowers in the field?"

"You are impossible." Garrett swung an arm around Ashby and hugged him tightly. "I will miss you more than life itself while you are gone."

"So," Madeleine interrupted, "he has agreed to go?"

The two men turned to her.

"Who knows, Madeleine?" Ashby smiled. "Mayhap I will find as fresh a flower as you among the women of France."

Madeleine's brows arched. "And how many will you sip from before you alight upon the one true bud?"

Ashby let out an exasperated sigh. "I do not know how you live with the women in this family, Garrett."

They all laughed and then Garrett said solemnly, "If the place suits you . . . if you find an affinity with the grape . . . mayhap you could remain there indefinitely and manage the vineyards alongside Pierre."

The idea intrigued Ashby more than he was willing to admit. He shrugged nonchalantly. "Let me first get there, Garrett. I have yet to see a sunrise in France."

"Then let us meet on the morrow to discuss the details. It will involve a new strain of wine that I have an idea for, mixing the red grapes with white ones. Would you be agreeable to leaving the day after that?"

Ashby smiled. "I am at your service, Lord Montayne. Wherever you wish me, there I will go."

CHAPTER TWO

MARIELLE DE LA Tresse contained the excitement that filled her. Finally, a visitor that was not Marc. Someone who could take the boredom from her days and nights. Jean-Paul promised that she could plan entertainment and a small dinner or two while Ashby fitz Waryn stayed with them, talking, as most visitors did, of the grape. The Englishman represented an English nobleman who owned the neighboring vineyard, managed by the Bouchard family for several generations.

She had liked Robert and Cadena Bouchard from the moment Jean-Paul introduced her to the couple. While a bit gruff, Robert was a fine storyteller, weaving fantasy with the everyday into magical stories. Cadena had taught Marielle much about herbs and spices. She'd tried to pass along her new knowledge to the chateau's cook but the stolid woman merely grunted and prepared what she intended to in the first place.

Pierre was another matter. The Bouchards' son was so serious, seldom speaking. He reminded Marielle of Sister Clotilde, the quietest of the nuns at Sisters of Merciful Heart. Thank goodness her convent days were well behind her although Monteville was often as silent as a tomb. The quiet drove her to distraction.

She fingered the twisted rope of gold and garnets that hung from her neck. It was Jean-Paul's latest gift to her, one of a hundred he had presented her with during the last seven years. He'd promised her diamonds upon the birth of their first child.

Neither the diamonds nor the child seemed forthcoming.

Marielle stood, restless, and stared out the window. She'd already discussed with Cook all the menus for fitz Waryn's visit. She knew the great hall was set for their visitor's welcome. New rushes covered the floors, their sweet smell wafting through the air. She'd picked fresh flowers only an hour ago and had placed them in the English visitor's bedchamber. She was dressed and perfumed, eagerly awaiting the new company.

Marielle perched on the window seat in front of her and looked down the road as far as she could see. After a quarter-hour, she was rewarded with a glimpse of horses in the distance. It would be their guest, certainly accompanied by Pierre Bouchard. Jean-Paul might also have joined in if he'd seen them from the vineyards. Most likely, though, her husband would not return to the chateau until work ceased for the day. She almost hoped he wouldn't. She was eager to speak with this Englishman and find out what had gone on in the outside world as of late. Maybe fitz Waryn had even been to London or Paris. How she longed to see those magnificent cities one day.

She doubted that day would ever come.

If she had it to do all over again, knowing what she knew now, she would steal away from her parents' house, never to return. The nuns hadn't wanted her at the convent after she'd been exiled there for ten years. Mother Superior and all the Sisters of Merciful Heart nuns had tried to push her toward the holy life. It was a pity they hadn't practiced more of the holiness they preached. If even one of the nuns had shown her any personal kindness, Marielle might have tried to fit in and take her vows.

Instead, they returned her to her parents' care and the long days and nights of her father's badgering and her mother's complaining. No wonder each of her siblings had left by the time she'd returned home, seeking a trade in another town or fleeing into the hands of the first man that asked for their hand in marriage.

Marielle should have seized an opportunity and left. She was fairly tall for her age. She should have cut off her auburn tresses and worn a man's tunic and pants, trying to pass herself off as a young boy for a time. She might have found work as a servant to a great nobleman, traveling far and wide with her master and seen all the world had to offer.

Instead, she'd willingly gone with Jean-Paul de la Tresse. In her inexperience and immaturity, she mistook the sad air about him, romanticizing how heartbroken he was at the death of his wife the year before. When he'd wanted her to come to Monteville, she assumed it was as a servant. Eager to please, she offered to cook or clean or weave tapestries, her only skilled accomplishment from her convent days.

Jean-Paul had taken her as a bride instead. Marielle was certain that Agnes, the first wife, had died of neglect. She learned all too quickly the unhappiness Jean-Paul wore was a mixture of boredom and indifference. She'd been eager to marry him and escape her father's house, never dreaming she'd become a caged bird at Monteville. Thank the Sweet Christ her husband was often gone on business. It was the only thing that helped her retain her sanity.

Marielle rose and made her way from the bedchamber to the floor below. From there, she went outside into the cool, sunlit morning to await the riders. Within minutes, three men on horseback entered the courtyard. One was Donatien de Toulouse, Monteville's overseer and Jean-Paul's right-hand man. The second, as expected, was Pierre Bouchard, looking slightly out of sorts, as if the ride to Monteville was an interruption he barely tolerated.

But it was the third rider that most interested her. The nuns always chastised her for her immense curiosity but they were no longer the ones who made the rules in her life. She was *la Comtesse* of Monteville. Marielle regally moved down the steps to greet fitz Waryn.

He swept off his horse with a grace that belied his size. He was far taller than any man she'd met and possessed a lean yet athletic frame. She was drawn to his long, muscular legs tucked into black boots which gleamed in the sunlight. His handsome face radiated strength and good cheer. As he bowed to her, his blue eyes twinkled with mischief.

"I take it you are the Comtesse de la Tresse." His white, even teeth shone in a wide smile, a direct contrast to Jean-Paul. Her husband rarely smiled and, at two and forty, was missing several of his teeth.

"I am Ashby fitz Waryn, man of business for Lord Garrett Stanbridge the Earl of Montayne of Stanbury."

Marielle's eyelashes fluttered instinctively,

surprising her because they'd never done so before. She curtsied to her guest. "Please, call me Marielle. We do not stand much on formality at Monteville."

Fitz Waryn took her hand in his. His touch was light but decidedly masculine. It also made her instantly aware that she was a woman and he a very handsome man. Marielle looked into his eyes of azure, her mouth gone as dry as brittle bones.

He gave her another smile, pleasant and yet at the same time sensual. Sweeping a quick kiss across her fingers, he said, *"Enchante,* Marielle. And please, you must call me Ashby."

The name fit him. Marielle returned his smile. "We are honored to have you stay at Monteville, Ashby." She liked the way his name rolled from her tongue. "Your French is quite good."

He beamed. "I was brought up at Stanbury with Lord Montayne. His mother had us speaking French from an early age, though Garrett didn't use it much. Still," he added, "it wasn't until Garrett married the Bouchards' daughter a few years ago that I had a true feel for the language. Madeleine drilled me like a tyrant before I journeyed here, especially since it's her native tongue."

"Well, you may tell her that you have done justice to it." Marielle turned to the others.

"*Bonjour*, Pierre. It's always nice to see you."

Pierre mumbled something in return, no louder than a mouse confronted by a hungry cat.

She turned to their steward. "Thank you, Donatien, for bringing Ashby here." Glancing at their visitor, she added, "Jean-Paul said he would mostly likely visit with you when we sup this evening. Until then, I am sure Donatien can answer any of your questions. Come, let us go inside the chateau and allow you to wash."

She led the trio into the darkened hall and signaled for water and towels. The men soaped and rinsed their hands before being seated. Since it was past the midday meal when their workers had eaten, Marielle had only one trestle table set out for them to dine on.

"Monteville is quite a becoming estate," Ashby commented. "The land is lush and your *chateau* is full of charm. And you, my lady, are the jewel in its crown. Rarely have I seen such beauty."

Marielle's face flamed, unused to any form of flattery. As the youngest of seven children, no one had paid attention to her at home. When she'd been sent to the convent as punishment, the nuns had not tolerated vanity in any form. The only way she'd learned she was pleasing to the eye was when Jean-Paul told her so and then pursued her with determination in the space of a single afternoon. She'd regretted that his passion had all been in the chase, for once caught, he rarely gave his young wife a second thought.

"I thank you, sir," she said meekly. "I fear your long journey to France may have addled your brains, nonetheless."

The Englishman took a sip from his wineglass before replying, "I've been here a good week, Marielle. Long enough to recover from any strain my trip could impose. As for the ride here, it was merely a snap of the fingers." He snapped his fingers as he spoke.

Marielle winced involuntarily. A chill passed through her, settling in the pit of her belly. Jean-Paul usually ignored her but when he wanted her for something, he would snap his fingers loudly. The staccato sound always washed over her, covering her in dread. She tried to dispel that feeling now.

"I am glad you have come to join us. Would you care for more of the duck? Mayhap some more fish?"

She settled more into her role of hostess after that, letting the men speak of wines and the weather and what prices next year's crop might bring. Before long, the meal ended. Pierre excused himself, saying he must return to the grapes. Donatien, too, begged forgiveness to go about his duties.

That left Marielle alone with Ashby. She had studied him surreptitiously throughout the meal.

She liked his easy manner and relaxed grace, whether it was conversing or spearing a tidbit of meat with his knife. The fact he was so handsome that he took her breath away made her realize she grew warm. Marielle pushed a loose tendril back. Why, she hadn't experienced infatuation since her brother Renaud's friend, Guy, had been underfoot years ago. Guy, who never looked at her as more than a pesky little sister, while she worshipped the ground he trod upon.

Many a night, she had endured Jean-Paul's hasty lovemaking by closing her eyes and picturing that young image of Guy as her lover—not her husband with his sagging middle and hairy back and foul breath. Jean-Paul may have gruffly claimed to love his wife when pressed but Marielle did not reciprocate such feelings. She found it increasingly difficult as the years passed to be around him, much less share his bed on the rare occasion he snapped for her appearance.

Yet now, at the ripe old age of three and twenty, this Ashby fitz Waryn had her heart doing somersaults, like the monkey she'd seen at the faire two years prior. She longed to lean over and kiss him, a gesture Jean-Paul found distasteful. Because of her husband's opinion, Marielle had never been kissed.

She knew this childish attraction she felt toward their visitor must be quashed. To act upon it would be dangerous—not only for her, but for Ashby himself. In the meantime, she would continue to enjoy the rare company of a visitor. She couldn't remember the last time a man eyed her so appreciatively yet respectfully. This Englishman would be amusing to have around.

"Would it be possible to walk about and show me some of the grounds?" Ashby asked.

"I would be delighted to be your escort."

They went out into the afternoon. A cool wind had picked up since the men had arrived.

"Here, let me return for your cloak," he told her. "I'll only be a moment."

Before Marielle could protest, he went back inside the castle. Little tingles pricked her spine. She threw off the warning signals and clasped her hands together to still their trembling. In less than an hour, Ashby fitz Waryn had paid her more attention than she'd received from a man in her entire life.

Except for Marc.

"Here you are." Ashby draped the cloak about her. As when he'd taken her hand upon first meeting, Marielle sensed a quick spark between them. Because of it, she avoided meeting his eyes. Instead, she tied the cloak tightly about her, nervous and unsure what to do.

"If I may?" He took her arm and guided her through the inner bailey and beyond. His casual air and dozens of questions soon had her laughing, recounting humorous incidents of life at Monteville. Marielle admired his easy charm. She also liked how he didn't speak down to her, as if she were a child, which Jean-Paul frequently did. Rather, the Englishman spoke to her as *la comtesse* should be addressed.

They walked to her garden, where she planted the flowers and herbs that Cadena Bouchard recommended when Marielle first came to Monteville as a young bride. She pointed out the differences between rosemary, fennel, and thyme. They sat on a bench in the garden and talked for what seemed like hours.

Marielle had never known a more perfect afternoon.

"I find you a delightful companion, Marielle," Ashby told her. "You are intelligent and beautiful. You have such a natural curiosity, as well."

She laughed. "You should have heard what the good sisters said about me."

"Were you convent-raised?" he asked.

Marielle nodded. "My parents, Gautier and Blanche, had six children before me. They hoped the nuns could take my nosiness and quick perceptions and mold me into something God would look upon with favor."

"And did He?"

She laughed. "I shall simply say that Mother Superior and I came to same conclusion. It was not meant for me to have a vocation within the

Church."

"So you were a misguided novice?"

"No, I never even made it that far. The sisters took me in at five years of age. By that age, I was already a difficult child. Always into trouble. I seemed to have a knack for being in the wrong place at the wrong time.

"I was only allowed to stay because they found me intelligent. The good sisters kept hoping I would come around. That the day-dreaming would cease and the mischievous deeds would end." She grinned. "They never did."

Ashby took her hand and gave it a friendly squeeze. "I find you perfect the way you are, Marielle."

"So does her husband. My brother," a voice said from behind them.

CHAPTER THREE

ASHBY TURNED LAZILY to look over his shoulder while gently releasing Marielle's hand. Before him stood a man of about five and twenty, with dark hair and even darker eyes, thanks to the anger sparking within them.

He stood and gave the man a quick bow before extending his hand. "Ashby fitz Waryn. As a visitor to Monteville, I am happy to make your acquaintance."

The man hesitated, obviously thrown off-balance by his gracious gesture. Awkwardly, he pushed out his hand and received Ashby's. Ashby maintained his friendly smile but flinched inwardly at the weak, clammy hand. The man was short but stout. Someone should have taught him how to better present himself.

"I am Marc de la Tresse, brother to Jean-Paul."

Marielle rose and while she did not stand close to him, Ashby sensed the change in her. They had spent the afternoon together in conversation and he'd never felt more in tune with a person as he did the comtesse. Though physically she was the most beautiful woman he'd ever met, with rich, auburn hair and sparking violet eyes, he'd become enchanted by her zest for life and keen intelligence. The time in her company had passed quickly, full of witty conversation. Her demeanor now had totally changed. She was wary and stared at Marc de la Tresse coolly. Ashby couldn't help but wonder at her relationship with this brother-in-law.

"We were not expecting you so soon, Marc. Did the business in Paris go well?" Marielle asked.

The Frenchman shrugged. "'Tis neither here nor there," he said rudely. He seemed to have gathered his poise as he glared at Ashby. "Do you always go about caressing the hands of married women?"

Ashby answered cheerfully, "Only the ones that show any interest in me at all."

Marc de la Tresse was left speechless by the remark, so Ashby added, "Unfortunately, Marielle displays remarkably good sense and sees me for the flippant fool I am. If you saw me holding her hand, it was merely to impress upon her my gratitude in spending such a delightful afternoon of conversation before I begin the bothersome task of talking business."

His answer further perplexed the newcomer but Ashby could tell Marielle was ready to burst out in laughter. To cover for her, he asked, "Would you care to direct me to your stables? I always like to check on my horse after a bit. Make sure the animal's settled in, you know. I would not want to return a surly horse to the Bouchards."

Placing a firm hand on Marc de la Tresse's shoulder, he said, "Come along," and guided the man away from the garden. He did, though, turn and look over his shoulder, wanting to make sure Marielle was all right. "Thank you for your fine company today, my lady. I look forward to seeing you when we sup tonight."

De la Tresse led him a good quarter-mile before they reached where the horses were stabled. He seemed reluctant to leave Ashby on his own, possibly fearing an Englishman, and this one in particular, would stir up trouble with any Frenchman he passed.

Ashby purposely took his time fawning over the borrowed horse from the Bouchards, whose name he couldn't remember for the life of him. He crooned to her "Oh, Girl," and "My Sweet" enough times to get a rise from his companion. He rather enjoyed each twinge of disgust.

Ashby didn't care for this man. He would learn why once he spent enough time in de la

Tresse's company. He possessed a sixth sense when it came to people. He would discover why her brother-in-law's presence bothered Marielle and what the relationship was between the brothers de la Tresse.

All in good time.

MARIELLE DRESSED WITH care for the evening meal. She knew Jean-Paul liked for her to look impressive when guests were present in the chateau, showing off the pretty baubles he bestowed. More than that, she wanted to look her best for Ashby fitz Waryn.

She gazed at her troubled expression in the small mirror she'd received only last year for her birthday. Why did she feel Mother Superior looming over her shoulder, ready to scold her for her interest in Ashby? It wasn't as if she'd actually flirted with the handsome Englishman. She had been on her best behavior.

Well, mayhap she smiled a bit too readily at his quips. In one afternoon, she'd laughed more than she had in a lifetime. Still, no harm had been done. She simply saw to their guest's amusement while her husband was detained in the vineyards. Besides, Ashby was a charming, witty man. What woman wouldn't laugh at his observations or reward him with a ready smile when he offered a compliment?

Still, a cartload of guilt seemed parked at her doorstep. Simply because she found the man immensely attractive did not mean she would act upon that attraction. Sisters of Merciful Heart had driven that into her head. She would never be disloyal to her marriage vows, no matter how miserable she became. Others might stray from their sacred promises—but Marielle never would. Ashby, for all his flirtatious manner and charm, did not seem a man to press himself upon a woman who did not wish for that attention.

Marielle doubted he ran into many females who did not desire him. The truth was that he was a sophisticated English nobleman who had merely been a polite guest. He would never find a convent-bred girl such as her attractive. It seemed ridiculous even to speculate about such matters.

Yet Marielle smoothed her lavender surcoat, hoping it would bring out the color of her eyes even as she tried to downplay the vain gesture. She'd only met one person with eyes her shade of violet and that was her *grandmere*, now dead these past ten years. Marielle was the only one of more than twenty grandchildren who could lay claim to such color. The sisters often blamed the violet shade when it came to her pranks. They seemed to associate her being different with the troubles she caused.

She left to check with Cook on tonight's supper. It would be grander than usual, on account of their guest, but lighter fare than the midday meal. All seemed in place as the vineyard workers began arriving. Marielle greeted many by name and, as always, wished she could be more a part of the close-knit household. Jean-Paul, though, had different ideas for his comtesse. He commanded her to be apart from his retainers, as befit her noble position. In bowing to his wishes, Marielle found herself totally isolated from any friendships that might have otherwise formed naturally over the course of time.

She often lamented that she'd never made a single friend, other than her twin. After Arielle's death, when Marielle had been sent to the convent, no one befriended her. From ages five to fifteen, she'd never grown close to any of the nuns, much less the few girls who came to live at the nunnery in order to take their vows and become Brides of Christ. Her passion for knowledge, coupled with her naughty behavior, marked her for isolation from the convent's residents.

She'd hoped that by coming to Monteville that things would change. She longed to go into the vineyards and help tend the vines and harvest them when they ripened. What she wouldn't give to stomp on the grapes in merriment as the laborers of Monteville did each year. She was used to hard work. The sisters believed in strong toil as the entrance into heaven and Marielle always did more than her fair share of labor around the convent. It had continued once she'd returned to her parents. With her mother's poor health, all the cooking and cleaning had fallen to Marielle. It proved difficult to come to Monteville and have servants wait upon her hand and foot. The only kind of work Jean-Paul approved her doing involved weaving tapestries. Despite the wide arrays of colors and threads at her disposal, even that grew old with time.

She was grateful for the times her husband spent away from Monteville. On those occasions, she tended her garden in her oldest, plainest tunic, dirt smeared upon her cheeks and caked on her hands. Some of her happiest times were spent in those gardens. She prayed Jean-Paul never discovered her secret.

Her husband entered their bedchamber and spied her. As he approached, she couldn't help but see the thinning hair and deep lines of dissatisfaction and self-indulgence etched about his mouth and eyes. At least he'd bathed for once. Thank God Almighty for small blessings. Maybe their guest's presence had some influence on Jean-Paul.

"Have you met Lord Montayne's man?" Jean-Paul gestured and Marielle poured wine for him into a pewter cup.

"I have. He speaks fluent French."

"Excellent. It will be easier to deal with him. English is a tiresome language." Jean-Paul drained his drink and set the cup aside. "Shall we?"

He offered an arm to his wife and they went downstairs to the great hall.

"Did fitz Waryn speak to you of any business?"

Marielle laughed. "You must be joking, Husband." She sobered at the harsh look Jean-Paul gave her. "No, my lord. He spoke at some length to Donatien and Pierre Bouchard. He did ask me to take him about the grounds. I showed him around the chateau and all parts of the inner and outer baileys."

"Indeed, Comte, we spent an enjoyable afternoon together. Your wife is well-informed regarding the workings of Monteville." Ashby bowed before them. "I am Ashby fitz Waryn, come from Lord Garrett Stanbridge, the Earl of Montayne of Stanbury. It's a privilege to meet the noble owner of such a vast estate. I look forward to seeing your lands and the vineyards themselves in the days to come."

Jean-Paul greeted Ashby. "You must have Donatien show you the vineyards. I fear I have been called away on business and leave at first light. I will return in two days' time. When I next see you, you will be much more knowledgeable about the grape and its care."

Her husband glanced to her. "Amuse fitz Waryn while I am away. Keep whatever entertainments you have planned in his honor. He and I will do our business upon my return."

Marielle curtsied. "Yes, my lord." She glanced around, noting the meal was ready to begin. "Come and sit. The others await us."

She, Jean-Paul, and Ashby moved toward the dais where Marc was already seated. Her husband greeted his brother stiffly. They had never been close but things looked unusually strained between them as they gathered near him. Marielle hoped Marc would have the good sense not to cause a row in front of Ashby.

Or drink too much.

Most Frenchmen knew how to hold their drink. They knew to taste their wine, to roll it about their tongue and enjoy its many, subtle flavors. They let it enhance their meals. Not Marc de la Tresse. He washed down those same meals with multiple bottles of wine. Jean-Paul remarked upon more than one occasion how Marc's taste buds were dulled by his careless habits. Always left unsaid was if Marielle could not produce the expected heir, then Monteville would fall into Marc's hands someday. Jean-Paul always noted it would be a shame if the master of Monteville had not the skill to judge the vintages produced.

The meal ended and Rennier, the troubadour Marielle engaged for the week, proceeded to play several ballads. They told of unrequited love and the glory days of France. She hoped Ashby enjoyed the musician's playing and inquired so when Rennier rested his voice for a few minutes.

"Do you find our troubadour to your taste?"

Ashby smiled, the firelight playing across his strong features. "He's very talented but not the best I've heard."

"Who would that be?" she asked, curious since Rennier possessed one of the finest reputations among all troubadours in France.

He chuckled. "Why, Lady Madeleine, Countess of Montayne. Formerly Madeleine Bouchard."

"A woman?" Marc frowned. "What right has a woman to take the place of a man?"

"Oh, I believe Madeleine could take the place of the nightingale itself." Ashby looked back to Marielle, a wistful look in his eyes. "Not only does she sing from her soul, but Madeleine also is a fine storyteller. She weaves absolute magic for her audience. I have heard her a thousand times over the years and she still amazes me."

Jean-Paul grunted. "Robert Bouchard has a bit of a reputation as a teller of tales. Is there any relation between the pair?"

"Yes, Comte. Madeleine is his daughter. She is now wife to Lord Montayne and mother of the earl's son, Cynric."

The conversation continued but Marielle did

not join in. She thought of the look upon Ashby's face when he spoke of this Madeleine. Was he in love with her? Surely not, with her being the wife of Lord Montayne.

More than anything, at that moment, Marielle wished a man would look at her the way Ashby had looked when he spoke of Lady Montayne. She desired to love and have the love of a good man, but fate had other things in store for her. Jean-Paul had wanted her, even marrying beneath his station to have her, but no spark ever grew between them. Marielle found she cared more about her garden and her books than she did her own husband.

At least they gave her comfort and pleasure, things Jean-Paul never could.

Rennier continued playing for another hour before Jean-Paul stood. "It's late," he said to the troubadour. "You may play for those assembled tomorrow."

He dismissed the musician and bid Marc goodnight, as well. Marielle watched the two men depart.

"A pleasant sleep to you, fitz Waryn," Jean-Paul told Ashby. "I assume you have settled into your room."

"Yes, Comte. Marielle has been most accommodating. I thank you both for your splendid hospitality."

At the mention her of her name, she looked

up just as Jean-Paul snapped his fingers. She flinched inwardly at the sound.

"Come along, Marielle. I have need of you." He strode off, knowing she would follow without question.

As she made to leave the room, her gaze connected with Ashby's. The Englishman wore a deep frown on his handsome face. She glanced away and started after her husband.

But Ashby touched her arm as she passed, halting her progress.

"Is something wrong, Marielle?" he asked softly. "I have seen you recoil twice now when your husband snaps his fingers at you."

Tears welled in her eyes. "Please, Ashby. It is nothing. Do not involve yourself."

"But if he mistreats you—"

"I beg of you. Say nothing. It would only make it worse for me. Goodnight."

She hurried away, dread filling her as she crossed the great hall. Yet despite knowing it was the wrong thing to do, she turned back because she sensed Ashby's eyes upon her. She inclined her head to him and left the room.

Tonight, instead of envisioning Guy during the dreaded marital act, Marielle wickedly knew she would picture Ashby fitz Waryn instead. It would be the only thing that would see her through her wifely duty.

CHAPTER FOUR

ASHBY AWOKE EARLY, the guest bedchamber dark and cool. In the corridor outside the room, he heard the stirrings of the chateau coming to life. He arose and dressed in gray breeches and silver hose. Both his tunic and cotehardie were of a darker slate. He slipped on his black boots while he pondered on the strange dreams that had plagued him. He rarely dreamed but when he did, he constantly awoke to vague images that dissipated and a feeling of unease. Usually, he attributed any discomfort in his sleep to the times he was on the road since he slept like a babe when under Stanbury's roof. It troubled him, though, that he couldn't remember anything this morning other than the sense of dread that blanketed him. He hoped the dreams didn't foreshadow any problems he might encounter at Monteville.

As he combed through his hair, he wondered if Marc de la Tresse visited his visions sometime during the night. If so, those would have been nightmares. The man troubled him like no other he'd met. It stemmed from his faulty handshake, one that Ashby would have never trusted, but it was much more. The younger de la Tresse brother's eyes darted about at all times, as if he looked for conspiracy in every corner.

He also never seemed to relax. Ashby watched with interest as de la Tresse ate last night's meal. Marc glared at each bite he brought to his mouth as if it were poisoned. He also cast odd glances in his brother's direction, almost as if he looked for fault with the comte.

What disturbed Ashby the most was when Marc peered at Marielle. He gazed at his brother's wife with a hunger that no man should show—especially in the presence of that woman's husband. Ashby would have thought Marc was haggling for a showdown over Marielle if he hadn't seen how utterly Jean-Paul ignored his striking young wife.

Ashby pitied Marielle when her husband barked at her. The Frenchman never bothered to converse with her. Instead, he spit out short, pointed commands. Even then, he spoke condescendingly to her, much as if she were a child. The final blow came when he'd snapped his fingers at Marielle and commanded her to follow him like a trained dog. The poor woman appeared as if she was headed to her own funeral.

He fastened his jeweled girdle low on his hips and prepared to leave the bedchamber. He tried to clear his head of any thoughts of Marielle de la Tresse. She was a beautiful woman in what he feared was an impossible situation. Unfortunately, she wasn't the first to find herself in such circumstances. It was rare when love grew between a married couple. Marielle was trapped in a web of her own making—or one her parents had seen to on her behalf through an arranged marriage. Ashby could not concern himself with any problems in the household between his hosts. He would simply be a gracious guest, conduct his business, and be on his way back to England and Stanbury. He couldn't afford to be caught up in the lives of the inhabitants of Monteville.

Much less a flirtation that could prove dangerous.

Despite her years of marriage, Marielle seemed an innocent to him. He'd wager she'd never given consideration to a love affair. She wouldn't know how to proceed. If he displayed any interest in her, she would take it seriously. He refused to toy with an innocent's affections and he certainly couldn't leave her to face any consequences.

Yet he couldn't shake her image as he made his way down the stairs to the chapel. He'd inquired of its location yesterday and for the time morning mass was said. Madeleine had been firm with him on this point.

"I do not care whether you are interested or not, Ashby," she proclaimed. "A good guest in Bordeaux will attend mass each day of his visit. Daydream of your village conquests or traveling the English countryside while you are there, but you will go to daily mass. Is that understood?"

Ashby smiled as he recollected her words. Only Madeleine dared speak to him in such a manner. She had him as well-trained as Garrett. Funny how two of the strongest willed men in England meekly submitted to her every whim.

He genuflected and slid into a pew halfway from the altar. About fifty people gathered for the mass. He nodded at the man on his right. It was Donatien de Toulouse, Jean-Paul's overseer. He'd listened carefully to the man's opinions yesterday, glad to learn Donatien was full of knowledge and willing to share it. Garrett would be pleased at the results of this trip to France and what Ashby had learned.

As expected, he spun a few reveries while the priest droned on in Latin. How was a man expected to pay homage to God, the Highest of all Liege Lords, if he couldn't understand a bloody thing said? That was only one sticking point Ashby found about the Church. He'd rebelled entering the priesthood from the time he was four. That was when his brother, Ashland, informed Ashby he was destined to serve the Church as a third son. Ashland was eleven at the time and already full of himself and his position as future lord of the castle.

Probably because Ashland deemed it would come to pass, Ashby fought his brother's words tooth and nail. He'd been so insistent that in three years' time, his father, Walter, sent him off to foster with Ryker, his old friend from their days of war. It had been the best decision—probably the only good one—that his father ever made concerning his youngest son.

Mass ended and Ashby made the Sign of the Cross. He followed the group up the stairs into the great hall, where loaves of bread and tankards of beer waited for the occupants of Monteville to break their fast.

He watched Marielle make her way over to him, a jar in her hand. He offered his hostess a smile.

"Might that jar hold sweet butter or even sweeter honey, Comtesse?"

She pursed her lips. "I so wanted to surprise you. Yes, it's honey. We only bring it out for our special guests." She set the container on the table. "Please, enjoy your humble meal. I promise you the next meal will be much grander."

He hesitated and then asked, "Will you join me in breaking my fast?"

"No," she told him. "I have far too many things to do this morning. I must meet with the servants on the day's duties and then with our steward, Etienne. Then I will look over the supplies our butler has purchased and see to their placement in the pantries."

"I hope you will have time to work in the midday meal." He grinned at her shyly, unsure why he suddenly felt like a callow youth and not the experienced man he was.

Marielle colored slightly pink. "Oh, I would not ignore a guest of my husband's. You can be assured I will cease my labors and see that you receive a proper meal in good company." She glanced away and then back to him. "I see Donatien. I will send him to you. He is eager to show you our vineyards this morning."

She signaled the overseer to join them. "Donatien is well-versed in all manner of the grape. His family has lived at Monteville close to three hundred years. Feel free to trust any advice he gives you." She curtsied to him and left the hall.

RELIEF WASHED OVER Ashby as fast as the sudden downpour that hit while Donatien showed off the Monteville vineyards. They rode over three hours around the property. Ashby was impressed by the efficiency of their operation. It was much larger than the one run by the Bouchards. Ashby questioned whether Garrett should make an offer for a part of the Monteville land that connected with his own property that the Bouchards managed, one of the items he'd been tasked to negotiate with Jean-Paul de la Tresse. After having met the comte and seen the organized manner in which Donatien ran things, he doubted they would be willing to part with any small portion of de la Tresse land. Still, it couldn't hurt to inquire, especially since Garrett had shown interest in blending certain grapes for a new vintage. He would propose the purchase according to Garrett's instructions before his time at Monteville came to an end.

Although he'd been intrigued by Garrett's suggestion to stay in France indefinitely and help Pierre Bouchard oversee the Montayne vine-yards, Ashby knew Madeleine's brother would resent any interference, especially coming from a man who came only knowing how to drink wine, not grow and nurture the grapes.

It would also leave him in too close a proxim-ity with Marielle de la Tresse. Ashby found his mind wandering from Donatien's detailed explanations all morning, only to find it hovering around images of Marielle. He couldn't remem-ber ever having been so taken with a woman.

Except mayhap Madeleine. Even then, he'd realized from the start she was meant for Garrett.

Ashby never thought he'd find a woman with the exceptional looks, grace, and wit of Madeleine, Countess of Montayne. He constantly reminded himself that even if he did, he would have nothing to offer this vision of loveliness. That meant marriage and settling down would always be out of the question. He would be happy with no less than someone Madeleine's equal or better, so he'd been safe these last few years.

Until now.

Marielle de la Tresse had captivated him in no uncertain terms. It wasn't just her beauty, though that alone made a summer day pale by comparison. She carried a *joie de vivre* about her, a coupling of mischief and zest and quiet charm that made her irresistible. Marielle was like no other woman he'd ever met. She was set apart from those he'd dallied with in his typical fashion. Ashby never placed his heart in the hands of another, always keeping his affairs light and carefree. Wasn't it his luck he would discover such a rare treasure, only to find she was married, and unhappily at that.

No, leaving Bordeaux as quickly as possible offered him the only respite from the sudden longings that Marielle de la Tresse brought to him. Regrettably, the less time spent in her company, the better.

The rain drove them back to Monteville's stables, where they handed off their reins to the stable master and walked through the bailey to the castle steps. Servants greeted them with towels and promises of hot water to be sent upstairs. Ashby barely had time to doff his sodden tunics when the water arrived. It warmed him considerably.

He changed into fresh clothes and gave the servant who arrived with his water the sodden ones. The boy promised to place them near the fire to dry and then reminded him to hurry to the great hall for dinner, which would be served within the next few minutes.

An empty dais greeted him. He waited a moment as serfs came in from the vineyards and begin gathering around the trestle tables, pulling them away from the walls and to the center of the room. Finally, he decided to take his seat. Marielle joined him almost immediately.

"I apologize for my tardiness, Ashby."

Just the lilt of her voice caused a stirring within him. He gritted his teeth and forced a smile. Mayhap if he looked out over the crowded hall he could find an attractive, willing wench to meet his needs and take his mind from its pointless wanderings. He spied a few likely candidates and decided he would approach them discreetly after the meal.

The servants brought a single trencher and set it before them. He raised a brow.

"Is your brother-in-law not joining us?"

Marielle shrugged. "Marc comes and goes as he pleases. Sometimes, he is gone for days or even weeks, and then he turns up without a word as to where he has been. Other times Jean-Paul will send him on some small errand. And again he will be gone forever. When he is present at Monteville, he comes to meals infrequently at best."

She sighed. "I have no control over a grown man's lack of manners."

Ashby sliced their trencher in half. A pretty maid ladled choice bits of meat and gravy over the bread. As was custom, Ashby offered Marielle the first bite.

"For you, my lady. Hopefully, neither my manners nor my French are lacking. I fear I butchered a few phrases this morning. Donatien questioned me several times before I could make myself understood."

Marielle chewed the venison carefully. She pressed a cloth to her mouth and then sipped from the silver wine goblet before her.

"I fear Donatien was speaking to you about things which you had no background or reference point. England is much too cold to grow grapes, or so I am told."

Ashby slipped a piece of the meat onto his

own knife and brought it to his mouth. "England is cold much of the year. The castles are always drafty. The winds can grow quite fierce at times." He paused. "But there is nothing like an English spring anywhere. I would lay odds on that."

"I hear Paris is lovely in the spring and fall."

He cocked his head. "Have you ever seen it?"

"No," she replied. "I did grow up in Libourne, which is a fairly large town. Just as Paris, it has a walled gate and marketplace with main roads leading to it in a spoke fashion."

"I thought you were brought up in a convent."

It surprised—and pleased—her that he had remembered that detail about her.

"You have a good memory. The convent was located just outside Libourne so, occasionally, I would be allowed to go into town to see my parents or brothers and sisters. I remember the color and the excitement." Her eyes danced with mischief. "The nuns always warned me about the corruption, though."

Ashby laughed. "Sounds like the nuns of my acquaintance."

"My father was a merchant there. He sold carpets from the Far East. He also worked with others and sold their shoes and gloves and hats in our shop."

"Do you remember living with your family or were you too young?"

Marielle shook her head. "I remember some things. Trade started at dawn. Our shop was open in the front. Dozens of carpets were displayed, though a storeroom in the rear held many more. My father wore a long, dark robe that was required of all merchants in town. At night, my brother, Gustave, would place me upon his shoulders and shutter the front, then we would retire upstairs to our quarters."

"You sound as if you still miss it. I would think your life would be so much more enjoyable here at Monteville with servants to wait upon you."

She sat silent for close to a minute, her excellent posture more than likely a holdover from her days with the nuns.

"I would rather work in a shop or hire out as a domestic as my sisters did," she told him quietly.

Her admission surprised him. "I do not know you well, Marielle, and wouldn't wish to judge you harshly but it's obvious that your marriage to the comte enabled you to rise into a different class. You no doubt have luxuries here that your father could only dream of giving you."

Her angelic face did not match the bitter tone of her words. "Since I had no vocation for the Church, the good sisters returned me to my parents, noting my numerous faults. My parents had no dreams of providing me with anything.

They only wished to have someone take me off their hands. All six of their children had left home by the time I arrived again and I'll tell you, they weren't pleased that I was back, another mouth to feed when they had thought the Church would assume responsibility for me.

"The day Jean-Paul came to my father's shop, he was immediately taken with me. He told me he married his parents' choice the first time and now that they were dead, he would make his own decision and please himself. He thought I would please him. My father let me know I was to accept the comte's generous offer of marriage. He thought a connection to the de la Tresse family would bring him more business than before. Frankly, I was eager to be gone."

"But you made the wrong choice?" he asked.

She laughed, low and musically. "Does a woman ever have a choice? I came here. Much as I would like to sew and cook and even stomp the grapes into wine, my husband treats me as if I am as breakable as glass. I am allowed to weave tapestries for my enjoyment. No more, no less."

She moved closer to him and lowered her voice, taking him into her confidence. "My secret pleasure is to read. I read all the time. If Jean-Paul knew, he would instantly put a stop to it. He would not understand an intellectual curiosity, especially from a woman. He already feels I am overeducated. That the nuns indulged me too much in my love of learning."

Marielle drew a sip of the wine from the goblet in front of them before she spoke again. "My husband thinks me a child, the malleable girl he married years ago. I would give anything to have a craft and seek membership in a guild. I fear I am not meant for the life I lead."

Her words surprised him. "If you were free to do so, what kind of craft might you wish to pursue? Would you see yourself as a metal worker? A candlemaker? What about a carpenter or cobbler?"

She contemplated his words and then said, "It would be hard for me to decide. I have so many interests. Perhaps a tanner, who treats animal skins so that they become leather. So many items are crafted from leather. Shoes. Gloves. Outer garments. Even musical instruments. I do enjoy working with my hands. It might be enjoyable to be a clothmaker, using a loom, or even a tailor who cuts the cloth and sews clothing for others."

She frowned. "Of course, both tanners and tailors are always men." Her lips twitched with amusement. "But if a woman could pursue any craft, I think I might choose to be an apothecary."

"Why so?" Ashby encouraged, seeing Marielle come alive at the idea.

"Apothecaries specialize in medications and they treat a wide variety of ailments and illnesses. They are at the heart of a community because so many come to them for treatments and seek their advice."

She paused and then revealed, "You have seen my secret garden. A neighbor's wife helped advise me what to plant when I first came as a new bride to Monteville. It has many flowers and all kinds of herbs. I tend to it when Jean-Paul is away. He would never approve of the time I spend in it. But if I could, I would use the herbs there not only in cooking. I would discover their medicinal worth and use them to treat the sick and hurt."

Marielle shook her head, sadness blanketing her. "What good is it to speak of these things, Ashby? Yes, I should be pleased that I was able to leave my parents' household and come to such a grand estate as Monteville. They no longer have to be concerned about me. I have a husband who is quite wealthy. I will never go without food or shelter. I should be more appreciative of all I have been given."

Her mouth trembled. She seemed so lost and alone, despite her station and titled husband.

"Mayhap if you have a child," he suggested.

"A child?" Her voice quivered with emotion. Ashby longed to touch her face or stroke her hand, to somehow bring comfort to ease the sadness now cast across her features.

"I have longed for a child more than anything in this world. Someone to shower my love upon.

To spend my days and nights with. I have endured my husband's touch a thousand times and still have no babe in my belly or my arms."

She stood, a look of horror crossing her face. "I cannot believe I have spoken to you of such things. Pray forgive me," she mumbled and fled the room.

Ashby picked at what remained of his meal, the ache in his heart heavy.

CHAPTER FIVE

MARIELLE BIT HER tongue as she crossed the great hall, the better to steady her emotions. Why had she poured forth like a river that bursts its dam? She'd played foolish pranks in the past and let her tongue run away with her when she was a child but nothing of this magnitude had ever occurred.

What must Ashby fitz Waryn be thinking? How could she face the Englishman again?

And what would he tell Jean-Paul?

She raced up the stairs to the solar and bathed her face with cool water from a basin. She breathed deeply in and out, over and over, until the rushing blood stilled within her. She must repair the damage and quickly. Jean-Paul would be furious with her for betraying such private matters to a mere stranger.

Yet Ashby fitz Waryn didn't seem a stranger

at all to her. The few hours she'd spent in his company invigorated her. It was as if she'd known him all her life and yet they would never run out of things to say to one another. She wondered if it was because he took her for what she was, the chatelaine of Monteville. Although that was her assigned role in life, Marielle always believed she was a pretender. Her husband ignored her for the most part, not allowing her to be a life partner to him. Consequently, the people of Monteville overlooked her. They weren't disrespectful toward her. They merely paid no attention to her.

The Englishman unthinkingly awarded her with respect, as her position required. He was not dismissive in any way. In fact, he treated her as the woman she longed to be. Marielle mused upon how sad it was when a virtual stranger esteemed her more than her own husband did.

As she patted her face dry, Marielle stole a glance into the blurred glass. Her reflection was as white as a ghost, with troubled eyes. That would never do. She pinched her cheeks until her fingers ached. At least it brought some color to them.

She returned to the great hall in order to repair the damage she'd caused. She didn't know how but she would need to smooth the situation over. The rounds of cheese and fruits had just arrived, the last course in the meal. Calmly, she surveyed the room. A woman stood before the dais, engaged in conversation with Ashby. Even from this distance, Marielle read her sensual body language. It was Lisette, a flighty servant whom Marielle guessed was trying to arrange a tryst for tonight. Lisette wasn't one to let a handsome man slip past her.

Stopping to check on a table or two, she gave a word of encouragement and passed along a few compliments. She finally came to their seated guest. As she arrived, Lisette flounced off, obviously not happy with the answer Ashby had given her. Marielle's heart gave a small leap that he hadn't succumbed to the vixen and her dark beauty. She ignored its fast beats and seated herself beside him once again.

The look he gave her was subdued. His good manners again shone. Most men would have questioned her outburst or possibly initiated a seduction with her revealing her unhappiness. She expected neither from this Englishman.

"May I offer you some cheese?" Ashby lifted one of the two rounds lying upon the table and sliced a neat piece with his knife. She accepted it, thankful for another moment in which to collect her thoughts.

He cut open an apple and placed half before her before biting into his own section. They ate in companionable silence before she ventured an apology.

"I fear I have badly neglected my duties as hostess," she said lightly, hoping Ashby would forget the episode from before because she could think of nothing to erase her previous outburst. "With Jean-Paul gone and Marc nowhere to be had, I would be remiss if we did not spend the afternoon together."

He chewed thoughtfully before replying, "Your duties of this morning have been completed?"

Marielle nodded. "Yes. I had planned a different entertainment for your pleasure this afternoon but, with the rain, I am afraid we shall have to cancel the hunt until tomorrow."

"As you wish." His tone was pleasant but he seemed to walk upon eggshells now. She needed to set him at ease and return to their former camaraderie.

"Do you play backgammon?" she asked.

Ashby's face lit up. "I am champion of Stanbury at the moment. We play for fun each year after the winter crops are planted and more time is spent indoors. Madeleine organizes a tournament just after the Christmas season. It gives the people something to look forward to after the feasting has come to an end."

"Would you care to pass the afternoon thus engaged?"

He nodded with enthusiasm and gave her a smile. "I hope you are accustomed to losing, my lady. It will become a familiar feeling to you in the next hours."

They retired after the meal to her chamber. It was connected to the solar itself. Jean-Paul rarely wanted his wife to lie abed with him after a bout of lovemaking. He normally banished her to her own room, which she looked upon as a haven. Rarely did her husband venture past its door. She had books hidden in all sorts of places. Regularly, Marielle juggled the housekeeping accounts in order to save money for a new book. When she was desperate, she would trade in one of her older ones, one that she wasn't as fond of, though it always proved a difficult decision if she had to give up a favorite companion.

She had a servant light a fire, as the wet October afternoon turned not only dreary but quite cold. That was one thing she'd never gotten used to—the bitter cold. It was as if the chateau drew it into her walls and then breathed gusts of it up innocent spines. A fire in her chamber was one indulgence Jean-Paul never chastised her for. He'd told her she must keep her fingers from a chill, the better to complete her tapestries. If she lived long enough, she might finish enough to line every wall at Monteville.

The thought depressed her.

A peace descended upon the room as they played. Talkative at first, Marielle told Ashby of some of the jokes she played upon the Sisters of

Merciful Heart nuns in her years at the convent. He told her of fostering with Ryker Stanbridge at Stanbury and his great love and respect for his friend, Garrett, his liege lord who'd sent him to Bordeaux to learn more of the grape.

"It's rare to find such a companion as Garrett," Ashby shared. "We are more brothers than friends, truth be told. His mother, Lady Edith, always made me feel a part of the family at Stanbury. Garrett and I have been through battle and lost loves and spent great times of joy together."

"You sound as if you miss him a great deal."

Ashby moved his piece, frowning as he did. "Indeed, I look forward to my return to England. As Garrett's man of business, I will first stop in London before returning south. But I am eager to see Garrett and Madeleine's children again. Lyssa enjoys when I take her hunting and Cynric loves nothing more than to throw rocks into the pond. It's his greatest joy in life to heave a pebble as far as he can into the water and then squeal with loud delight at such a witty accomplishment."

"It seems you lead quite a domestic life at Stanbury." The picture Ashby painted made her long to see the castle and surrounding lands.

"Stanbury is my home. I miss it when I'm gone. I adore the children and enjoy entertaining them."

They fell silent, finishing their game and

another two. Marielle took two of the three games and Ashby voiced his delight over her wins.

"God's teeth, Marielle, but you are quite the player. I have not seen another woman with such determination and luck since Madeleine. Mayhap you and the comte can one day visit England. You might be crowned the new champion of Stanbury."

Marielle put away the board. "I would like nothing better than that but I have not left Monteville since my marriage seven years ago."

Ashby looked perplexed. "Not even to visit your own parents?"

She shook her head. "Jean-Paul sees them on occasion when he is in Libourne upon business. He wishes me to stay home."

He nodded. "Of course. Someone must run the chateau in his absence. I know he is only to be gone a short time this trip but it's good he has you to oversee all things and deal with the peasants' legal matters while he is away as all good wives must do."

Marielle's jaw dropped in surprise. "Do you jest?" When he frowned at her response, she added lightly, "My husband would never trust me to make such fortuitous decisions while he is away. That is what Etienne and Donatien are for."

She brooded a moment and then spoke hesitantly. "Not having come from this class, I . . . I did not know this was a practice among the nobles."

Ashby started to say something but she saw he thought better of it.

Marielle realized she'd once again revealed too much and sought to divert his attention. "Come, let us not ruin a pleasant afternoon with such foolish talk." She indicated a chess set on a table nearby. "Are you up for a game of chess?"

He rose and brought the set to them. With a twinkle in his eyes, he said, "Only if you will let me win."

She laughed richly, a sound so unfamiliar to her that it gave her pause. Marielle was glad she'd gone back to the great hall to speak with Ashby. His company had made the afternoon pass quickly. She felt certain his remaining time would be without incident.

Until Marc appeared in the doorway.

Marielle's insides tightened. She stopped breathing. The room filled with a sudden tension as palpable as the rain that cascaded down the windowpane. Marc knew not to come here. This chamber served as her retreat. She never invited guests to it. In fact, she had surprised herself by bringing Ashby. Yet somehow he was different. She wanted him here. She did not want her brother-in-law to set foot in her sacred place of refuge.

"May I watch?"

She couldn't refuse his request without seeming churlish. "Of course. Have a seat."

"I shall stand," he replied and went to the fire. He turned his back on them some minutes before he faced them again.

Marielle found her concentration waning. Marc never ceased to have that effect on her. Her throat thickened. Her breathing became labored. Usually, he stood much too close for comfort, his eyes lingering over her in an unseemly way.

With Ashby present, she sensed only his eyes upon her now but she refused to meet them. *Think of the game*, she commanded herself. Still, when she moved her queen, her hand trembled slightly. She hoped Ashby would not notice and say something with Marc present.

Marielle swallowed, her mouth gone dry. Her nose began tingling. She prayed the sneeze would stay in. Either God had no time to answer such trivial prayers or He had a poor sense of humor about Him. At her expense.

She sneezed.

She sneezed again.

The third time capped the series. Rarely did they come in less than a trio. She dreaded what she would hear next.

"My God, Marielle! Do you have to bellow so before you sneeze? An ass sneezes more delicately than you. I am surprised the walls of Monteville have not come crashing down from the strain of holding up against one of your sneezes. France would do well to take you into battle next time against England. One sneeze and all the pretty little English soldiers would run for their lives."

Marielle glared at Marc through watery eyes. They always teared up after one of her gargantuan sneezes. Yes, she knew they were unseemly, especially for a female, but she had no control over when they came, much less their intense volume. If she had a small gold coin for every time Marc berated her after one, her treasury would far outweigh that of the king's.

She chose to ignore Marc's cutting comments and returned her attention to the game. Ashby's eyes remained fixed upon the board, his face deep in concentration. It was almost if he hadn't heard the exchange. She knew that to be impossible but what a gentleman he was for casually continuing the game, not missing a beat.

He made a few moves before softly calling out, "Check."

Oh, how had she gotten into such a bad situation? She usually did so well at chess.

Ashby lifted his arms high above his head in a stretch. "I am afraid I tire, Marielle. Mayhap we could finish this game at a later time? Or even start afresh tomorrow?"

His face was full of concern and his tone was kind. She understood he was trying to help her save face. "A guest is always accommodated at Monteville, sir."

She rose. "Would you care to rest before we sup? I could show you back to your room."

"Only if I have a book to read. Does Jean-Paul have a library I might peruse?"

Thank Sweet Jesu for Ashby's perceptiveness. She knew he realized how badly she must want out of this room.

"It's a small one but adequate. Let me take you there."

She stood. Marc stepped into her path. "A word, Marielle?"

She looked over his shoulder at Ashby. She could think of no gracious way out of his request. Ashby came to her rescue again.

"I shall await you in the corridor, Marielle. I fear I would never find this library since Monteville is so grand."

"Grander than Stanbury?" Marc inquired, his tone sarcastic.

"I find both houses to be majestic. Fortunately, I have lived at Stanbury for more than a score, so even in my follies, I have actually learned the library from the great hall and can distinguish solar from privy."

He bowed to them. "I leave you to your privacy."

The minute the door closed behind him, Marielle turned on Marc. "Do you wish to alienate our guest? You have been rude for so long that you no longer know when you speak thus."

Marc moved menacingly toward her. She held her ground but her legs shook. She locked her knees, hoping that would still the trembling. Marielle raised her chin defiantly and glared up at him.

He gave her a sardonic smile. "You seem quite taken with this Englishman, dear sister. Mayhap I should share that with Jean-Paul."

"That I am doing my duty as hostess to his guest? You have nothing else to say, Marc. I have only done what my husband wished in his absence."

He took her chin roughly. "You play with fire, Marielle. If you want to be burned, why not let me singe you?"

She jerked away from him and he gave a malevolent chuckle.

"You want Monteville and will more than likely possess it one day, Marc. If we have no son, then I will gladly vacate the premises and leave it to you."

His gaze roamed over her face and dipped lower to her breasts, a lascivious smile lighting his face. Suddenly, he reached out and snagged her wrists, yanking her toward him. Marielle stumbled into his chest and then tried to jerk away but his fingers only tightened until she feared he might crush her bones. She quit struggling, hoping he would come to his senses and release her.

Looming above her, he licked his lips, as if he were ready to feast upon her. Fear filled Marielle. Marc had never gone this far before. She longed to call out to Ashby, who waited for her just the other side of the door, but found her throat tight with fright. No sound would come out.

Marc continued to look at her, his gaze intense. She could see the longing on his face and feared he might try to kiss her.

Or more.

She hadn't liked Marc from the moment she met him. He was ill-tempered and volatile. Spoiled for a grown man. Disrespectful of Jean-Paul and everyone around him. Her way of handling her brother-in-law had been to avoid him as much as possible. Now, though, she truly feared him for the first time.

Would he dare take what belonged to his brother?

She prayed he would not.

He lowered his face until his nose almost touched hers. Marielle held her breath, hoping he wouldn't try and kiss her. It was bad enough having to endure Jean-Paul's touch. The thought of Marc was even more repulsive.

Just as he moved as if to kiss her, she swallowed and managed to say, "I warn you. I will tell Jean-Paul if you dare touch me," hoping that thought might scare him away.

It didn't.

Marc's mouth slammed down onto hers in a punishing kiss. Marielle tightened her lips, trying to withstand the ugly, unwanted assault. She struggled to free her wrists but saw that only enflamed him so she stilled. Held her ground. Waited for him to cease.

When he raised his head, he also dropped her wrists. Immediately, Marielle stepped back and began rubbing them, trying to get feeling back into them She knew they would be bruised—and she would have to hide this from her husband and the world.

"I cautioned you not to touch me," she told him, her voice shaking with emotion.

"You think you will dare to tell Jean-Paul about this?" he asked lazily. "I think not. If anything, I would make sure he blamed you. That *you* were the one who tried to entice me. You were the one to break your marital vows and force yourself upon me, his loyal and faithful brother. Who might Jean-Paul believe? Me—or you?"

Marc chuckled. "That is if you think that husband of yours truly cares what you do."

His cruel words stung. Most likely, Marc was right. Marielle didn't believe Jean-Paul cared for her. If he did, it was more like a once-prized possession which at one time he had valued and still wouldn't want broken or defaced.

Loathing for Marc filled her and she said, "You may have Monteville. But you will never, ever have me. Do you understand?"

"Believe whatever you wish, Marielle," he told her. "Time will tell."

CHAPTER SIX

THE HUNT WAS on. Ashby was ready to smell the outdoors once again and move his legs after the day of rain yesterday kept him cooped up inside the chateau. He'd tried to read some from the book Marielle loaned him but reading French was infinitely more difficult than speaking it. It made so much more sense to hear the musical words. The worst part was the difficult spelling. He swore that half of the letters in each word were not pronounced, a good three or four dangling from the end for show.

Last night's entertainment had gone well. Rennier, the same minstrel, performed, followed by a trio of mimes. Those gathered enjoyed watching the group and imitating some of the gestures from their seats. The leader even pulled Ashby up and he good-naturedly pantomimed alongside them.

After breaking his fast this morning, he spent a few hours cloistered with Donatien, looking at drawings of various vines and discussing different vintages. The vineyard manager freely shared his knowledge, which Ashby appreciated. He had much to tell Garrett upon his return. Ashby had decided that Garrett should make a return trip to France himself and initiate some of the practices at Monteville in his own Bordeaux vineyards. Pierre, though a thorough and dedicated manager, was very set in his ways. Ashby knew any suggestions he made to the Frenchman to alter anything would be ignored. It would take Garrett's specific orders—in person—before anything changed at Chateau Branais.

Ashby saddled his horse. He was most comfortable when performing his own tasks, especially when it involved a horse. Several years before, a squire had readied Ashby's horse for battle when he took too long telling a lovely maiden goodbye. The fool hadn't fastened the saddle properly and Ashby found himself unseated during the first charge. It bruised his pride more than his body although he'd broken a rib as he fell unexpectedly. That same rib gave him a twinge every now and then, which was a good reminder to him. He'd always looked after his own horse ever since.

He mounted the horse he'd borrowed from the Bouchards and followed the stable master and his assistants as they led the other horses from the stables. He saw Marc de la Tresse and three other men whom he'd seen in the great hall at meals. He cantered toward them.

Instead of properly introducing him, Marc gave Ashby a surly look and remained silent. An awkward moment passed before Ashby filled the gap.

"I am Ashby fitz Waryn, come from Stanbury in England. My liege lord, the Earl of Montayne, owns the vineyards at Chateau Branais. I have come to Monteville to learn more about vineyards and the process of winemaking."

The oldest introduced them all. "*Bienvenue*, Ashby. I am Gaudin." He motioned to the two men standing next to him. "This is Gregory and Jacques. We are knights of the comte and are pleased you have come to Monteville."

Marielle trotted over on a white palfrey to join the assembled group. "I see you have met our fellow hunters. Are you gentlemen ready?" Her eyes shined with eagerness.

He looked from her to the other soldiers. "Do you three have any advice? From the looks of the comtesse, I fear we are in for an invigorating ride."

Jacques laughed aloud. "La comtesse is fearless in the saddle. She had never ridden before she came to Monteville but she took to it like dew upon a flower."

Ashby noted the look of scorn Marc tossed Jacques' way.

Marielle flashed Jacques a smile. "You're very kind, Jacques. I must thank you, as my teacher, for all your patience in our riding lessons."

She whirled her horse around and galloped across the bailey. Ashby assumed that was the sign the hunt had begun. The men followed her through the gates of the chateau and down the open road next to the vineyard. He wondered where they headed.

Marielle turned over her shoulder and waved them on. Ashby spurred his mount to catch her. He pulled alongside her, noticing how well she sat in the saddle. He found himself sitting taller, wanting to impress her, though God knew why. She was a married noblewoman, but one of the most desirable women he'd met. She was intelligent, quick-witted, and had a playful nature. He could imagine her as a girl, giving the sisters at the convent fits.

They turned off the main path into a wood and slowed their horses considerably due to the denseness of the forest. Marc pulled up next to them. Ashby longed to knock some sense into the man, especially after his diatribe on Marielle's sneezes the day before. What an inconsiderate oaf. He dare not imagine what would next come out of the man's mouth.

"The way you ride that horse, Marielle,

people will think you are the spawn of the Devil himself. You might think to ride in a more seemly fashion, especially in sight of guests."

"Oh, I admire Marielle's riding, Marc," Ashby said easily, coming to her defense. "It's not often a lady can ride so admirably. I know this visitor is in awe of her skill."

Marc frowned. He had to fall behind them as the path narrowed even further. Ashby despised the Frenchman's critical manner. He couldn't remember a single pleasantry coming from de la Tresse.

"There!" Marielle cried. Ashby caught sight of a medium-sized fox racing away and took off after it. He could hear the others behind him. He really didn't want the fox caught. That's why he'd put himself between the poor creature and the riding party. Ashby never understood the fun in chasing a small, defenseless animal. It was different to place food on your table but killing for sport had never appealed to him.

As the fox shot across the ground like a bolt of lightning, Ashby veered off to the left. He led the group in the opposite direction the fox had taken. Eventually, they slowed and circled their horses around.

"We were within striking distance," Gregory said. "I wonder where the creature disappeared to."

Gaudin pointed over his shoulder. "He could

have turned that way. Anyone game?"

Both Gregory and Jacques nodded. The three knights took off in the other direction. Ashby thought the fox had had plenty of time to hide from its hunters with the head start it'd been given. Marc hesitated, looking at the riders as they headed away.

As Marc stared after them, Ashby caught a smile playing about Marielle's lips, coupled with a wicked gleam in her eyes. He knew to be prepared for what would come next.

"I think he's this way!" she cried and took off at breakneck speed. Ashby, knowing something was afoot, easily followed. It took a moment for Marc to react, though, since Marielle's words caught him off-guard. He started after the pair but soon fell behind.

Marielle led them on a good chase, as they dodged tree limbs and old stumps, bushes, and the carcass of a dead wolf. She finally slowed her horse and looked around.

Seeing only Ashby, she sighed. "Thank the heavens we are rid of him." She slid from her horse and took its reins in her hands as she patted its flank affectionately. Pulling an apple from her pocket, she offered it to the horse, who snapped it up and munched noisily.

He dismounted and asked, "So do you often run away from your brother-in-law? Is he so great a threat?"

She shivered. "My best advice to you is to keep a fair distance from Marc de la Tresse. He is jealous to his core of all that Jean-Paul has. Fifteen years separate the pair, with a slew of stillborn babes between them. When Marc was only five, his mother died. Jean-Paul had recently wed Agnes, his first wife. They raised Marc as their own child since they had none. I fear Jean-Paul has never come to accept Marc as the grown man he is, much less Marc finding it kind that his brother saw fit to look after him so well."

"You said Marc is jealous of all Jean-Paul has. I know Monteville is one thing." Ashby paused. "Are you another?"

Marielle frowned, an angry blush staining her smooth, pale skin. "I have repeatedly told Marc to keep his distance from me. He makes me . . . uncomfortable."

"Have you shared that with your husband?" he asked softly, wanting more than anything to take her in his arms and give her solace.

She crossed her arms tightly as if she wanted to protect herself. "No, I would never trouble Jean-Paul about such matters. I can handle Marc." She turned to stroke her horse's neck and cooed endearments to the animal. Ashby wished she would do the same to him. Guilt washed over him at the thought.

He'd had more than enough light o' loves over his lifetime. His soul now burned for more.

He witnessed the looks that passed between Garrett and Madeleine. The happiness they shared. Watching his friends made him desperately want the same joy in his own life. But he'd never come close to acting upon it since the right woman had never come into his life.

He thought he might go mad because he couldn't put his arms around Marielle here and now. Stroke those auburn curls. Taste those rose-budded lips. Every bone in his body cried out to him that this amazing woman was the one meant for him. Yet she belonged to another, a man of power and great wealth, with land as far as the eye could see and a lofty title to go with it. Even if Marielle was given a choice, she would never choose someone like him.

Anger at his foolish longings made him say in a tone more harsh than he intended, "Are you ready to move on?"

Marielle's head turned at once. She looked at him oddly. Her violet eyes burned with unshed tears.

"I'm sorry to bark at you so, Comtesse," he quickly apologized. "May I aid you in remounting?"

She nodded, a faraway look in her eyes. "Yes, please, if you would be so kind."

Ashby went to her and placed his hands around her waist. Marielle steadied herself by placing her own hands atop his forearms. He looked deeply into her eyes and caught sight of both fear and longing in them. He hesitated a moment, wanting to steal a kiss but the gentleman in him refused to yield to such temptation.

He lifted her gently onto her saddle, reluctant to release his grasp on her. He felt a slight tremble run through her and broke his hold. Quickly, he strode to his own horse and mounted but Marielle had already fled the glen they'd stopped in. Ashby took a deep breath and started after her. She knew the terrain, though, and used that knowledge to leave him quickly behind.

He wished she'd slow down. The ground was still damp from yesterday's rains, which made it slick in some spots. Twice, his own horse faltered and he adjusted his speed accordingly.

Not so Marielle. He could see her in the distance simply because of the scarlet and gold surcoat she wore that flashed between the trees. He breathed a sigh of relief as she exited the woods and galloped across the open field.

Then her horse stumbled, as if it had hit a hole in the soil. It wobbled and veered crazily, trying to regain its balance. She went sailing over the animal's head and hit the ground hard.

"Marielle!"

Ashby pushed his mount and reached her within seconds. He leaped from the saddle and bent down to where she lay still in the grass.

Turning her over to face him, he caught sight of a nasty bump already rising on her forehead. He touched it gently. Marielle frowned and a low moan escaped her lips.

His battlefield instincts kicked in. Ashby immediately checked her for broken bones. At first he remained dispassionate, concentrating on the task at hand. Yet with each passing moment, he became more aware of Marielle not as victim to an accident but as a woman, ripe and sensual.

Neither her arms nor her shoulders were broken in the fall. He could easily bend the joints at her elbows and wrists. One hand was badly scraped but every finger was intact. He took a deep breath and felt about her midsection, probing for broken ribs. His hand brushed against a full breast, instantly breaking his concentration. He cursed softly and continued, determined to see the task through, grateful she remained unconscious.

He pushed aside her skirts to her knees and continued his examination. He started at her ankles, moving up slender calves. His groin tightened and he fought the flood of emotion that poured through him. Ashby gritted his teeth and swallowed hard, bending Marielle's knees, finishing the last of the job with trembling hands.

Assured that she'd suffered no serious injury, he scooped her into his arms and held her close, a prayer on his lips for her to awaken to good health. He took her to his horse and managed to mount it with her in his arms. Ashby looked down at her still face, the long lashes swept down over those magnificent violet eyes.

Then succumbing to temptation, he bent and pressed his mouth softly against hers.

CHAPTER SEVEN

ASHBY RODE QUICKLY but carefully back to Monteville, which he could see in the distance. He didn't want to jar Marielle unnecessarily. He assured himself he'd seen men thrown in a similar fashion before. Other than the lump he'd spied upon her brow, she should wake with few problems. There'd been no broken bones and no bleeding. She would be fine.

Suddenly, she sneezed. Ashby pulled up on the reins, stopping his horse. Marielle opened her eyes for a moment and gazed at him, a frown wrinkling her brow. She sighed and her eyelids fluttered several times before they closed again. He spurred the horse on.

As he approached the chateau, he signaled to the man in the watchtower and the bridged lowered slowly. As he rode through the bailey, he cherished the last moments he held her close.

He'd never been in love. He hadn't really believed much in it until he'd witnessed Garrett and Madeleine together. Oh, he knew a handful of couples grew to love one another within their arranged marriages but he was used to more carefree emotions that he wore upon his sleeve. He rid himself of women and any feelings he had for them as easily as he changed tunics.

He thought back to some of the women he'd been involved with over the years. Few liaisons lasted beyond a fortnight. He'd been physically attracted to many of them, making love to them as a lute player makes love to his instrument. It had all been in the here and now, taking what he could for his own pleasure and returning as much of that pleasure as he could. No lasting feelings—no regrets—existed for him.

Until now. The woman in his arms held for him all that he ever desired. He enjoyed her mind as much as her beauty. She was someone he wanted to grow old with. Marielle was a woman who would never bore him. Why in Heaven's name must she already be wed? It brought a turmoil he'd never known before, misery to a life which had experienced no heartbreak.

Ashby dismounted and carried Marielle up the stairs to the chateau's entrance. The steward met them.

"La comtesse has taken a spill from her horse. Bring your healer to see to her needs."

Etienne nodded. "I'll find the comte, as well. He has just returned from his trip. In fact, he may be in his solar. Why don't you take la comtesse to her chamber?"

Ashby carried his precious burden up to her room, the now-bittersweet taste of the brief kiss still upon his lips. He placed her on her bed and ordered a lurking servant girl to set a fire. He tucked a blanket about Marielle, hoping to prevent possible shock.

Jean-Paul stepped through the connecting door, a glass of wine in his hand. He took a swig from it and belched loudly. "Good to see you, fitz Waryn. Thank you for bringing my errant wife home."

Ashby bristled at his uncaring attitude. He fought for composure before answering. "It could be serious, Comte. Mayhap you should come comfort Marielle in some small way."

Jean-Paul shook his head dismissively. "It's not the first time she has been thrown. It's merely another little mishap. Marielle takes far too many chances in the saddle. She has no more restraint than a child. I fear she will never mature."

His comments startled Ashby. *How dare he talk about Marielle in such a cavalier way!* She meant nothing more to de la Tresse than the plaything Ashby realized she must be to him.

"Do you mind if I stay with her a while? I feel responsible for her accident since I saw it happen.

We had become separated from the rest of the hunting party."

Jean-Paul shrugged. "Do as you please. Only make your way down by supper. Marielle has planned for a magician tonight." His eyes lit up at the mention of that. "I would not want you to miss such grand entertainment. And then we will conclude our business on the morrow."

"As you wish." Ashby kept his head bowed and his eyes lowered. He had no doubt of the rage that boiled within them. If he ventured to look at Jean-Paul de la Tresse, the man would be as good as dead. He was ready to strangle the nobleman at this very moment with his bare hands.

He wet a cloth and placed it over the bump, now big as a small hen's egg. Taking Marielle's hand in his, he noticed how cold she seemed. He wished the fire would spread its warmth faster. He wanted the healer to hurry and arrive. Ashby thought if only Jean-Paul could fall into his moat and drown, all Ashby's problems would be solved. He would sweep Marielle far away and keep her safe. Protected.

And loved. He would never let her go.

He took a deep breath and tried to still the tumult in his head.

MARIELLE COUGHED AND noticed how it made her head ache. She squeezed her eyes more tightly shut, willing the pain to flee. It didn't. Still, she realized she was warm and cozy in her own bed. Someone wonderfully masculine held her hand. She inhaled the air about her, picking up that scent she thought of as Ashby. It was full of the outdoors, clean and strong.

And totally irresistible.

His image filled her head. How unlike Jean-Paul Ashby was. She admired his strength and way of speech and quick wit. He displayed lovely manners and had a mouth that she longed to touch with just the tips of her fingers. Well, mayhap a quick touch of her lips to it, as well. She'd never kissed a man, though she'd longed for Guy to do so when she was young. The nuns would have called her longings wicked, but did not God bring into existence Adam and Eve to go forth and multiply across the face of His earth? If God invented kissing, surely He thought it fine to do so or He never would have created the idea.

Drowsily, she opened first one eye, and then the other. She was right. Ashby sat in a chair next to her bed, his hand wrapped around hers. She looked at him and was rewarded with a tender smile.

"How do you feel?" he asked.

She still wasn't sure. She tried to remember why she would be here but for the life of her she couldn't come up with a reason why.

He must have read her mind. "You fell from your horse, Marielle. I fear a hoof hit a hole and the creature lost its balance. As it fought to keep on its hooves, it tossed you from the saddle."

She nodded slowly. Pain sprang to her head immediately and she winced. "Is Jezebel all right?"

Ashby cocked his head. "If Jezebel is your horse, yes. The wicked little thing beat us back to Monteville. She's probably chomping on sweet hay and regaling her stablemates about today's adventure."

He grew more serious. "You'll be up and about soon. The healer has come and gone and pronounced you fine. No broken bones. Just a tap on the head. But you will need to stay abed for a few days. You'll need your rest."

She pushed her body back with her heels and gradually came to a sitting position. "I am a lost cause."

"No, you simply rode too fast. The rains from yesterday affected the ground. If you had it to do over again, I am sure you would slow down and pick your way more carefully."

Marielle thought how she'd been riding away from him, from all she longed for when she gazed at him. She'd been trapped in this mindless existence over seven years now. She tolerated it—until Ashby fitz Waryn arrived. With him came everything she'd ever wished for. When he left, and it would be soon, her life would become even more dull and dreary than ever.

"I wish I had fallen and broken my stupid neck," she told him, unhappiness washing over her in waves.

Ashby looked at her sternly. "No, Marielle. You must not speak that way." He tightened his grip on her hand and reached with his free hand to cradle her face with his palm. "You have too much to offer this world. Do not ever think of leaving it early."

She sensed a current running through them, binding them together for all eternity. His touch brought the same reaction each time. She knew in future nights when the loneliness hovered about her, she would remember this moment— their closeness, her hand nestled in his, his hand against her cheek.

Slowly, his fingers came around and cupped her chin. His thumb ran sensually over her lower lip. "You sense what is between us, even as I do?" he asked softly.

Marielle nodded. Her lips parted but no words came out. Ashby looked sadder than any man she'd ever seen, a look of pain and remorse that ran deep, etching lines into his face that hadn't been there previously.

As he brushed his thumb back and forth, he whispered, "And you understand much as I want to act upon this feeling, I cannot. For your sake."

Again, she nodded, her heart splitting in two. Minstrel's tales told of love at first sight but reality never measured up to those songs. Yet here she was, utterly, desperately in love with a man she'd met only two days ago.

"One kiss," she whispered. She did not want to beg. "Something to be treasured on those nights my longing for you is too great to bear."

Ashby hesitated. Marielle knew he would never do as she asked. As sensual a man as he was, he hadn't in him the ability to come between a husband and his wife, no matter how ravaged their relationship might be.

Instead, she reached a hand up to him and placed it around the nape of his neck, pulling him close to her. The instant their lips met, her bones melted. A sweetness greater than any honey she'd tasted poured from him. Marielle hungered for it. Without understanding why, her lips opened in invitation and his tongue swept against hers, becoming as one.

She became lost in the kiss, its warmth and desire enveloping her in a richness unknown until now. Time stood still. His fingers pushed into her hair, massaging her scalp, bringing a giddy tingling to her insides.

Marielle wanted him. She'd never felt desire—but she *would* have this man. Her fingers locked round his neck and sought to bring him closer but he resisted. He broke the kiss and looked at her with remorse.

"Alas, Marielle. I am contrite for my actions. Do not make me do something we would both regret."

"What might you regret, Ashby fitz Waryn?"

CHAPTER EIGHT

MARIELLE STEELED HERSELF and looked to the open doorway. Marc stood in it, his handsome face dark with anger.

"Regrets?" Ashby asked. He shrugged in the Gallic manner of those he'd witnessed around him. "I try not to focus on the past, de la Tresse. It's where all regrets hover like little hobgoblins. I prefer to look to the future."

He stood and bowed slightly to Marielle. "My only regret is challenging you, my dear comtesse, to race back to Monteville. I feel responsible for your unfortunate accident."

"No," she said quickly, taking up his strand of thought. "It was no one's fault but my own. I have won a reputation for being a bit too bold in the saddle. I thought I could win the dare. Please, rest easy, Ashby. I lay no blame at your door."

"Then I will bid you *adieu* until the morrow. I

know the healer will not allow you from your bed for this evening's festivities. I'm only sorry that you won't see the magician you hired work his magic."

Ashby walked to the door and good-naturedly slapped Marc on the back. "Shall we leave la comtesse to her rest now?" As he spoke, he guided Marc from the room and closed the door behind them.

Marielle's heart refused to be stilled at their leaving. First, thoughts of the tender yet passionate kiss she'd shared with Ashby continued to enthrall her. Before, she'd possessed no idea how quickly desire could spark between a man and a woman. All her silly childhood daydreams of Guy and her lackluster love life with Jean-Paul seemed to pale beside the single kiss she'd shared with Ashby fitz Waryn.

And what if anyone had seen them in their indiscretion? Marc appeared only moments after Ashby ended the heated kiss. Could he have witnessed it? The thought of what her brother-in-law would do or say to Jean-Paul caused her heart to beat erratically. Knowing Marc, he would simply use what he'd seen to blackmail her into doing the same with him.

The thought of her lips next to Marc's caused a deep disgust to rise within her. She loathed her husband's brother. Despite Marc's fine looks, he had a reptilian quality to him. He had annoyed her in the beginning when she'd first come as a new bride to Monteville. Now it ran much deeper. His penetrating looks greatly disturbed her. She would refuse to remain at Monteville once Jean-Paul went to meet his Maker. Already, she suspected her husband would not live many more years. He overexerted himself, working long hours. She'd seen his hands trembling at times, something he'd tried to hide from her. Once Jean-Paul was laid to rest, Marielle would have no reason to remain at Monteville.

She had few options. Going back to her parents' house and shop would begin a new nightmare, one she wasn't willing to accept. Returning to Sisters of Merciful Heart would be a wiser choice, though not ideal. The convent's abbess would take her in willingly, thanks to the wealth she would bring with her. Jean-Paul had gifted her with numerous pieces of jewelry over the years. The Sisters of Good Mercy would be more than willing to open their gates to a widow with such riches in her possession.

Those gates would provide her protection from any trouble Marc might cause. The nunnery would become her sanctuary from the world in general. Marielle still felt no vocation to the Church but she knew she would be given a place to live comfortably within the convent's walls when the time came.

How ironic that the very place she'd been

forced into by her parents so many years ago would be where she eagerly turned if Jean-Paul passed on without an heir. The thought saddened her, knowing it was likely that she would never hold her own babe in her arms. Instead she would spend her days living in a place that brought such miserable memories to her. Whenever she thought of the convent, Marielle couldn't help but think of her twin.

How she longed to make amends for poor Arielle's death. Yet in all these years, no one had ever mentioned her sister's name. Sweet, shy Arielle. Always wanting to be like her bold, brave sister. Always destined to remain a child in Marielle's mind.

She pushed aside the unpleasant memories. Her body throbbed still, as much from Ashby's kiss as the bruises from her fall. She drew the bedclothes about her and escaped into sleep.

"I FIND THAT impossible, fitz Waryn. For Lord Montayne to even think I would part with a rod of Monteville is out of the question. I don't care how much you're offering to pay."

Ashby quelled the disappointment that inadvertently rose within him. Garrett wanted more land to produce a new variety of wine, combining the reds from Chateau Branais with a white he would grow on the additional tract. He envisioned a new wine, different from anything yielded before.

Yet Ashby knew what Jean-Paul's response would be before he extended the offer. It bothered him nonetheless. He rarely failed Garrett in matters of business. He would not be eager to return to Stanbury with this news.

He took one more stab. "Lord Montayne is willing to part with—"

"I care not what some English lord thinks he will give me in return. I would have to be dead and buried before I give over any part of Monteville."

Ashby sighed inwardly. At least he'd steeled himself for this expected reply. He was still tottering gingerly about on other matters. Try as he may, he had not discovered if Marc de la Tresse saw him kiss Marielle yesterday afternoon. He'd tried to guide his conversation with de la Tresse without revealing anything the younger man was not privy to. All last night as they'd dined on venison and mutton, on starlings and chickens, he gently probed and pushed.

The Frenchman hadn't budged. Even deep into his cups as the evening progressed and the magician cast a spell over his audience, Ashby still couldn't guess if Marc had seen their kiss and was waiting to cause mischief later or if he'd arrived just after the kiss took place. Either way, it made Ashby uneasy.

Yet the younger de la Tresse brother had been present all morning as Ashby outlined why Garrett wanted to add the small piece of land to his property that was adjacent to Monteville. If Marc had witnessed anything amiss, surely he would have revealed it to Jean-Paul by now. Maybe it was the guilt eating away at him but a sudden idea occurred to Ashby.

What if Marc had seen their embrace and would continue to withhold the information from Jean-Paul after Ashby left Monteville? What if he used it to blackmail Marielle? The thought of her at Marc's mercy turned his stomach sour.

Ashby rolled up the scroll that Garrett had drawn upon, the better to show Jean-Paul his future plans for Chateau Branais and the new wine he wished to attempt using a part of Monteville land.

"I'm sorry we are not able to conclude a fair price and make this exchange," Ashby told the owner of Monteville. "Still, I must thank you for all your kindness and hospitality." He indicated Jean-Paul's vineyard manager. "Donatien has been most gracious in sharing his knowledge with me. I hope to implement several of his ideas in Lord Montayne's vineyards here."

Jean-Paul burst out in raucous laughter. "You would change Pierre Bouchard's mind on how to run Chateau Branais?" He slapped Ashby on the back. "That comment alone was worth your coming to stay at Monteville."

Jean-Paul looked to Marc and then Donatien. "Can you imagine Pierre altering his ways?"

Both men suppressed smiles and shook their heads. Donatien looked to Ashby and said, "If it's not the way the Bouchards did it a hundred years ago, then it will never occur at Branais. Pierre is more set in his ways than an old man such as Robert Bouchard. Now mind you, the Bouchards produce a fine merlot and a very decent cabernet but our way at Monteville has always been to continue to strive for something better."

Ashby inclined his head to the trio gathered around him. "I understand. I do thank you for hearing out Lord Montayne's proposal." He slipped the scroll under his arm. "I think I will return to the Bouchards now. Nothing else holds me here."

He looked at Jean-Paul and added, "Please give my best to Marielle. I know she is still resting. I would not want to disturb her. She was an excellent hostess during my stay. I hope to see you all again someday."

Jean-Paul walked him to the stairs. "You are welcome any time, fitz Waryn. Lord Montayne, as well. I remember him from his trip to France several years ago. He knew nothing of the grape when he arrived in Bordeaux. He left with quite a bit of knowledge."

"I will pass along your compliment, Comte. Good day to you."

Ashby went up the stairs and packed the few items he brought with him. Most of his belongings had remained at Chateau Branais during his quick visit to Monteville. He hated leaving without wishing Marielle goodbye but he thought it best. Marc obviously had seen nothing untoward or he would have spoken to his brother by now. Ashby thought it easier to leave quietly without drawing any further attention his and Marielle's way.

He also knew if he saw her again, his willpower would crumble. He would take her into his arms and do much more than kiss her. He wanted to possess her. That one kiss had already catapulted him into eternal damnation, for he now coveted another man's wife—and would until his dying day. He would even go to Hell gladly, the taste of Marielle always with him, for there could be no Heaven for him without her by his side.

Ashby wondered if he was forever condemned to be attracted to other men's wives. Madeleine had been married to Henri de Picassaret when he first met her. Not that she let that little tidbit escape. No, without knowing whom she spoke with on a deserted road to London, she boldly told him and Garrett that she was wife to Lord Montayne, not realizing that Garrett *was* Lord Montayne.

She might as well have been wed to Garrett. Ashby had never seen his friend become so intrigued and so possessive of a woman in such a short time as he did with Madeleine. Ashby hadn't stood a chance with Madeleine and had, in fact, moved aside with haste in order to enjoy watching Garrett's pursuit of the mysterious French maid.

Yet despite his deep friendship with Madeleine these last few years, Ashby increasingly found himself attracted to her in recent months. It was one of the reasons he leaped at the chance to come to France and put distance between them.

Now he'd met another French wife and fallen madly, utterly in love with her. He wondered if he always wanted the unattainable or if it was simply a strange quirk of fate. Regardless, he was gentleman enough not to act upon his impulses, no matter how they sang through his veins at the moment. Marielle's life was at Monteville with Jean-Paul de la Tresse, be it for better or worse. He would not come between the husband and wife.

Mayhap he should have joined the Church after all, he mused. That would have ruled out the possibility of marriage forever.

Ashby took one final glance about the room

where he had savored thoughts of Marielle most of last night. He closed the chamber's door behind him and turned only to find his way blocked.

"You would leave? Not even say *au revoir* to me?" Marielle's eyes glistened with unshed tears.

His mouth grew dry. All flippant remarks died upon his lips. God in His Heaven, he wanted this woman.

She looked in both directions then slipped her hand past his side, opening the door he'd just shut. He knew what she intended yet he was powerless to stop her. Ashby willingly backed into the empty chamber. Marielle followed him and eased the door closed behind her.

He dropped the satchel in his hands and moved toward her, pulling her into his arms even as his mouth came down hard upon hers.

CHAPTER NINE

MARC HAD ACCUSED her of playing with fire but Marielle suddenly knew what he meant. Her body was ablaze at Ashby's touch, molding itself to him as desire rushed through her. He groaned deep in his throat, causing shivers to dance up her spine.

He tore his lips from hers and trailed fiery kisses down the column of her throat. Her head fell back and he greedily took in more, then brought her even more tightly to him.

Breathless, Marielle wanted to tell him she loved him, wanted to shout it from the watchtower over the valley below. Yet his mouth was on hers again as he turned them. He pushed her against the door, his feet straddling her on both sides, trapping her, dominating her, causing her very blood to sing. His hands moved to her waist, the fingers slowly kneading her like a cat before they crept up to her breasts.

At his touch, the nipples flared to a life of their own, standing erect, aching for his hands on them. He moved over them gently yet firmly, his touch expert. What was she to expect? A man like Ashby fitz Waryn must have had many lovers over the years yet he was the kind of man who would please as much as he wanted to be pleased.

Slowly his thumbs began a circle that lingered lovingly, magically. They would have driven her mad had it not been for his mouth still on hers, his tongue probing, dancing, smooth as silk against her own.

Then, as suddenly as his onslaught had begun, it ended, his hands releasing her, his body moving away. Marielle's knees buckled without his support. He caught her before she fell, bringing her against him again, murmuring nonsense against her hair, stroking it, assuring her.

Finally, he stopped. He gripped her elbows and pushed her slightly away from him, studying her with a look of sadness no woman should ever have to face.

"Oh, Sweet Jesu," he whispered, his eyes roaming over her, as if he were memorizing her every feature. He bent and softly brushed his lips against hers once more and then stepped back.

"Forgive me, Marielle," he said, his words so low she strained to hear them. "God forgive us both."

With that, he reached down and retrieved his things and left the room.

Ashby was gone.

Shaken, Marielle stumbled to the bed he'd slept upon. She lay upon it, wanting her head to touch where his had rested. His fresh, clean scent assaulted her nostrils. The lump in her throat rose until she wouldn't have been able to speak if spoken to.

Gently, Marielle brought her fingertips to swollen her lips. She ran them over and over where he had kissed her. She longed to cry but, strangely, no tears fell. It was as if she floated through a dream world.

Silently, she stood and collected herself before she moved toward the door. She opened it carefully and looked out. She saw no one in the dim hallway. She made her way back to her own chamber without being seen and crawled into bed.

Dry-eyed, she stared at the ceiling and wished her husband were dead.

TWO DAYS HAD passed since Ashby fitz Waryn's departure from Monteville. To Marielle, it felt more like two decades. She did not come down that first night, thankful the healer ordered bed rest after her fall. Jean-Paul chose not to visit her and she was grateful for his absence by her bedside. She didn't want his image to dispel Ashby's. Marielle spent the night concocting wild daydreams of her and Ashby together, forever, living with adoring children surrounding them and the goodwill of all.

She awakened from a restless sleep to an ache that was more than physical. She thought it would be simpler to rip her heart from her breast than experience the pain she experienced. To make matters worse, Jean-Paul arrived in her chamber that afternoon. Her head pounded from lying abed. He opened the door that connected her chamber to the solar and inquired politely after her health.

Could he not look at her and see she was dying inside?

She courteously responded that she was better without much thought. Then he'd snapped his fingers and a chill rushed through her.

"I am so happy you have fully recovered, *ma chère.*"

His endearment sickened her as much as the gesture. When her husband snapped in such a manner, he wanted her physically.

Wordlessly, as if following her executioner, Marielle left her bed and joined him in his. At his first touch, she withdrew in mind and spirit. She lay there, unmoving, unemotional, while he rutted away, oblivious that she was miles away. She had never loved him and, after years, no longer even cared for him. He simply fulfilled his needs, using her, with no thought to her pleasure.

After he finished, he rolled off her. "You seem in much better health now. I will expect you to join Marc and me at supper tonight."

With another wave of his hand, she left him and returned to her chamber. She immediately called for hot water and scrubbed herself raw everywhere he had touched.

Now she sat upon the dais, a wooden smile plastered across her face. Not that Jean-Paul would notice it. He talked and drank and ate without needing any response from her or Marc. Marielle nodded occasionally, which was all Jean-Paul asked of her.

Before the servants brought the last course, she asked him, "Would you mind if I retire early? I still am feeling out of sorts."

He studied her a moment before answering. "You do seem a bit pale. You must not rush things, Wife. Get abed now and in the morning, I am sure you will have regained your full strength."

In a surprising gesture, he kissed her on the cheek and added, "I know how you love your tapestry-weaving. I would not want to keep you from it too long."

Marielle held her sanity and gave him a vacuous smile. If she had her way, she'd run through the castle this very minute and rip down every tapestry on its walls. Instead, she curtsied and left the great hall.

Once in her bedchamber, she undressed and climbed into bed, despite the fact that she knew sleep would be impossible. Her bed was fast becoming a refuge for her, an escape from the world. Maybe Hell would be living this day over and over again for eternity—the emptiness inside, enduring Jean-Paul's touch, the mindless supper.

She must have drifted off because she woke with a sudden start. Jean-Paul moaned, loudly enough for her to hear from the next room. Marielle tossed on a dressing gown and padded softly over to listen at the door. Another groan sounded and she knew her husband was in severe pain. She tightened the dressing gown about her and opened the door to go to him. A candle still glowed next to his bed. Marielle could see a fine sheen of sweat across his brow.

"What ails you, Jean-Paul?" she asked gently.

"Nothing," he growled back, his disposition sour. Since they'd been wed, he'd only fallen ill twice. He'd been surly and mean both times so Marielle kept her distance and let the healer tend to his complaints. Only afterward, when he was weakened by the effects of fever and vomiting, had she ventured to sit by him.

Tonight looked to be much of the same.

"Shall I call the healer to look in on you?"

He winced with pain. His stomach gurgled loudly. "No!" he roared. "It's just some stomach ailment. I will simply sit upon my chamber pot and let it flow forth from me. Be gone. I have no need of you or any healer."

Marielle flinched at his harsh words but tried not to take them to heart. Her father was much the same as her husband, not one to abide pain well or treat those around him with decency when ill.

"Call if you have need of me."

She backed away and returned to her own room, leaving the door slightly ajar so she could hear him if he cried out for her. She doffed her dressing gown and climbed into bed, lying there listening for him. She heard grunts and groans for over half an hour before the sounds subsided. Marielle crept back and peeked through the slit in the door.

Jean-Paul lay on his back, snoring softly, his face still contorted with the remaining pain he must feel. She was reassured that the worst of his discomfort had passed and shut the door completely before returning to bed.

Exhausted, she fell into a dreamless sleep.

A sudden shaking roused her. Marielle opened eyes heavy with sleep to find a dark shape hovering over her. A faint light came from Jean-

Paul's room.

"He is dead," the shadowy figure hissed at her. "I hope you are satisfied."

Marielle sat up, pulling the bedclothes tightly around her. She was very aware that it was Marc that stood next to her bed and that he held her dressing gown in his hands.

"Put this on." He tossed the wrap at her but made no move to turn away. Awkwardly, Marielle tried to bring it under the covers so she could slide it about her. In disgust, he finally walked away, back into Jean-Paul's solar.

Marielle quickly slipped on the dressing gown and tied its belt about her waist. She followed Marc and gasped when she entered the room.

Jean-Paul still lay on his back, his tongue protruding from his mouth, thick and discolored. His eyes were wide, staring blankly, fear etched into them. Marielle bit back the scream that threatened to fight free. She went to her husband's bedside and silently said a quick prayer as she drew the sheet over him.

"What happened?" Marc demanded.

"I . . . I do not know," she stammered. "He came to bed with stomach pains last night. He was irritable, as usual, when he was in less than full health."

She pushed a hand through her hair and shook her head. "He was up awhile with the pains and then he fell asleep. He was snoring peacefully when I last looked in on him."

Her brother-in-law looked at her grimly. "You know it was poison."

Marielle's heart lurched. She had guessed Jean-Paul's heart had finally given out. "Are you certain?" she asked.

"They will think it was you, Marielle."

"Me?" A thousand thoughts that whirled through her mind came to a screeching halt. "I did not kill my husband, Marc." She swallowed. *"I did not kill him."*

"It won't look like that to the world, my dearest sister. You have never cared a whit for my brother. You flirted outrageously with fitz Waryn. I would think that some might even surmise you broke your marriage vows for the Englishman."

She felt her face grow hot. "No! I did not!" she denied, but guilt poured through her. She may not have coupled physically with Ashby, but even to have allowed him to kiss and touch her was a sin. Jean-Paul considered her his property. To violate her in any way would have been just grounds for him to lock his wife away for all time.

Marc contemplated her words. "Mayhap there is a way out," he said cautiously.

"What?" she asked, sounding overeager even to her own ears.

"You would ask my help?" He studied her leisurely. Marielle's blush grew hotter. She clasped the dressing gown more tightly about her.

"Yes," she said, her voice but a whisper.

"I do not think you will be accused outright," he said slowly. "I would think Jean-Paul would be laid to rest before the rumors would rise in full force." He clucked his tongue. "Rumors can be so nasty, you know. It only takes a breadcrumb of truth before they spread."

A chill ran through her. Marc was now the comte, which made him all-powerful. Still, she couldn't appear weak to him, despite feeling more vulnerable than she ever had.

"Rumors are not facts, Marc," she said simply. "No proof can be produced that I poisoned Jean-Paul simply because I did not do so. You can attest to that. You are Comte de la Tresse now. If you vouch for me—for my innocence—then no one will dare cross you." Hating to grovel, she added, "I would so appreciate your support."

His eyes gleamed and, for a moment, Marielle thought he might have gone mad. Then she realized he merely gloated with the power that had been bestowed upon him with Jean-Paul's sudden death.

"Why would I proclaim your innocence, Marielle?"

"Why wouldn't you?" she countered boldly though panic flitted through her.

"Should I explain what will happen to you if I

claim you poisoned my beloved brother?" he demanded sharply, causing her to wince.

"You were a common woman. Not one of the aristocracy. Mayhap I will proclaim you are a witch who placed a spell upon my brother, forcing him to wed you. Would you care to burn at the stake?"

Marielle wrapped her arms tightly about her, trying to stop the abrupt shudders that had begun with Marc's threats.

"Or I could say you were merely a commoner who married far above her class, seeking wealth and position," he mused. "Who are you really, Marielle? The low-born daughter of a carpet trader. A woman who has produced no sons for her husband. One who was plucked from obscurity in order to bring Jean-Paul the heir he longed for. Yet no children resulted from your marriage. One in which you were unfaithful. Not only with fitz Waryn but perhaps a score of others."

His tone, full of malevolence, frightened her beyond measure.

"I can summon the magistrate, Marielle. You said so yourself. I am the powerful Comte de la Tresse now. I share the tale I wish with the magistrate. What will it be? One of unfaithfulness, malice, and murder? Or one of support for my beloved brother's poor, youthful widow? The choice is yours."

He took a step closer to her and brushed a lock of hair from her cheek. Marielle stood her ground, not backing away from him.

"I think it best to protect you—and the estate—we should marry immediately."

"What?" His words blindsided her. "Are you mad?"

He smiled, the light playing shadows across his features, making him more ominous than ever before. Suddenly, Marielle's heart told her that Marc had poisoned his own brother.

All to claim her and Monteville.

He took her chin in hand and said, "Oh, yes, I'm quite serious, Marielle. Never more so."

"But . . . but . . . there would be talk. I mean, if we were to wed so soon after Jean-Paul's death."

Marc held her chin firmly. "There might be some but it would die down. As long as things continue to run smoothly as they have in the past, most people will be perfectly content to continue as they have before."

His fingers tightened on her jaw to the point of pain but she remained stoic.

"I trust that you will make the right decision, Marielle. The one in your best interest. You have no wish to burn at the stake as a witch. Or hang for murder. You will wed me because no one would believe your story. Everyone would believe mine."

He loosened his grip and his fingers caressed her cheek. "You will be mine, Marielle. You will provide me with physical pleasure multiple times a day. You will give birth to my heir. I believe we will be blessed with many children.

"Or your days on this earth shall be numbered."

She understood Marc held all the power. He could make his assertions to the magistrate. His lies would break her. Yet she fought capitulating to him, the idea of spending the rest of her life with such a loathsome man controlling her every action terrifying.

"And if I choose not to wed you?" She tried to keep the defiant edge from her tone but heard it come through nevertheless.

He stroked her cheek lightly. "I would hate to be the one that started—or confirmed—any rumors we just discussed." His eyes glittered with both lust and greed.

"So what will it be, Marielle? Will you wed me or suffer the consequences?"

CHAPTER TEN

MARIELLE TOOK A calming breath as the priest chanted in Latin. His tones soothed her like nothing else had since Marc came to her bed with his offer of marriage. The thought made her stomach queasy again, though no food has passed her lips today.

Many vineyard workers and servants had gathered to see Jean-Paul de la Tresse put to rest. He'd been a steady figure known to his people. Marielle had desperately wanted to get word to Ashby yesterday when Marc made it known that Jean-Paul died in the night despite the ministrations of his fair wife. She guessed Marc knew she would try to do so when she suggested sending a rider to the Bouchards with the message of Jean-Paul's sudden death.

"No, my Marielle," he said in gentle tones. "The Bouchards need not come to the funeral mass. Robert and Pierre were not especially close to Jean-Paul."

"But Cadena—"

"Cadena Bouchard could comfort you no better than I." His gaze pierced her. "I would think that family would be all you wanted right now." He put a reassuring arm about her and she forced herself not to shy away.

"Maybe if *Maman* and—"

"I did send word to your parents. I know it's been years since you have seen them. At their age, though, it would be far too long a journey for them to undertake. Besides, we will bury Jean-Paul long before they could arrive."

Marielle had pleaded with Marc. "Mayhap I could go for a short visit to see them." She hoped he would think they would marry upon her return.

He said as much. "I suppose I see no harm in a brief visit. Then you would return home for our marriage?" He brooded upon that for a minute. "That might be acceptable."

They'd left it at that. Marielle was in a quandary. Should she go to Libourne and then refuse to return? She could take her jewels with her and after seeing her parents, she could go directly outside the city to the nuns at Sisters of Merciful Heart. Once inside, Marc would have no way of forcing her to the altar.

Oh, why hadn't her husband given her a son?

Marielle wouldn't be in such a difficult position now if that were the case. With no heir, the Monteville lands and title of comte now reverted to Marc, Jean-Paul's closest male relative. As custom allowed, Marielle should be able to live her remaining days in her home under Marc's protection. With Marc threating that she might be implicated in Jean-Paul's death, though, she must leave for the nunnery and the sanctuary it provided.

Yet what her heart cried out for her to do was head straight for Chateau Branais and find Ashby fitz Waryn. She was free now. They could return to England and marry. Marc de la Tresse be damned!

Sudden doubts plagued Marielle. Would the dashing Englishman even want to wed her? Even though he acted as a gentleman and stopped their indiscretion after two searing kisses, they had been passionate ones. They moved Marielle to her very soul. Surely it was not a simple flirtation on Ashby's part. No two people could share such an experience without wanting to be together forever. Could they?

She must proceed as if she knew Ashby had definite feelings for her. She must believe that he would act upon those feelings once he knew she was now a widow, especially one in danger of being falsely accused of murder. If her instincts proved incorrect, then she hoped the dashing

Englishman would see her to the convent's gates.

The trouble was how to get word to Ashby without arousing Marc's suspicions. Surely, he would find out if she said she were going in one direction and then took another. Marc had already mentioned providing her with an armed guard to escort her to Libourne. It would leave in two days' time though it would head in the opposite direction of the Bouchards and Chateau Branais.

Her mind continued its scattered whirl through the rest of the funeral mass and burial. Marielle thought things hopeless. Marc remained closely by her as they returned to the chateau and he now escorted her into the great hall for the midday meal.

"I find I must go to Biarritz for a couple of weeks. Business of Jean-Paul's which is unavoidable. A messenger arrived just this morning. Will that trouble you, *ma chère*?

Marielle's heart almost leaped from within her from sheer joy. She tamped down her excitement and calmly replied, "You must attend to the business at hand, Marc. Jean-Paul was very conscientious about all affairs regarding Monteville. I would expect you to do no less."

He led her to the dais and sat beside her. "Then I will do as my brother's widow requests. Do you still plan to visit your parents?"

Marielle frowned. "I may. I may not. I hate to

leave if you are to be gone, too. Whatever you think best, Marc. I trust your judgment."

She knew she'd fed his ego as he visibly puffed up. "I would see no problem with you going as planned. In fact, it might do you some good."

Marielle sighed. "It will take me a day or two to have my things prepared for the trip. I must think of gifts to bring both of my parents. I would not arrive without them."

"Do as you see fit." Marc drained the wine from his cup and motioned a servant for more.

She contained her growing excitement and listlessly stared at the trencher. "Marc?"

He turned and studied her. "What is it?"

"I find I have no appetite after burying my husband. I would rather go and lie down for a while. I can always have something brought to my chamber later if I grow hungry."

"Suit yourself. I will leave after this noon meal at any rate."

"Thank you."

Marielle rose and walked slowly across the great hall, wishing she could skip across as a child might. She ascended the stairs to her room and shut the door. Only then did she break into a smile.

First, she must pack. She wouldn't carry much in the way of clothing. She would take her small casket, however. Every piece of jewelry

Jean-Paul had given her would go in it. Marielle nervously paced her room, collecting her thoughts. Then she went to the window and looked down into the yard. She would wait for Marc to leave before she acted.

Thoughts of her brother-in-law bursting in upon her with some last minute instructions caused her to pause. She had no lock upon her chamber door, and even if she could lock it, she might raise Marc's suspicions. No, she would still her racing heart and gain control of her emotions. She would plan what must be done as soon as Marc left the walls of Monteville.

She only waited a quarter-hour before she saw Marc ride out with three other knights accompanying him. It was safe to put her plan into action.

Quickly, Marielle assembled what she wanted into the container. Everything fit nicely. She removed a small leather satchel which would easily hold the casket. No one could see it with her cloak wrapped about her and she could tie it to Jezebel's saddle.

She then removed her surcoat and cotehardie and placed a second kirtle over the first she already wore. She replaced the cotehardie and then layered another one on top of it. The surcoat went back on top of it all. It was a bit bulky but once her cloak was placed over it all, it would be easy to hide her extra layers of clothing.

Marielle looked about her chamber, wishing she could take her books along. They would be too cumbersome, though. She took out one from under her pillow and stroked it fondly. Many times, it had served as a close friend during her lonely hours. With regret, she slipped it back into its hiding place and went to the window.

All she needed now was for Ashby to cooperate. She pushed that thought aside. If he refused to aid her, she would then make her way to Libourne and go to her parents as originally planned. She wanted to see them once more before she went to Sisters of Merciful Heart.

Marielle made her way downstairs and told a page to go to the stables and have her horse saddled. She passed Etienne and thought it best to tell him her whereabouts.

"I am going to pay a call to the Bouchards and inform them of Jean-Paul's death. Marc had not thought it necessary but I would like them to know."

The steward nodded. "They will be grateful for your visit, la comtesse."

"I'm also to visit my parents in Libourne."

Etienne nodded. "Le comte informed me of your plans and asked that I have a guard assembled to accompany you the day after tomorrow."

"Thank you."

Marielle left and found the horse already

awaiting her. Thanks to its close proximity, she had never taken a guard with her on her visits to Chateau Branais. She looked about for anything out of the ordinary, trying to determine if anyone was watching her. Fortunately, Marc had no close friends at Monteville. His rudeness toward servants and knights alike now worked in her favor. She doubted he would have anyone spying on her actions while he was gone. He wasn't bright enough to have thought of it in the first place. If he had, she was confident no one would follow through. Things might change as he assumed the reins of Monteville upon his return but, for now, Marielle felt safe.

"Have the watchman lower the bridge for me," she told the eager page who held her horse. "I go to visit with our neighbors, the Bouchards, and plan to tell them of my husband's death."

The boy was off and running before he'd even helped her mount her horse. Marielle tied the heavy satchel containing her casket to the saddle and then used the steps leading down into the bailey to mount Jezebel. She settled herself nicely and held her head high. She wanted to draw no suspicion and strove to act as if nothing were out of place.

As she approached, the bridge was lowered for her. She gave a wave to the guards along the wall-walk and in the tower and set out at a gentle trot. She passed workers in the vineyards and waved at a few of them, too.

Marielle kept repeating to herself under her breath, "You are calm. You are tranquil. You are in control of this situation. You can do this. You must do this." The words did soothe her and she began to relax as she rode further away from Monteville.

That estate and Chateau Branais literally touched one other so it was difficult to tell when she'd left the first behind and come upon the latter. She did see riders on the road before her. She recognized Cadena's horse before she did Cadena herself.

Marielle waved to them and spurred Jezebel on. They met in the middle. It was both Cadena and her husband, Robert. Marielle looked at her old friends for the first time with new eyes. These two were the parents of the wonderful Madeleine, Lady Montayne, whom Ashby seemed to admire quite a bit.

"Oh, my dear," said Cadena. She leaned over and hugged Marielle carefully. "I am so sorry to hear about Jean-Paul. It was sudden, was it not?"

"Yes. He complained of jarring stomach pains that night. By morning, he was dead."

"One of your workers told one of ours. We just now heard the news," Robert Bouchard said gruffly. "We would have come to the funeral mass this morning if we'd known earlier."

Marielle bit her lip. She needed to be diplomatic. It was a very tricky situation to let the Bouchards know how she valued their friendship without seeming to turn them against Marc.

Robert scratched his chin in thought. "Never mind. Your silence confirms what I told Cadena. We weren't informed because of that bloody Marc de la Tresse."

Bloody? Marielle wasn't sure exactly what that meant, other than it had been Marc's fault.

Cadena threw her husband a look. "Robert, you are not to use that word outside the house. I have warned you about it before."

Robert looked surprisingly sheepish. Marielle glanced back at Cadena.

"I have told you I hail from England originally, my dear. Well, I taught Robert a word or two of English that he had not previously known. Let us say he is not very happy with Marc de la Tresse at the moment."

"*Zut!* Of course, I am not happy with the oaf. Not telling his own neighbors his brother has passed away? Unthinkable." Robert cleared his throat. "Anyway, we were on our way to see you and express our sincere condolences for such a loss."

"Thank you," Marielle said quietly. She treasured the Bouchards and wished she had seen more of them over the years. If their Madeleine was as gracious and kind as her parents were, she deserved Ashby's praise.

"I was on my way to see you. And your guest," she added.

"Ashby?" Cadena smiled. "That boy would charm the horns from the Devil himself. I am sorry to say he has just left us to return to England."

Marielle's smile faltered. "He's already gone?"

"Yes," Robert said. "He left about the same time we did from Branais. He was headed up to Pauillac. He will take the Gironde from there to the Bay of Biscay and, from there, make his way to London."

She took a deep breath. "Then I must plead with you not to mention you saw me or gave me that information."

Cadena's eyes narrowed. "And why is that?"

"It's much too long to tell now, Cadena. Suffice it to say Marc plans to force me to wed him in a few weeks. I am foolishly pinning all my hopes on Ashby to help extricate me from that situation."

She knew she was blessed with these friends when Robert quickly asked, "Shall I ride with you on the road he took? Ashby could not be more than ten minutes ahead."

"That is kind of you, but no. I do not want anyone blaming you for helping me to escape."

Robert looked upon her in a fatherly manner. "Then I shall send a servant to Monteville in two hours' time and tell them you are dining with us tonight. That we have extended an invitation for you to stay the night and share your sorrows with us."

Marielle looked at him in surprise. "You would do that for me?"

Robert's lips trembled. "I made a mistake years ago with my own daughter, Madeleine. I sent her into a marriage with a man so horrible that she eventually fled his home."

He took Marielle's hand in his. "I would not see another such marriage come to pass."

Robert reviewed with her once again which way to ride as Cadena stroked her arm as a loving mother might.

"May the Living Christ be with you," Cadena called out and Marielle spurred her horse on.

If ever her riding skills came in handy, this would be the one day, the one hour, she would most need them. She whispered her own prayer in her mind and rode as if the Devil himself pursued her.

CHAPTER ELEVEN

ASHBY RODE AT an easy gait, his horse responsive to direction. The infected hoof that afflicted Lightning had healed during his time in France. He was glad to be on his own mount again and not a borrowed steed. He would need to ride a little over twelve miles to reach Pauillac, where a small vessel awaited him.

Garrett insisted on keeping the ship there. Relations between England and France were strained ever since Edward claimed the French throne over Philip. The Flemish rebellion and subsequent alliance with England only aggravated matters. Though Garrett deemed it safe enough for Ashby to travel to Bordeaux, he wanted a quick means of escape for his friend in case he found himself in dire straits. With England's domination of the Channel, Ashby knew he would be safe once he boarded the ship for England and it pushed away from France.

While his body might return to his home-land, Ashby would leave his heart in France's wine country, in the hands of a woman he barely knew and yet loved with a fierce passion. No woman had come close to stealing his heart before now. With just a few impish smiles, Marielle de la Tresse had taken his very soul into her hands.

And he would never see her again.

Of course, he promised the Bouchards he'd come again, bringing Madeleine and Garrett and the children with him when he called. He told them a thousand stories of their daughter and her happy life at Stanbury. Robert and Cadena already seemed like family to him. He would regret not seeing them in the future.

Yet how could he? He could not trust himself to land on French soil again—else he'd foolishly challenge Jean-Paul de la Tresse to a duel. He had wild fantasies about sweeping Marielle away with him. That was an impossible dream. Where would a third son, landless and untitled, take a married, wealthy comtesse? If his heart wasn't breaking, the situation would almost be comical.

No, he would return to Stanbury and contin-ue his work for Garrett. He knew his place there. He would keep his hands and his mind busy. He would make do. Ashby idly thought about a comely widow in the village nearby. Mayhap he would pay a call upon her when he returned.

He shrugged the idea off, the thought leaving his mouth like sand. No woman appealed to him at this moment. He doubted one ever would.

Sudden hoof beats interrupted his thoughts. Immediately, Ashby was alert. He pulled around and stilled his horse, peering down the road he'd just ridden. He saw a single horse in the distance, a small dot on the horizon. The rider was skilled; the speed, incredible.

He questioned what kind of man would push a horse in such a manner. It put him on edge. Was it a rider with news for the king? Had England made a sudden move against France in their dormant war? Would he be caught up in the turmoil?

His eyes followed the form as it approached, his hand poised atop his dagger. He crouched low in the saddle until, suddenly, his heart tossed wildly inside his chest. He recognized Marielle coming toward him. Ashby slipped from his mount to await her arrival. No thoughts formed clearly in his head. He wanted to reprimand her for coming. What kind of excuse would she give, riding out alone with no guard, so far from Monteville? He shuddered at the consequences of her foolish actions.

Before he could chastise her about such a dangerous act she was there, sliding from the saddle, her face a mixture of panic and relief. She fell into his arms and clung to him tightly, breathing heavily, gripping him as if her life depended upon him. Tremors ran through her as if she'd been chased by death—and barely escaped it. Ashby had seen men like this after a battle, their ragged emotions worn on their sleeves, their legs barely holding their weight.

He wrapped his arms around her, willing his warmth to surge through her. "Are you all right?"

"No!" Marielle withdrew from him, her eyes wide, almost fearful. "You must take me with you," she demanded. "Jean-Paul is dead."

"What?" Ashby grabbed on to her shoulders, shaking her. "What did you say?"

"Jean-Paul was poisoned." She took a deep breath. "I believe Marc had a hand in it."

Though his mind reeled at the accusation, Ashby turned rational. He lowered his hands and calmly asked, "Why do you think that?"

Marielle frowned. She shook her head several times before she spoke. She squeezed her eyes tightly shut, as if trying to see something.

"I have always disliked Marc," she ventured softly. Her eyes opened and she continued. "He has always made me feel . . . unclean. He looks at me as if I am . . ." Her voice faded, but Ashby knew exactly what she meant.

"Go on," he prodded gently.

Marielle bit her lip. "He woke me very early to tell me Jean-Paul had been poisoned. I saw the body. I don't know what a poisoning would look like but I know my husband's death was unnatural."

She hesitated a moment. "Marc insinuated, at first, that I would be blamed. That rumors already swirled about. He said I had flirted with you. He even accused me of breaking my marital vows."

Ashby drew in a sharp breath. Marielle looked at him sympathetically and took his hand.

"A comte is like a king on his own estate," she explained. "Everyone from peasants to merchants do whatever is in their power to please him. Marc is already drunk with power now that Jean-Paul's title and wealth have passed to him. Whatever he says will be believed by the local authorities. He told me he would summon the magistrate and tell him one of two things."

"What?" he asked, afraid to hear the choices, which wouldn't be choices at all.

"Marc first said he would accuse me of witchcraft. Of casting a spell upon Jean-Paul in order for him to take me as his wife. If he does this, his claim alone—with no proof produced—would be enough to see me burned at the stake."

He squeezed her hand, words failing him.

"Or he said he would claim I had murdered Jean-Paul. That I was an unhappy wife who engaged in affairs and wanted to be free of my husband. Once again, it would take no evidence of this action. The accusation of a comte would be enough to see me swing from a gibbet. Either way, my life will end painfully. No one will care that I am innocent of any charges. Marc will have spoken. That will be enough to see me gone."

Ashby's head swirled with the choices Marc de la Tresse had offered Marielle. He had known English lords held immense power but a French comte seemed to have even more sway in France.

"Of course, he gave me a much different choice than dying. He said I must marry him to end the rumors. That he would protect both me and Monteville. No harm would come to me under the blanket of his protection because I would be his wife." She paused and gazed into Ashby's eyes. "At that moment, I saw within him a greed that would stop at nothing. I knew how deeply his jealousy ran. How much he despised Jean-Paul and how he'd longed for Monteville for so many years."

She dropped his hand and turned away. "And how he hungered for me."

Ashby placed his hands upon her shoulders again. She lay a hand atop one of his. "I have seen desire in his eyes for many years yet I convinced myself nothing could possibly come of it. I had my husband's protection. Marc might have been jealous of his older brother but he was also afraid of him."

She gazed up at Ashby, grinding out her

words. "I should have warned Jean-Paul. I could have done something. I—"

Marielle burst into tears. Ashby drew her to him. Great sobs racked her body. His cloak grew damp from her tears. She cried for some minutes. He comforted her the best he could, murmuring nonsense as he stroked her hair.

Finally, she composed herself. "That is why you must take me away with you. Far from Marc. From France. If I refuse to marry him, I dread what my life will become." She paused. "If you choose not to aid me, I shall take sanctuary in a convent."

Ashby remembered she'd spent much of her life in one. How she had as little calling to the Church as he did. A woman of her intelligence and beauty should not be locked away from the world. He knew her to be a good person but not pious as a nun should be. Marielle would wither and die in that kind of environment.

"What I fear most is that Marc will kill me," she added. "That my refusal to marry him will drive him far over the edge. He is a volatile, angry man. If I stand up to him and reject his idea of our marriage, he is the kind to take matters into his own hands. I would be beaten. Abused. And murdered. He would take pleasure choking the very life out of me."

Her final words made up Ashby's mind. If he'd wavered before, she'd now convinced him.

Knowing his gut's reaction to Marc de la Tresse from the beginning, he would not put it past him. Marielle had good reason to be frightened of such a man.

He might regret his actions later but he would take her to Stanbury. Madeleine fled years ago from an impossible situation. She would be sympathetic to Marielle's predicament.

"Come," he said simply.

Marielle brushed aside her remaining tears. "I know I am asking much of you, Ashby. I turned to you because you are my only hope. I realize I am leaving behind everything I have ever known. But I know I must in order to survive."

She went to her horse. Ashby lifted her into the saddle and handed her the reins.

"Thank you" she said, her voice still thick with emotion.

"I always hand a lady her reins," he said lightly, hiding his own emotions.

He mounted his horse. Turning to her, he asked, "I must know—are we in a hurry? How soon will you be missed?"

Marielle sniffed. "Marc left for Biarritz after we dined midday. He said he would be gone a couple of weeks. I told Etienne that I was going to visit the Bouchards and inform them of Jean-Paul's death. Robert is sending a message that I will stay with them overnight. I won't be missed until sometime tomorrow when I don't return."

Ashby thought quickly. "Then match my pace. I want to be on our ship at Pauillac and down the Gironde before they even think to look for you this way."

He spurred on Lightning, knowing she would follow. He only hoped he did the right thing.

For the both of them.

Chapter Twelve

MARIELLE WANTED TO fling her arms about Ashby, grateful that he decided to allow her to accompany him. She even hoped for a quick kiss when they reunited but he'd taken the situation seriously and had been all business. They'd ridden at a good clip and now approached Pauillac.

Ashby signaled her and they drew up. "I will take you to the ship first. Do not speak to anyone, either in town or once you are on board."

He gave her a sympathetic look. "I must sell Jezebel. There's no room for her aboard."

She winced at his words but knew the wisdom of them. She hadn't thought that far ahead. She hadn't known if he would aid her escape from France or not. She couldn't imagine what lay ahead. He'd made no declarations of love. Given no offer of marriage, though he knew her to be free now.

Maybe she had assumed too much. What had been the blossoming of love for her might only have been a mere dalliance on his part. And yet, when she thought back to those kisses, his touch—he had not faked the deep emotion behind them. She hoped once they were on English soil he would press his suit. Nothing stood between them now.

If not, the casket filled with precious jewels would provide for her future. She would make her own way. It might be in a foreign land but anywhere would be better than a life in bondage to Marc de la Tresse.

"I understand," she told him. "Thank you for warning me."

The remaining minutes before they reached the city were hard for Marielle. Jezebel had become her closest friend since Arielle. She'd made no friends during all those years in the convent. She did see Cadena Bouchard sporadically ever since she'd come to Monteville as a bride but it wasn't the same. Jezebel listened to her problems and showered her with unconditional love. Marielle regretted having to leave the horse behind.

They entered the city. She tried to curb her excitement. It had been years since she'd been in a place so large. The teeming crowds, the smells from the stalls, the buildings packed closely together—it all reminded her of her past. She thought how she and Arielle had played hide and seek in their youth and grew wistful for such simpler times, two girls laughing in the endless day that stretched before them.

Ashby led them to the harbor. He waved at a man aboard a small ship.

"Wait here a moment." He climbed from his mount and looped the reins around a post before joining the man on deck. They spoke for some minutes. The man looked around Ashby at her several times, curiosity etched on his craggy features. Finally, they shook hands. She assumed they struck some bargain regarding her passage.

Marielle untied the leather bag containing the casket. Ashby rejoined her, helping her from the saddle. She knew she would be sore after such a long ride.

"Say your goodbyes. Bartholomew has given me an idea of where to sell your horse."

She nodded and turned to stroke the palfrey. "Be a good girl," she whispered to the animal. "Thank you for being my friend." Before she broke down in tears, she turned away and asked, "Where am I to go?"

Ashby secured Jezebel's reins and then took her arm. "You'll board now. Bartholomew will show you where to stay."

He gave her arm a squeeze. "It's a very small boat, Marielle. I am afraid the quarters are tight, indeed. Practically every bit of space is used up for the return." He gave her an apologetic smile and turned to go.

"Wait," she told him. She returned to Jezebel and gave the horse one quick pat, tears stinging the backs of her eyes. Without a backward glance, she walked toward the ship. The man called Bartholomew gave her a helping hand.

"Good day to you, my lady. I hear you're going to England to visit the master at Stanbury. You'll love England. The greenest grass you've ever seen and birds that sing like the Blessed Virgin."

He led Marielle past a few crewmen and down below.

"Here's the place you'll stay. Sir Ashby will be back before you know it. There's no headwind to speak of and that's a good sign."

Marielle had no idea what Bartholomew spoke of but thanked him and closed the cabin door. The cramped room was full of chests and boxes stacked sky high. She saw nowhere to sit— not a chair or bed in sight. She wondered about the canvas strung from two ends. Might that be something to sit upon?

She placed her casket atop a large crate and tried to figure out how to best approach the canvas. She finally decided backing into it would be the best idea. She tried it, only to find her feet swept up in the air. She was thrown back and gripped the sides in panic.

The canvas started swaying gently, rocking her as if she were a small babe. Marielle saw the good sense in it. This is what the men must sleep upon when at sea. It enfolded her and, for the first time since Jean-Paul's death, she felt safe. She relaxed and closed her eyes.

"MARIELLE?"

A gentle shaking interrupted the most wonderful dream.

"Go away," she muttered, ready to sink back into sleep.

She was peacefully drifting off again when a retching sound startled her. She sat straight up. She saw Ashby bent over a wooden bucket. Immediately, she slid from her canvas cocoon and went to him.

He lifted his head and wiped his mouth with a cloth. She'd never seen a man's face look green in her life.

"You are ill," she cried.

He smiled feebly. "It happened on the way over. I have heard it does to some. I have been up and down rivers before, but the Channel is much rougher."

He gagged again and bent over the bucket for

several minutes. Marielle stood helplessly nearby, not sure what she should do. Gradually, she noticed the boat's movement, the swell of water under them, rocking them gently.

Ashby raised his head once more. "I think that's all of it," he said with great effort. "I beg your forgiveness at such a disruption."

He made a motion to go but Marielle doubted he would make it very far.

"Come." She guided him over to the canvas. "Lie down. I shall see about finding you something to drink."

He grimaced. "I do not want anything now. Except for the bloody boat to stop pitching and lurching so."

Marielle wondered why he put up such a fuss over so little motion. She rather enjoyed the feel of the boat swaying. She stood by his side, holding his hand as he once held hers after she'd carelessly ridden Jezebel too fast.

Ashby protested at first, saying he would go to the cabin next door. Marielle put her foot down and insisted he stay with her for now. She settled him upon the hammock and he fell into a restless sleep. The greenish color faded and then he looked pale as a ghost. A knock at the cabin door interrupted her worries.

Bartholomew stepped in. "Got two tankards of ale and a bit of bread and cheese for you." He looked over at Ashby. "Poor lad. Same thing on the way over. It's always the big blokes that you'd not expect it from."

"What is wrong with him?"

Bartholomew smiled. "He's got seasickness, my lady. Fells the best of them. Sir Ashby will be fine once we dock. Some just can't take it out on the open sea, that's all. You seem fit and fair as a good sailor should be."

"Yes," she agreed. "I am not bothered at all by the boat's motion."

"Well, you might try and bathe his face with some water. It's in the barrel over here. Just pop the top so. If he can get a bite of bread or two down him, it will help settle his belly some. I'll check on you later." Bartholomew left the cabin.

Marielle found the water. A small dipper floated inside the barrel. Lacking any better ideas, she tore a small piece off her kirtle. Her tunics and surcoat covered it as it was. She used this to soak up some water and wrung it almost dry.

Returning to Ashby's side, she bathed his face with the damp cloth, repeating her action several times. He continued to sleep, a slight scowl marring his handsome face. She brushed his blond locks from his forehead, feeling for fever. He had none.

After a few minutes he woke, groaning, griping his side.

"You need to sip a bit of water," she told him. "Bartholomew says it will make you feel better."

He looked at her skeptically but raised up and let her bring the dipper to his lips. She encouraged him to drink slowly and was proud that she got a few bites of bread down him.

His seasickness continued for the entire journey. Marielle had no idea how long they were in the cabin. She could hear the wind whistling at times. At other times, the swell of the waves caused the boat to pitch to and fro. Those were the worst times. Ashby would motion for the pail. He was not the strong knight with the witty tongue that so impressed her that first day at Monteville.

Yet even in illness, he possessed a boyish appeal, as well as expressing his need for her. She talked to him, telling him a few stories about her days terrorizing the nuns at Sisters of Merciful Heart. Twice, she even sang to him, one a lullaby she remembered from childhood and the other a song she'd heard the peasants singing in the vineyards at harvest time. She even hummed some of the chants from the chapel services she'd endured as a child.

Marielle didn't know how much of this he heard. Ashby drifted in and out. Twice more, Bartholomew brought ale and bread, liberally dashed with encouragement.

"He'll be fine, my lady. He's a strong one. We've just happened on rough seas this crossing. He wasn't half as bad on the way over. I think staying on land in the future would be my best advice to him."

The sailor was the only crewman Marielle saw. The one time she'd indicated that she might go up for some fresh air, Bartholomew stopped her.

"No, my lady. Sir Ashby would have my hide scraped clean if I let you above."

She was puzzled. "Why?"

The man shook his head. "It wouldn't be right. Sailors are a rough lot. You want nothing to do with them. It's better you stay safe and sound below with the master. We'll be in London before you know it."

Marielle went to the cabin next door that Ashby had referred to, only to find it more cramped than the one they occupied. It also had no hammock. She returned and tried to get some sleep leaning against the stack of chests but her back rebelled. Knowing Ashby would most likely be unaware of her presence, she climbed into the hammock next to him.

Unfortunately, she was very aware of him. Marielle had turned her back to him but as their weight hit the center together, it pushed them close. She doubted she would be able to fall asleep, thanks to Ashby's very nearness. She didn't lack for warmth, though. The ship was quite cold but he radiated a heat unlike any she'd ever known. She checked him again for fever until she realized this was his natural state. It made for a toasty time, especially after Bartholomew brought a blanket for them to share.

Reality would set in soon. They had reached the Thames. Marielle immediately sensed the difference between this and the Bay of Biscay and the English Channel. She knew from Bartholomew that they would arrive in the early hours of the morning. Going against everything the nuns had drilled into her, Marielle decided to enjoy these last few hours on the boat. Ashby slept peacefully now. She knew he would soon recover his strength and good cheer. She might never have this opportunity again.

She turned toward him, snuggling closely. Her cheek rested upon his chest, her arm across him protectively. This tiny cabin, this hammock, and this man had become her haven from the world.

Marielle drifted off to sleep, content.

CHAPTER THIRTEEN

ASHBY AWOKE FEELING warm and secure. He pulled the woman closer to him, her curves heating his loins. He heard a soft mewl, as if she were a kitten, and grinned.

Then his eyes shot open. He had no idea where he was or who lay in his arms. It wasn't the first time that had happened to him but as he looked about, he panicked. He tried to think back to yesterday and drew a blank. Slowly, he turned his head to view the bundle of pliant flesh that snuggled next to him.

It was Marielle de la Tresse. Her long, auburn hair spilled around her shoulders. Her breasts pressed softly against his chest. His hands itched at the thought of caressing them.

Had they made love and he didn't remember? How could he forget such a thing? If simply kissing her made Heaven and Earth move, surely time would have stood still as he loved her.

Then he realized what had occurred. He'd been ill from the waves' motions. The seasickness struck him during the crossing when he'd left London for France and, apparently, had repeated itself. Bits and pieces flooded back. Marielle bathing his face, talking and singing to him, warming him.

He looked about the cramped quarters. The cabin was jammed with an assortment of odds and ends, with nowhere to sit and hardly any room to stand. The poor woman had no choice but to sleep with him. She began to stir. He remained perfectly still, willing himself to breathe evenly and deeply, as if he were still asleep. He did not want to embarrass her in any way after she'd cared for him so. He would take his cue from her.

Marielle stretched against him, bringing him immediately to the breaking point. He wanted nothing more than to pull her into his arms and make sweet love to her. Yet he was the perfect soldier, in full control, disciplined enough to remain unmoving.

She yawned. He swore he could feel her lashes, soft as a butterfly, opening and closing against his neck. Her scent was everywhere, filling his nostrils, his entire world. And yet, he kept motionless.

"Oh," she yawned again.

Ashby could hear her tongue as it ran over her dry lips, moistening them. He'd heard of men being tortured before, drawn on the rack, their muscles ripped in half. It couldn't be half as bad as what he suffered through now.

"Hmmm," she sighed against him and finally sat up. She brushed back his hair from his forehead and placed her palm flat against it.

"No fever," she murmured to herself. Her hand moved to his cheek. "Everything will be much better, Ashby," she told him softly. "We will soon be in London."

Marielle eased from the hammock and replaced the blanket over him. He longed to cry out for her to return. Never had such emptiness filled him when a woman left his bed. What was it about her that he so desired?

He heard stirring about the cabin, imagining what she might be doing. She finally came to him and shook him gently. He allowed his eyelids to flutter a few times and then lay still against his cheeks once again.

"Wake up, Ashby. We must try and get some food in you."

He opened his eyes and tried to look groggy. She was the prettiest sight he'd ever awakened to.

"Marielle?" It surprised him how hoarse he sounded.

"Don't worry," she reassured him. "You haven't spoken since yesterday when we left

France. We'll be in London soon. Here, sit up. Have a cup of ale that Bartholomew brought earlier."

She patiently helped him sip small bits of the ale until the cup was empty, feeding him bites of bread in between. His stomach gurgled loudly, making him aware of how empty it was.

Marielle giggled. "Bartholomew said once we are upon land, you will be weak a day at most. He said your appetite would return almost immediately. By this time tomorrow, all this will be but a fading, bad dream."

Ashby knew it to be true. He'd been ill on the journey to France but he'd been his old self almost as soon as he'd set foot upon land, ravenous and ready to take on the world again. Now his only complaints were his head hurt and his joints ached from disuse.

"The only good part is that you stayed with me."

She blushed. He didn't realize he'd spoken aloud.

"Now what was I to do? There was no one else to watch over you. I'm glad to have been of good service. After all, you are helping me escape an intolerable situation."

That was true. He hadn't thought much beyond getting her on the boat and taking her to Stanbury. There, she would be cared for, kept safe, far away from Marc's clutches. But if

Marielle were there, then he must go elsewhere. He could not stand to see her on a daily basis and want her as badly as he did now.

Ashby cursed his dismal luck. He'd never wanted for much and had been happy in his service to Garrett. Now, he wished for all the things that life hadn't given to him, the things that would make him worthy enough to woo Marielle. She deserved far better than him, especially with the kind of life she'd lived up until now. He would work out the details before they reached the Montayne estate but he would not stand in her way of finding freedom and happiness with a man who could give her all the things she deserved.

In the meantime, he had much to accomplish in London during the next few days. It would give Marielle time to adjust after their journey.

He laughed aloud.

"What?" she asked, eyeing him curiously.

"I was thinking that you might need time to recover after our voyage when you look fit and ready as ever. I am the one who needs rest."

She hesitated and then said, "What are our . . . your plans?"

Ashby sat up. His head protested the sudden movement but, already, he was feeling more like his usual self. They must have left the Channel and been sailing down the Thames for him to feel as well as he did. The violent rocking of the boat was now but a gentle swaying.

"I must stay in London a few days," he said in answer to Marielle's question. "There are some people I must meet with before we journey to Stanbury."

"Madeleine's home?"

"Yes, Madeleine and Garrett's estate. It's several hours' ride to the south of London. In the meantime, we will stay at Garrett's London home. Oh, Lord Almighty!" he proclaimed.

"You are ill?" she asked, concern wrinkling her brow.

He shook his head. "No. Far from it. It just hit me that you will meet Maude."

"Maude? Who is she?"

Ashby laughed. "You will see."

THEY SAID THEIR goodbyes to Bartholomew, Ashby already joking as he always did. The change in him amazed Marielle. No one would guess by looking at him how ill he'd seemed just hours ago.

The London docks teemed with people and rats, both scurrying as if late to important appointments. Ashby aided her as they disembarked from the small vessel. As they reached solid ground, he dropped his small bag and fell headfirst. Marielle gasped and bent to aid him, thinking him ill again, only to see him kiss the earth. She started laughing.

He looked at her sheepishly and offered her a hand as he raised them to their feet. He retrieved his bag as she held her satchel.

"I swore that when we reached land, I would kiss the ground and never take it for granted again. I never want to see another boat as long as I live. Garrett must find another man to see to his business in France. My sailing days are officially over."

"Here, Sir Ashby. Over here," a voice called out.

Marielle turned to see a tall, thin man waving in their direction. Ashby returned his greeting and led her over his way.

"Good day to you, John. Thanks for retrieving Lightning. How do you fare?"

The man named John bobbed his head up and down. "Fair to middling, I'd say. My wife's in that way again. She can be a real terror in that state."

"Will this make five or six children, John? I am afraid I've lost count."

The servant's laughter filled the air. "More like eight. At least I think it will be eight. I might have lost count myself!"

Both men chuckled. Marielle saw nothing funny about losing track of how many children one had.

"This is Madame Matesse. She comes from France and will be visiting Stanbury shortly."

Ashby had told her he thought it wise to avoid use of the de la Tresse name for the time being. He'd asked Marielle what her maiden name had been before they'd boarded the ship in France. Now she understood that she would be known by Matesse. It felt right to her. She had longed to return to the girl she once was. With Jean-Paul's death, all things were possible.

"A pleasure to have you visiting our fair land, my lady. Stanbury's a right pretty place. The earl and countess will be good company to you."

"Have you been with them long?" she asked, making polite conversation as they headed across the docks.

"My father's father was head groom at Stanbury. My father took his place. I am in charge of Lord Montayne's London stables."

"Do you hope to return to Stanbury one day?" she asked.

John nodded. "That I do. London's a bit cramped for my tastes but this is where Lord Montayne has need of me."

"It's a fine job you do, John." Ashby turned to Marielle. "I have never met a better groom than John. He has a way with horses like none other. He but whispers in their ears and they are as putty in his hands."

John halted their progress. "Seeing as how I didn't expect a guest, Sir Ashby, I didn't bring another horse." The servant gave a coin to a small boy who'd obviously watched the animals for him.

"I'll let Madame Matesse ride my horse and I'll return by foot."

Ashby studied the horses a moment. "No, John. Madame Matesse will ride Lightning with me."

He gave a quick smile to her. "I promise I am a steady rider who does not take many chances."

"Unlike me?" she asked under her breath, but a smile played upon her lips.

"Very good, sir. Maude asked me to stop at market to pick up some fresh fish for you."

Ashby licked his lips. "I already feel my appetite returning. Maude does spoil me. I hope fresh eels will be part of your shopping?" he asked John hopefully.

"Yes, Sir Ashby. She knows you and Lord Montayne can't get enough of eels in saffron sauce."

"Then we shall see you back at the town house. I will rub Lightning down myself." He gave his horse an affectionate pat, causing Marielle to miss Jezebel.

John nodded and mounted his horse. Ashby took his traveling bag and tied it on the back of the horse. He turned to Marielle.

"You packed awfully light."

She blushed. "I was in a hurry." She handed over the satchel that contained the casket holding her jewels. She still wore the two sets of clothing since she had nowhere else to put the spare change of clothes.

Ashby took the satchel from her. "Forget what I said about traveling light. I am surprised you were able to lift this. Do you travel with your most precious books?"

Marielle thought it best if he believed so. "You know how I am about my books."

"Then you shall adore Stanbury's library. It will make you feel right at home." He attached her satchel to the saddle and mounted his horse, holding a hand out to her. "Come. Let us go."

Marielle slipped her hand into his, and he hoisted her up in front of him.

"This could be a bit uncomfortable, so search about and find a position that feels right."

She scooted a little bit and Ashby's arms came around her. "Here, lean into me." He brought her against him. "There. Will that do?"

Will that do? Marielle's heart pounded so loudly, she expected to see it pop from her chest any minute now. His very nearness brought a giddiness to her belly unlike any she'd ever known. She'd lain next to him in the hammock but only she'd been aware of their bodies pressed together. Now they were both awake and positioned together and the heat he emitted would probably scorch her cloak, roasting them both alive.

"Yes. I am fine," she said meekly, afraid to say more.

"We will reach Garrett's place in about three-quarters of an hour. Relax now, while I point out all the sights of London to you."

He made good on his promise, telling her about the different places they passed. Marielle heard the words rumbling from his chest but they held no meaning for her. The only thing that mattered was being next to him. His arms were closely about her, meeting to hold the reins. He smelled of leather and horse and something wholly masculine that rocked her world. Each breath she inhaled took in a little more of him, until she was filled with his essence.

"We've reached our destination," he told her.

Marielle looked up at a large house, impressed by not only its size but its beauty.

"What a marvelous home!"

"This? It's nothing compared to Stanbury. Now that estate is a marvel to behold."

They rode onto the property and straight to the stables. A groom greeted them.

"I will be back in a moment," Ashby told him. "I have missed my Lightning. I want to rub him down myself."

Ashby eased her from the saddle before untying her possessions and his. "I want to take you into the house and let you get acquainted with Maude before I return to the stables to care for Lightning."

He led her up to the house and stepped in. The fresh smell of pine enveloped Marielle.

"Maude's been on a cleaning streak again," he commented.

"And when have I not, you arrogant, winsome boy?"

Startled, Marielle turned and saw the tiniest woman she'd ever seen coming their way. Ashby dropped their things to the ground and went to the servant. He swept her into his arms, spinning her around until she grew quite pink in the cheeks.

"Put me down, you fool, or I'll knock you from here to Wales."

He laughed and set the woman down. She swayed slightly but held her ground. Then she caught sight of Marielle and cocked her head.

"You're French, I daresay."

Ashby gave an exasperated sigh. "Maude, you are trying to sound clever now. You know good and well I am returning from France." He turned and indicated Marielle. "Allow me to introduce Marielle Matesse. She is a recent widow and neighbor to the Bouchards at Chateau Branais."

Maude's face lit up. "Do you know my Madeleine?"

Marielle shook her head, a bit put out. Judging by Maude's face, she was as taken with Madeleine as Ashby.

"No, she was gone by the time I arrived at Monteville."

"Marielle's going to visit Madeleine and Garrett at Stanbury," he informed the servant. "I am off to care for Lightning. So you two get cozy. Be sure to only say good things about me, Maude."

"Oh, all right," the servant grumbled good-naturedly.

Ashby left with a wink and a wave. Maude turned and studied her up and down a full minute without saying a word, closely scrutinizing her, especially looking long into her eyes.

Marielle was so taken aback that she said nothing in return. The longer Maude took in sizing her up, the more she felt Maude delved into her very soul.

Finally, the servant took her hand and drew her into a small room where a fire burned, its warmth enveloping the room. She led Marielle to a seat and took the one next to her, drawing her chair up close to Marielle.

"So, tell me, dear. How long has my boy been in love with you?"

CHAPTER FOURTEEN

MARIELLE WAS TOO stunned to reply. She shook her head, no words coming from her lips.

Maude took her hand. "Don't deny it, child. It's written plainly across his face."

She shook her head. "You are mistaken, Maude. I lost my husband only a fortnight ago. Ashby has merely been a guest in my home. We hardly know one other."

The older woman contemplated Marielle's words before she spoke. "Be that as it may, the boy's smitten with you. I've known him since he was a wee one, getting into all sorts of mischief with Master Garrett." She snorted. "Ah, now, he's another one, too, who brought me a girl from France. Couldn't take his eyes off her, he couldn't, not for one minute. He'd been married before but it had never been like that between him and his wife."

Maude squeezed her hand. "I know those boys as well as if I'd given birth to them myself. I know what's in their hearts. The master loves Madeleine with all his soul. I see the same between the two of you."

Marielle's face grew hot. "I am grateful to Ashby for helping me leave France. I was in a difficult situation there."

"Just as Madeleine was. Oh, my boys. Two peas in a pod, they are. Both drawn to troubled, beautiful women."

Marielle burst into tears. She hadn't thought her feelings for Ashby would be so transparent. Yet here was a total stranger reading her most intimate thoughts.

Maude wrapped Marielle tightly to her. "Now, child, you'll be fine. My Ashby will take good care of you. Whatever troubles you have, he will solve them. He's a good man, that boy. Of course, he doesn't know he's in love with you just yet."

She pulled away, startled by the servant's words. "What?"

Maude chuckled. "Oh, dearie, you're a young one. I can tell you from experience, though, ain't a man ever known he's in love before the woman knows. Men fool themselves and lie to their hearts, but the feelings? They're inside them, all the same."

The tiny woman stood. "Let's dry your tears and get you some hot water to freshen up. John will be here soon with the eels and I'll have my hands full then."

She led Marielle up a stairway and to a chamber done in shades of blue. "Have a little cry if you must then banish the tears away, child. The time for sorrow is over. You're with Ashby now. He'll be good to you."

She turned to go but Marielle caught her hand. The servant turned back. "Maude," she said, her voice just above a whisper, "I think I fell in love with him the moment I saw him."

"Most women do," Maude replied, "but you're something special. I saw it . . . in his eyes."

Marielle sought some reassurance. "Was it wrong of me? I was still married."

"Not happily, I fear. If you were, no one—not even my sweetest Ashby—could have turned your head."

She nodded. "You are right. It was a loveless union. And now that Jean-Paul is dead . . ." Her voice trailed off, her future still so uncertain.

Maude patted her hand. "You must give things time. Give your soul time to heal. Give time for my boy to come around and acknowledge his feelings for you." Maude grinned. "He will—or I'll blister his arse but good."

Marielle laughed. Already England seemed

like home but, then again, anywhere she was with Ashby would be so.

"THAT JUST ABOUT does it, Maude." Ashby took the servant into his arms and held her tightly. He loved the old woman, despite her bossy ways. She spoke to him and Garrett like no other, not even Madeleine. She'd had her hand in raising them and Ashby was the better for it.

He released her. "I will tell Marielle we are ready to leave for Stanbury."

"Not just yet," the servant cautioned.

Ashby frowned, wondering what Maude was up to.

"You can wipe that puzzled look off your face, Ashby fitz Waryn. We're going to talk before you leave."

"But Marielle—"

"She'll wait. I want to know why you've been avoiding me."

To emphasize her point, Maude began tapping her foot. He knew from experience the gesture was not a good sign of what lay ahead.

"I haven't avoided you, Maude. Naturally, I attended to much business these past few days. Still, I have done justice to every meal you cooked. We sat around the fire and talked each night. We—"

"It's that *we* you keep mentioning. You haven't spent a moment alone with me."

Ashby laughed. "Come, Maude. You shouldn't pout. I never dreamed you would be jealous of Marielle."

"Should I be?" She stared at him intently.

"No," he said lightly. "You will always be my number one lady, Maude. No others come close."

She frowned. "That's not the answer I want from you."

Ashby grew serious. "What answer do you need?"

Maude gestured for him to sit. He did so. Reluctantly.

"You're in love with that girl, Ashby fitz Waryn."

Immediately, he shot to his feet.

"Sit back down, Master Ashby. I'll say my piece and you'll be civil while I do so." Her glare was enough to take him twenty years back. He sat as told.

"I don't know if there's anything's between you. I haven't seen sight of it but I sensed it from the moment you came in together."

Maude sighed. "It's your happiness I want. I see you look with envy at Master Garrett now. You're ready for a wife and family, my boy. It's time for you to settle down."

Ashby stared at her. In a flat voice he said,

"And you judge Marielle to be the woman I should settle down with."

"No. You're the one who's chosen her," Maude said quietly. "I've come to know her well in the time we've spent together. I see what's so special about her. You see it, too. There's a spark between the two of you. You belong together. Don't walk away from love, Boy." She gazed at him steadily. "I did once. My life was never the same."

Ashby looked at Maude with new eyes. He wondered about the mistake that she must have made, years and years ago, one which she obviously still grieved over.

She was right—yet he refused to heed her words. He had nothing to offer Marielle but love. It wouldn't be enough. It was enough that he safely removed her from France. He would entrust her into Garrett and Madeleine's care. That was all he could give her.

Yet to silence Maude, he said, "I will think upon your words, Maude. Marielle is a fine woman. Mayhap when she has done with her mourning, there could be a future for us."

"God's teeth!" proclaimed Maude sharply. "You still think you can look me bald in the face and lie through that winsome smile of yours?" She spat upon the ground in disgust. "You haven't learned a thing. If you weren't so big, I'd turn you over my knee right now and paddle your arse black and blue."

She stood, arms crossed over her chest. "I'll smile and make nice in front of Marielle. I won't embarrass her or you when we say our goodbyes. But I won't have a civil word for you in the future if you don't marry that girl."

With that, Maude flounced off, her shoulders squared. Ashby was surprised no steam rose from her, so heated were the words she'd spoken.

"Ah, she's been mad at me before," he reassured himself aloud. "She will get over it."

He went to fetch Marielle to set out for their trip to Stanbury but his heart was heavy.

CHAPTER FIFTEEN

"THERE. IN THE distance. That's Stanbury."

Marielle heard the pride in Ashby's voice as she turned to view the Montayne estate. It was breathtaking. She couldn't imagine living in so grand a castle.

Ashby spurred Lightning on. She sensed his eagerness at returning home. She envied him the feeling. She'd never had strong ties nor fond memories to anywhere she lived. The convent had no sense of family within its cold walls. By the time she returned to her parents' home, she possessed few clear recollections of it. With all her brothers and sisters gone, it did not seem like a place she belonged.

And Monteville? The chateau had never been welcoming. She'd experienced nothing but isolation and loneliness there and she'd never seemed to fit in. She became a caged bird taken out on occasion for Jean-Paul's pleasure. She had no friends within its walls and had certainly never been a true chatelaine of the castle in any real sense while living there.

What did her future hold? What lay in store for her at Stanbury? How would she be treated? Panicked, Marielle suddenly wondered what they knew of her.

"Ashby?"

"Yes?"

"Do Lord and Lady Montayne know I am coming? Do they know my circumstances? I cannot believe I just now thought to ask this, and here we are, practically upon their doorstep."

He laughed, the rich sound that she'd grown to love. "I sent a messenger ahead, Marielle. I will let you choose what you wish to reveal to them. All my missive said is that I was bringing a visitor from Bordeaux and to prepare a bedchamber."

Her belly knotted. Her idyllic time with Ashby was about to end. She'd enjoyed the evenings in London after he returned from business. They would dine on Maude's heavenly meals and then talk far into the night. She dreamed of them as a couple, longing for his companionship.

And love.

Yet there'd been no walks in the moonlight. No stolen kisses in the shadows. He'd not acted in a loving manner toward her since they set foot in

England. Kind, yes. Solicitous? Always. But he'd shown none of the fire of desire since they'd left France. It was as if he banked it, holding at bay the dizzying emotions from before. Must he seek Garrett and Madeleine's approval first? She knew Ashby's attachment toward them ran deep. As a knight in service to Lord Montayne, would he be obligated to seek their permission before pressing his suit regarding her? Is that how custom ran in England?

Or had she read more into his actions than she should have? She'd set out with two plans in mind. She knew she could always go to Sisters of Merciful Heart for sanctuary but instead she'd followed her heart—and the more dangerous course—by first reaching out to Ashby for help. Since he so willingly committed to aiding her, and because she was now widowed, she assumed he would take care of her. By wedding her.

Had she been wrong about him?

Now, she would be among strangers while he would be surrounded by those he cherished. He was coming home, whereas she was being set adrift. The thought frightened her so much that she began to tremble.

Ashby slowed and then halted his horse. "What ails you, Marielle? You are shivering." He pulled her cloak more tightly about her and pulled her against him, his warmth enveloping her, soothing her.

"You have nothing to fear. Garrett and Madeleine will welcome you with open arms. They are the two most generous people I know. You will be safe, Marielle. Marc is but a bad memory that will grow more distant as time passes."

She wished she could stay with him forever this way. Why did they have to go to Stanbury? She would be watched and weighed. Everyone there would judge her. See if she were good enough to be a part of Ashby's life. Worse, she was beyond frightened because she dreaded meeting Madeleine, the Countess of Montayne. Ashby spoke so highly of the countess. Marielle knew she could never live up to such an ideal woman. Why even bother?

The worst thing was that she had no control at this point. She might as well make the best of the situation and put on a brave face.

"I'll admit to a few qualms. I am a bit nervous when I meet new people. I will be fine."

"Of course you will," he murmured in her ear, sending chills through her. "That's my girl." He urged on his horse again. Within minutes, they reached their destination.

He called a greeting to the watchtower as the drawbridge lowered. They entered the outer bailey to cheers from every direction. Marielle saw the smiles around them. It was obvious Ashby was much-beloved at Stanbury. He cantered along, waving, shouting salutations coming from the left and right.

"Almost there," he told her. They entered the inner bailey. Marielle spied several people waving from the top steps. A young girl came galloping down those stone steps, followed by several others at a leisurely pace.

"Ashby! Ashby!" the girl called.

He sprang from the horse and quickly pulled Marielle down. He turned as the girl leaped into his arms.

"You are finally home," she cried. "I have missed you ever so much."

"And I you, Lyssa, even more so."

She pursed her lips. "You are just saying that. Madeleine says you always tell every female that, be she young or old."

Lyssa turned, her arms still locked around Ashby's neck. "Who have you brought home? Papa said there would be a visitor."

Marielle sensed a sneeze coming on. No, not now! Not when she was about to be presented to the Montaynes.

Yet out it came, a single one, but one she judged to be among the loudest in her lifetime. She winced and smiled sheepishly, her eyes now watery.

The girl studied Marielle a moment, her head cocked as she inspected her. "She is very pretty, Ashby. I think she is as pretty as Madeleine. But she will have to work on her sneezes. They will frighten poor Luke up a tree."

"Forgive my daughter's impertinence," a nearby voice said.

Marielle turned. "You must be Lord Montayne." She curtsied to him. "I am Marielle . . . Matesse."

"I am happy to make your acquaintance, my lady. Any friend of Ashby's is a friend to us all. Please, call me Garrett."

He turned and took a woman's elbow. "I would like to present to you my wife and son. This is Madeleine and Cynric. I am sorry the aforementioned Luke is unavailable to greet you as well. He no doubt lingers in the stables, finding plump mice for his supper tonight, though I doubt he would share—even with company."

Marielle was unnerved by Lord Montayne's glibness. She'd just begun to realize that Luke must be a cat. Marielle gathered her wits and her manners about her as well as her English skills and said to the woman, "It is a pleasure to meet you at last, Lady Montayne. Ashby has spoken often of you." Marielle was surprised at how calm she sounded, for her heart pounded rapidly.

Madeleine moved to greet her. The mistress of Stanbury was stunningly beautiful. She was very tall, almost as tall as her husband. Marielle didn't know women could be that tall. Madeleine's hair was the color of sun on summer wheat. Her eyes sparkled with good humor and patience. A small scar on her cheek was her only flaw, yet it did not detract from her considerable beauty.

"A great pleasure to meet you, Marielle. Your English is remarkable."

Marielle blushed at the compliment. "Sisters of Merciful Heart insisted language was the key to peace. I speak four of them but I am self-conscious about it. I rarely get enough practice in any of them."

Madeleine laughed, a husky sound. Her smile was genuine, lighting her face. "Mayhap you can help me. I am trying to teach Lyssa and Cynric French. You never know when it will come in handy."

Cynric buried his head in his mother's shoulder. "Oh, you devil," his mother cooed. "So, you play shy with Marielle?" She looked at her son with love and back to Marielle. "Do not let him fool you. He will lull you into thinking he's something he's not."

Madeleine bent and set Cynric down. With a spontaneity that surprised Marielle, Madeleine stepped to her and gave her a warm embrace and kissed her on both cheeks.

"I am so glad to have you here, Marielle. I cannot wait to hear about France. Although I love England, I find I do miss Bordeaux at times."

All Marielle's misgivings were dispelled in that moment. "It's wonderful to be here. I will catch you up on all the news of the neighbor-hood."

Madeleine looked at her quizzically. "The neighborhood?"

"Yes," she replied enthusiastically. "I know your parents. Cadena and Robert."

"*Mon Dieu!*" Madeleine's eyes filled with tears. She squeezed Marielle tightly and then flung her arms about Ashby as he handed Marielle her satchel.

"Oh, Ashby, you have brought me a treasure from heaven." She kissed his cheek and looked to her husband. "Marielle knows my parents!" she exclaimed.

Madeleine linked her arm through Marielle's. "We will leave you gentlemen to attend to your own business. We have much to discuss and I am sure poor Marielle is tired after that long ride."

"What about me, Madeleine?" Lyssa piped up. "I am not a gentleman."

Marielle noted the fond smile Madeleine gave the girl. "I will leave you in charge of the men, Lyssa. See that they behave properly, as gentlemen should."

"I want to help Ashby rub down Lightning."

Garrett laughed. "The child is mad for horses, Marielle. Ash encourages her in this." He ruffled Lyssa's hair affectionately. "We'll go down to the stables and keep Ash company while he tends to Lightning."

Garrett swung Cynric upon his shoulders. The boy squealed with delight. Marielle watched Ashby do the same with Lyssa as he took his reins in hand. The four of them began walking toward the stable, Lightning in tow behind them.

"Let's get you a hot bath, Marielle. I know how dusty that road from London can be." She gave her instructions to a servant and then led Marielle into the castle.

"You have a lovely home, Madeleine." She looked about her at the tasteful furnishings. Stanbury seemed much more a home than Monteville. It had a lived-in look, very comfortable and yet elegant.

"Come, we shall go to your chamber. I can help you unpack."

Marielle fidgeted. "I only have this small bag of books. I left France . . . rather abruptly."

Madeleine eyed her wisely. "I understand. When I fled my husband, I carried my beloved lute and a change of clothing. I did not want to be slowed in any way."

"My husband is dead," Marielle said quickly.

"Yet you felt the need to leave France." It was a statement, not a question.

She made an instant decision due to her rapport with Madeleine. She would tell the countess the truth. She could not enjoy her hospitality otherwise.

Madeleine opened the door to a chamber that

was light and airy. Fruit sat on a platter. Next to it was a bottle of wine. Marielle suddenly realized how parched she was.

"Let me pour you a glass," Madeleine told her. "Then I shall leave you to bathe and rest a bit."

She poured a glass and handed it to Marielle. "The hot water should be here soon. Is there anything else I can get for you? Maybe later we can chat about Chateau Branais. I so long to hear about news from home."

"Please. Share a glass of wine with me. I want us to talk . . . about why I am in England."

Madeleine studied her. "Marielle, it's enough that Ashby brought you to us. You are his friend. We offer our friendship, as well. You are not obligated to tell us anything. We are comfortable starting from today. If need be, leave your yesterdays behind you."

Marielle's eyes filled with tears at such open acceptance. "He told me how generous you would be. I found it hard to believe that someone could accept a stranger so totally, no questions asked."

"That is our way," Madeleine said gently. "I, too, once was troubled. I had nowhere to turn. Stanbury proved a refuge for me." She smiled wistfully. "That was long ago. I do not often think of those times. When I do, I realize how fortunate I am to be with Garrett now, to have our children and our home and family and friends.

"Love saved me, Marielle." Her steady gaze pierced Marielle's soul. "It will save you, too."

A knock at the door interrupted their conversation. Servants brought in buckets of hot water, filling the tub, setting out soap and towels. Madeleine thanked them and shooed them away. She poured liquid from a vial into the water. Marielle caught a whiff of roses as her hostess stirred her hand in the water.

"Shall I leave? Or would you let me help you? I know when I have come from London, I am so weary that I can barely lift a hand. I could wash your hair for you."

Marielle recognized the offer of friendship. "I would gratefully accept your help."

The countess helped her to undress. She made no comment about the double layers of clothing Marielle wore. She eased her guest into the steaming water.

"Just soak a bit. We will have your clothes washed. You are a similar size to Edith, Garrett's mother. She would be more than willing to let you borrow a few items of clothing. I will be back in a few minutes."

Marielle stretched in the water and rested her head against the edge. The hot water seemed to lift the worries weighing upon her. Instead of embarrassment at borrowing clothes, Marielle was thankful for Madeleine's gracious offer. Stanbury was everything Ashby had said it would be. She smiled and let her thoughts drift.

Strong fingers gently massaged her scalp. Marielle realized Madeleine had returned and had begun to wash her hair. In her hands she sensed strength and competence.

"No one has ever done this for me before. It feels wonderful."

Madeleine took a bucket and rinsed Marielle's hair. "Then we need to spoil you a bit."

She reached for a cake of soap resting on the towel and began to lather it.

"Actually, I do not need spoiling. I enjoy hard work. I am unsure of my plans at the moment but I am willing to do whatever needs doing while I am at Stanbury."

"You are our guest," protested Madeleine.

"I cannot sit and do nothing. I would earn my keep while I am here, however long that will be. I do not want to inconvenience you and I certainly do not want to be bored."

Madeleine smiled. "In that case, you can help me care for Cynric. He is a handful, and I tire easily these days."

Marielle looked at her questioningly.

"Yes, my monthly flow was due three days ago." She eyed Marielle with a gleam in her eyes. "I am never late."

"Congratulations!" Marielle proclaimed.

"I have not told Garrett yet. For all his gruff ways, he worries quite a bit. I would rather be farther along before he knows. He will coddle me and be simply impossible. He was when I carried Cynric. I am sure he will react the same this time round."

"So Lyssa is . . . not yours? I noticed she calls you Madeleine." Marielle paused. "Oh, forgive me. That was rude of me to mention."

"There is nothing to forgive. Lyssa is not my child by birth but I love her as much as Cynric." Madeleine chuckled. "I may have fallen in love with Lyssa before I did Garrett."

"She is a darling girl."

"And growing up all too fast, I am afraid. I think she fancies herself marrying Ashby one day since they both love horses so."

A sinking feeling filled her. Marielle reached for the towel and stood. She wrapped it around her and carefully asked, "So Ashby would wait for her?"

"Lyssa will always be a child to Ashby. He indulges her and spoils her. He would never marry her."

Madeleine took a comb and ran it through Marielle's hair thoughtfully. "It will take someone of great beauty and intelligence to capture his fancy. A woman of grace and wit, full of integrity and perseverance. Someone closer to his own age that will fascinate him and drive him to madness."

Madeleine placed a hand on Marielle's shoulder and gave it a gentle squeeze. "I have brought clothes from Edith for you to wear tonight. She was napping earlier when you arrived. Here, try this and see how it fits."

Marielle looked to the bed where Madeleine had laid out several things. She saw a smock and kirtle, along with a pair of hose and shoes. A cotehardie of pale blue with a surcoat of bright blue lay next to the other items.

"Edith has many other things for you to choose from. In all honesty, she tires easily of clothes. You will be able to take and keep what you need without worry."

She ran a hand along the surcoat. The color was rich, the fabric a soft velvet. The cotehardie was made of silk.

"I cannot accept such generosity, Madeleine. These are far too valuable."

Madeleine placed her hands on Marielle's shoulders. "Listen to me. You are a strong woman who has been in a terrible situation. Edith has clothes she has not worn for months and even years. Please take what is offered with no protests.

"Besides," Madeleine grinned, "I think Ashby will find these clothes bring out the color in your beautiful eyes."

Marielle's cheeks grew hot. "I—"

"It will not work, Marielle. Ashby has never been serious about a woman in his life. Yet he brings you here. To Stanbury. He has feelings for you, Marielle. I only hope those feelings are returned."

"I am grateful—"

"Shush now!" Madeleine commanded. "The charming Ashby fitz Waryn has fallen for a remarkable woman. That woman is you, Marielle. He is just too blind to know it yet. But between the two of us, I wager you two are wed well before a year has passed."

CHAPTER SIXTEEN

"SO YOU JOURNEYED a long way and the trip was unsuccessful," Garrett said. "Else you would be crowing like a rooster."

Ashby shrugged and looked about the great hall, choosing his words carefully. "Jean-Paul de la Tresse was not an easy man. From the moment I met him, I knew the venture to be doomed."

Garrett placed a hand on his shoulder. "Yet you doggedly tried, Ash. It's all I ever ask from you. Let it rest, my friend."

Ashby frowned at him. "You think I am troubled by failure?"

"It has crossed your path so infrequently, I was not sure you would even recognize it," Garrett quipped. "Still, I thought you had a better chance than I at finagling the land from Jean-Paul."

"The two of you did not get along?" Ashby

thought a moment. "That surprises me. In fact, he was complimentary on how much you learned about wine when you went to France on your extended visit several years ago."

Garrett chuckled. "No, Jean-Paul and I got along fairly well. It was his wretched brother I so disliked. The pup was not even a score and yet he knew all. I have never met a more churlish individual. If I had judged my visit to France solely on meeting Marc de la Tresse, I would have fled Bordeaux and swum back to England. In haste."

Ashby chuckled at the picture of his friend paddling back home. "I received the same impression. Marc de la Tresse has not changed at all since you met him. He now will run Monteville."

"Jean-Paul is dead?"

Ashby heard the surprise in Garrett's voice. "Yes. It happened a few days after I left Monteville. I returned to stay with the Bouchards, trying to sound Pierre out on some of the methods Donatien has successfully used in the Monteville vineyards."

Garrett shook his head. "Pierre is loyal but obstinate. He will cling to the old ways to his grave. That was one reason I wanted to try the new vintage on new land—and put someone else in charge of the venture." Garrett looked at him hopefully. "Possibly you."

Ashby thought about the trip over the water that must occur for him to set foot in France once more. He balanced that with the pain of seeing Marielle every day. Wanting her—yet never being able to have her. No, the sea voyage would be but a few days of misery. If Garrett were still willing to finance the venture, he intended to take him up on his offer. A new land. A new life. He couldn't ask for more.

Though every day he would mourn Marielle's absence in his life.

Ashby leaned closer to his friend. "I think it's a splendid idea. Of course, we would not be able to use adjoining land to Chateau Branais but I looked around the neighborhood extensively. After what I learned from Donatien, I believe a few available tracts nearby would suit your purpose in developing the new vintage you desire."

He set his jaw in determination. "If you would like me to return and pursue those possibilities, I will."

"Let me think on that." Garrett leaned back in his chair. "Tell me more about Jean-Paul's death. This interests me."

Ashby lowered his voice. "This is to go no further, Garrett."

"You have my word."

"Marielle is Jean-Paul's widow."

Garrett glanced over casually at Marielle and

back to him. "Why is she here then? Had they no issue?"

"None. Marc woke her and took her to her dead husband's body. He told her Jean-Paul had been poisoned. And that she might be blamed for it."

Garrett frowned. "She must have been terrified."

"Oh, the story gets better. Marc thought for Marielle's protection and for the sake of Monteville that they should wed. Immediately. He insinuated if she refused, he would start the rumors that she had murdered her husband."

Garrett fell silent for some minutes. Finally, he said, "At least she had the sense to leave. That took great courage. But had she a lover? Had she given anyone reason to suspect her of murder?"

Ashby swallowed. "Marielle believes Marc murdered his brother. To claim her and Monteville. She said he aggressively pursued her under his brother's very nose for years. She is repelled by him. She also thought she had little chance to prove his guilt—much less her innocence."

His friend studied him carefully. "And she came to you for help."

Ashby nodded. "She did."

"Is there something between you?"

Ashby ran a hand through his hair. "If it were another time and place, I would marry her on the morrow."

Garrett's jaw dropped. "You? Marry? Oh, God. I never thought that would ever happen. I'm delighted to hear that. What is stopping you, Ash? If you'd like, you can be wed here at Stanbury in the morning."

When he didn't reply, Garrett stared at him until Ashby felt his very soul invaded. "Marielle is free now, here in England. As your wife, Ashby, she would be under your protection. Sweet Jesu, man. If love has come to you at last, then grab it. And hold on for dear life."

Garrett gripped his arm. "Whatever is in the way, move it. Or I will move it for you. You are my dearest friend and brother-in-arms. I would see you happy at any cost."

"You are happy, Ashby?"

The two men turned to see Madeleine smiling down upon them.

"You two have been thick as thieves in this dark corner ever since we supped. I would think you would not wish to ignore our guest."

Ashby looked to where Marielle sat in front of the fire on the far side of the great hall. She was on the floor with Lyssa and Cynric. Even at this great a distance, he could see the contented look upon her face as she played their games.

"Garrett, go take Marielle a glass of wine and rescue her. Lyssa has quite talked her ear off. In fact, your mother went to bed with a headache. I have no doubt it was Lyssa's nonsense that drove her there."

Garrett stood and kissed his wife gently. "Anything else you wish me to do, my love?"

She smiled at him. A pang of jealousy stabbed at Ashby's heart. He thought the world of them, his two closest friends, but what existed between them was something he yearned for more than he'd imagined. He took a swig from his tankard of ale.

"Go be a charming host and let me visit with Ashby. I have not had two seconds alone with him since he returned." She looked at Ashby eagerly. "You must tell me all about my parents and Pierre."

Garrett excused himself. Ashby launched into detailed descriptions of how Robert and Cadena looked and what they talked about during his visit. Yet as he spoke, it was as if Madeleine listened to him with half an ear.

"You make a good pretense at being attentive but your mind is elsewhere, Madeleine."

She blushed. "You know me too well, I fear." She began toying with the folds in her skirts. Ashby immediately became guarded. Madeleine rarely played games of feminine wiles. She was up to something.

But what?

"Ashby? How well do you know Marielle?"

He hadn't expected that question. Should he

say he knew the way she tasted? Or how her curves fit perfectly against him?

Instead, he shrugged. "I know a bit about her. I visited her home while in Bordeaux. We spent some time together. She has a quick mind and is a skillful chess player. I know she loves to read and was raised in a convent. Why?"

"No particular reason. I have been drawn to her. She has been at Stanbury less than a day yet I feel she is the sister I never had."

"You were not close to Pierre, were you?"

Madeleine sighed. "No. My brother is more than half a score older than I am. He was born an old soul, I think. Both *Maman* and Papa have a gaiety about them. They love music and storytelling. Pierre? He is . . . *pratique*. Practical. For him, there are no amusements. Only work. We are very different."

Ashby lay a hand over hers. "I know Marielle has been very lonely. Life in the convent was harsh. She had no friends there. Mayhap she may stay at Stanbury indefinitely and become your companion."

"That would be nice for now but surely she will want a life of her own. A husband. Children. A home. Things all women want."

He tamped down the bitter rush that coursed through him. "Yes. What all women want," he said evenly, masking his true emotions.

Madeleine smiled at him. "It's so good to

have you home, Ashby fitz Waryn. I have missed you. As always. I do not know what we would do without you."

He stood. "It's always nice to return to Stanbury. I bid you a good evening."

Ashby skirted the edge of the great hall. He visited with a few friends but found his eyes straying back to Marielle time and again. She seemed so at ease, so different from the woman he'd met back in France. At least he'd accomplished one good deed by bringing her with him to England.

Lyssa and Cynric came to tell him goodnight. Garrett and Madeleine left to put them to bed. By the wicked gleam in Garrett's eye, Ashby knew that Garrett had his own plans for putting Madeleine to bed and keeping her busy once there. He assumed they would get very little sleep this night.

He gave the family time to make it up the stairs and to their rooms before he quietly did the same.

"Ashby?"

Marielle called his name. He had wanted to avoid her. He was angry with himself for the feelings he had, feelings he would refuse to act upon. He was afraid he'd snap at her if he spoke to her, so great was the tension that ran through him. Relaxing his features into a pleasant pose, he turned.

"Ah, Marielle. I bid you a good night."

"I wanted to thank you. Again. The people of Stanbury are wonderful, just as you said they would be. They have treated me with kindness and respect."

"Naturally. They are like my own family."

"I can see why. Even the clothes I wear tonight have been provided to me. Madeleine has thought of everything."

"She is a good woman. Garrett is a lucky man to have found true happiness with her. Unlike his first wife."

Now why did he say that? He didn't want to get into a conversation. Yet here he was, ready to pull up a stool and spout the Earl of Montayne's family history. Next he'd be telling Marielle how Garrett's father, Ryker, use to beat Edith senseless or how Ryker's mistress poisoned him out of spite in front of everyone in the great hall.

"Madeleine mentioned it when I asked if Lyssa was her child."

"Lyssa is the spitting image of her mother. She has more of Garrett's fire in her, though. Lynnette was very shy, very meek. Lyssa is quite the little minx. She worships Madeleine. You would think they were mother and daughter."

He stood there awkwardly, having run out of things to say. Their conversation died suddenly.

Marielle stood. "I think I will retire myself. Things are settling down."

Ashby looked around them. "Yes, Stanbury rises early. There is always much to be done. May I escort you to your chamber?"

She nodded. "I would appreciate that. I am not quite sure I could find it on my own as of yet. The castle is so large. Madeleine promised me a full tour tomorrow. I would be satisfied just knowing where the library is."

He offered her his arm. "Then let me show you quickly and then see you to your room."

She placed her hand into the crook of his elbow. Just the touch of her fingers lit a fire inside him. They walked down the corridor and he indicated the room.

"Here's the library. You need to see it in daylight to appreciate the full effect."

He opened the door. No candles shone from within. He longed to pull her into the darkness and into his arms. Oh, God, he would go insane if he didn't leave soon.

Tamping down the strong emotions running through him, he calmly said, "Well, now you know where to come. Let me take you to your room."

He led her down the dimly lit passage, his heart beating wildly. He stopped in front of her door. It was the bedchamber they used for special guests and he assumed Marielle had been placed there.

"There should be a candle lit for you." He

opened the door and saw the flickering light. He looked back at Marielle and, without thinking, said what he'd thought all night.

"You have beautiful eyes."

"Thank you." Her voice was faint. The darkness seemed to grow around them. He had to leave. He must force his feet to move.

"I will see you on the morrow," he said, more abruptly than he'd wished. He saw a puzzled look cross her brow.

Ashby turned and walked quickly along the corridor. He went down the stairs again and out into the night. The November cold surrounded him. He welcomed the chill. Had it only been two months ago that Garrett sent him to France? His whole world had turned upside down. He, Ashby fitz Waryn, who was always so steady and confident, now felt like a lost, lonely boy.

He strode to the stables and saddled Lightning. He decided it was time to pay a visit to the attractive widow in the village. Maybe she could take his mind off the bewitching Marielle de la Tresse.

CHAPTER SEVENTEEN

MARIELLE AWOKE TO hushed voices. She opened her eyes, trying to place where she was. The stable. That was it.

She'd come down after the midday meal and helped Lyssa feed apples to all the horses. The girl prattled on happily about this one and that. She'd finally taken leave of Marielle and begun following around the head stableman. Marielle, who'd been a little queasy earlier, was seized by a rush of dizziness. She opened an unused stall and sat upon the hay in it. She supposed she had fallen asleep.

She didn't sit up, though. As wrong as it was, she'd always learned a great deal from eavesdropping upon the nuns at the convent. Besides, she wouldn't want to make anyone uncomfortable by making her presence known now.

"He is being an ass, Garrett. You know that."

"I know, sweetheart. It's just Ash being Ash, though. He always wants to cut his own path. He has never done it any other way."

"Well, he has avoided her like the plague itself these last few days. If I were Marielle, I would want to know what is afoot."

"There's nothing wrong with her. In fact, he even told me if it were another time and place, he would wed her."

"Then why will he not act upon this? Surely, he must love her. Our Ashby has never wanted to marry before. He turns a score and ten next year. It's past time he settled down."

"You know why. It's been a sticking point between us for several years now. Ashby fitz Waryn is a stubborn man, Madeleine. I cannot change him. I can only hope he will come to his senses in France, being apart from her."

"You cannot be serious, Garrett. You're sending him to France again?"

"It's what he wants, my love. In a way, I understand why."

"You know Marielle will be brokenhearted. I will not see her hurt or unhappy, Garrett. She has become like a sister to me."

"Then we will keep her entertained until Ash figures out on his own that he cannot live without her. Until then, we must make the best of it. Now come, let us go back before a nice fire. I am chilled to the bone. You must be, too."

Marielle heard a giggle and then a heavy silence, followed by a few whimpers. She felt her cheeks heat, knowing what must be taking place between the pair. Though they'd been married over four years, Lord and Lady Montayne still acted as newlyweds. Marielle was especially glad she'd kept quiet for it would have been embarrassing to catch her hosts while at love play.

"Come, love."

She heard their steps receding and knew they'd left the stables. Hearing their conversation helped her understand that she'd done nothing wrong. She'd wondered during the past week what she could have done to drive Ashby away from her. He rarely spoke to her and yet she would catch his eyes upon her from across the room several times a day. She, too, found whenever he was in the same room with her that she was aware of him wherever he was.

So he did want to marry her. And yet he was returning to France, presumably on business again for Garrett. But why? She remembered how ill he'd been on the crossing they'd undertaken. How he kissed the ground once they'd left the ship. He'd sworn that he would never be caught upon the English Channel again—yet he was leaving Stanbury to do so once more.

It was because of her. What was so wrong about her that he must leave England?

Marielle sensed something so strong between

them that it frightened her and excited her at the same time. Garrett also referred to some problem between the two of them, one that had gone on for years. What could be so bitter between the two? On the surface, they seemed the closest of friends. Ashby always spoke fondly of Garrett, as if they were blood brothers. Despite that, something stood between them that prevented Ashby from ever marrying.

What could it be? It wasn't something Marielle could ask Madeleine about or her new friend would realize Marielle had overheard them. Should she approach Ashby before he left for France?

What if he never came back?

"ASHBY? A WORD?"

It was Edith. She motioned him into Garrett's study and closed the door.

"Have a seat." He did so and she took one across from him.

"You have been a member of this family since you came to Stanbury as a small boy," Edith began.

"Yes, my lady. You have always treated me as a son." He leaned over and kissed her cheek with affection, knowing how she'd given a mother's love to him without reservation.

"You also are an outrageous flirt." She patted her cheek where he'd kissed her and smiled at him.

"So what is this about? Am I to guess?"

She shifted in her chair. "Because we are close, I feel I can say these things to you. I like Marielle. I like her a great deal, Ashby. We have taken to each other as you and I did all those many years ago."

Edith looked at him intently. "I have seen the looks that pass between you. They are as heated as any Garrett has shot in Madeleine's direction. You need to marry her, Ashby, and be quick about it."

"No."

Edith cocked her head, studying him. "No? Why not? She is a lovely girl, full of wit and grace. You will have absolutely stunning children though I fear you would need to keep any daughters locked up, knowing there are men like you running about in the world."

"No," he repeated firmly.

Her color rose. He'd rarely seen Edith angry. Even when he and Garrett caused some mischief that led to problems, she had always been level-headed, never raising her voice at them.

"Give me a reason. And it better be a good one, young man."

Ashby knew he could trust this woman with

the truth. "I have nothing to offer her, Edith. She was married to a count in France. I have no title. Monteville lands stretched as far as the eye could see. The chateau she lived in would put most in England to shame. I can give her neither a grand home nor support her in the style she knows."

Edith burst out laughing. "Surely, you jest. I thought you knew women, Ashby. They have fallen at your feet since you were ten and two. I would have expected you to know more about what women want by now."

"What do they want, Edith? Absolutely nothing that I can give them. Why do you think I have never seriously pursued a woman in the past? I have only my name to give them. Nothing more."

She frowned at him, but then her face softened. "Women want *love*, Ashby. They want respect. They want to be the most important person in the world to their man and they want him to be the same in return. Money, land—none of it makes a bit of difference."

"It does to me," he said angrily and rose to his feet.

Edith stood and faced him. "I would not have thought you such a prideful man. Arrogant. Conceited. Even foolish. To throw away love for such vanity? I thought you would have known better."

She crossed the room and opened the door.

"You will regret your choice, Ashby. I only pray you will come to your senses before it's too late."

The minute she left, he went to his room and began to pack. He wouldn't stay at Stanbury a moment longer. His spirits were lower than they'd ever been. He'd moped about the estate without being able to think clearly for a week now. Twice, he'd ridden to the village to seek solace in the willing widow's arms, only to turn back before he arrived. He would leave immediately. Surely distance and time would conquer this lingering depression.

He ran into Madeleine as he descended the stairs. He gave her a quick kiss on the cheek. "I am off to London and France after that. Have you anything you wish me to take to your mother?"

She went white at his words. "Now? What about—"

"Where is Garrett? I have need to speak to him before I leave."

"He was in the bailey about an hour ago. Ashby, I wish—"

"Wish me Godspeed, Madeleine." He brought his arms about her and gave her a long embrace. "I must go," he whispered. "It's the only way."

He released her and hurried down the stairs. Garrett was with Lyssa and Cynric in the great hall. The minute Garrett saw him, bag in hand, he stood and met him.

"I'm leaving now, Garrett. I do not want to delay. Do you have any changes to what we discussed?"

"No." Garrett's face was troubled. "I only need to get you a pouch from my study. On all matters, you have my full authority. You speak for me. Tell the children goodbye. I'll only be a moment."

Garrett strode from the room. Ashby made quick farewells, promising Lyssa he'd return soon, not knowing if he ever would. He went to the stables and saddled Lightning then mounted up and rode him to the keep in order to claim what Garrett would give him.

Instead, it was Marielle that greeted him, her face without emotion. He slowed his horse as he reached her.

She looked up at him in the saddle, wordlessly handing him Garrett's pouch. They looked into each other's eyes and Ashby hoped he betrayed none of the longing he had for her at this moment.

"I see you were leaving again without a proper goodbye."

Immediately, he thought of that last time—and the passionate kiss between them. The kiss that haunted him by day and kept him sleepless at night. That was before Jean-Paul died. A moment of doubt flashed through his mind.

Had she murdered Jean-Paul to come to him?

Yet he remembered her fear of Marc and laid his brief doubts to rest.

"I will look in on your parents if you wish. Let them know where you are and that you are safe."

She nodded, her face resigned to his departure. "I will not trouble you now, seeing you are in a great hurry. Cadena knows the town of my birth. She will tell you how to reach my parents."

Marielle turned and walked away. Ashby longed to call out to her but knew it would only prolong the inevitable. He must have the courage to leave now, before more heartache occurred. He wheeled Lightning and cantered through the bailey.

As he rode out from Stanbury, Ashby knew his life would never be the same.

CHAPTER EIGHTEEN

"TWO DAYS HAVE seemed liked two years," Marielle complained to Madeleine.

"I know what you mean. When Garrett is gone, even for a day, I miss him terribly. I always try to stay busy to keep myself from moping about."

Marielle stroked the cat in her lap, its silky fur warm to her touch. She and Madeleine sat beside the fire in the solar. November was three-quarters gone and the day outside was cold and overcast.

Cynric let out a little moan and Madeleine went to where he lay napping. She stroked her son's head and smiled down at the boy. Marielle envied Madeleine in that moment. Her hostess had everything Marielle wanted—a husband who doted on her and children to love.

All Marielle had now was Luke, the cat. He'd taken to following her about the last two days.

Ever since Ashby left for France.

Madeleine returned to her seat by the fire. She reached across and rubbed Luke under his chin. The cat purred contentedly.

"Luke knows when anyone is out of sorts," Madeleine explained. "When I broke my leg, he often sat on the bed snuggled next to me. When I was carrying Cynric, I was violently ill every morning for three months. The little furball always kept me good company."

Marielle looked expectantly at Madeleine. "Does he keep you company now?" She was thinking how Madeleine revealed she may be again with child.

"Yes. He does after we sup at night. It's when the queasiness descends upon me this time around. I have been able to slip away without anyone noticing. Luke shows up and gives me comfort while I lose most of my supper. Fortunately after that, I feel fine. He goes off to Lyssa's bed and curls up, awaiting her arrival."

"Does Garrett know yet?"

"I have decided I will tell him tonight. I'm certain now. It's been six weeks since my monthly flow last came." She smiled contentedly. "He will be so pleased."

Madeleine shifted in her chair and looked at Marielle. "But enough about me. How are you doing since Ashby ran off? It's a child's way, not a man's. He has surprised me. For the first time since I've known him, I am disappointed in him."

Marielle sighed. "I know I must shake off this gloom but I cannot help it. I have no claim on him but, all the same, he has claimed my heart."

She brushed aside a falling tear. "I love him, Madeleine. I have never loved any man before. I cannot understand why he left. He seems to have feelings for me. I am free to return those feelings now that my husband is gone and yet Ashby has gone off with no indication if or when he will return."

Marielle quelled her rising doubts. She worried that she'd misread Ashby's attentions. She'd been left alone in a strange land, having to depend upon the kindness of strangers. If he did not return, she would be forced to face a future without him and move on to the convent and a life of boredom and regret for what might have been.

She pushed her fears aside and watched Madeleine carefully. Several times in the last two days, her friend seemed on the verge of confiding in her and yet, each time, she hesitated.

Madeleine stared off, as if she were far away from Stanbury. When she focused on Marielle again, it was obvious she'd come to some sort of decision.

"Ashby appears to be very self-assured. That is far from the truth."

Marielle sat up, thankful that Madeleine had

seen fit to speak to her honestly. "Why do you say that?"

Her friend absently twisted a finger around a lock of hair. "Ashby comes from a family of four. Ashland, the eldest, inherited when their father, Walter, passed on. Walter was great friends with Garrett's father, Ryker. The two men fought hard and drank harder. They were very heavy-handed men who abused their wives.

"His mother, Beatrice, died when Ashby was only three, in childbirth with his sister Faylinn. His mother is only a vague image in his mind, so you see, he grew up not witnessing a good marriage to begin with, either at home or here at Stanbury with Ryker and Edith."

Marielle began forming a picture of the young Ashby. He would have been raised knowing he would not inherit. He would have been protective of his younger sister. She knew Ashby came to Stanbury to foster when he was very young. He would have been out of sorts but Edith nurtured him as her own child.

"As a third son, he was promised to the Church, but Ashby refused to go along with that even from an early age." Madeleine chuckled. "Can you see him as Father Ashby, listening to confessions and comforting the sick?"

"I fear he would have flirted outrageously with all the women in his parish," Marielle said.

"But then attendance at mass might have

improved," added Madeleine. "With his blond hair and angelic looks, he would be so pleasant to gaze upon."

They both laughed at the thought of Ashby in a priest's robes, committed to the pious life.

Madeleine grew serious. "He has spoken very little to me of his home life before Stanbury. He considers this to be his home. Unfortunately, that's part of the problem, as well."

Madeleine now touched upon what Marielle had overheard that day in the stables.

"Garrett loves Ashby as his own flesh and blood. He has offered Ashby his own manor house so many times over the past few years that I have lost count. Beneath his carefree ways, Ashby is a proud, stubborn man. He feels with no title, no lands of his own, and no home to call his own that he would not be a husband worthy to any woman."

Marielle was stunned. "Surely, you jest? Many men are in his position. They marry with no qualms. Why, we could remain at Stanbury in a small cottage as other knights do. It's absurd for him to think women only want a grand home and a man with a fancy title."

Her friend shook her head sadly. "That's exactly what he *does* think. He believes he has nothing to offer you except his strong sense of honor. He is a man of his word. It dominates his world. Now you have come along. He is totally smitten with you. He told Garrett he would marry you under other circumstances."

Madeleine took her hand. "Don't you see, Marielle? He met a French comtesse, with a grand chateau and lands that extended as far as the eye could behold. One with jewels and servants that waited on her every need. He may love you but he would never want you to lower yourself from the position you held to join together with him."

She pushed Luke from her lap and stood. "It's absurd! I come from very simple stock. My father was a tradesman. My life in the convent was one of deprivation, not privilege. And my marriage was the most unhappy time of my life. Jean-Paul let me do nothing but weave tapestries and sit and look pretty for his guests."

She looked at Madeleine earnestly. "All those . . . things . . . they were not important to me. If I had Ashby's love and his babe in my arms, nothing else would matter."

Marielle began to cry. Madeleine came and placed her arms around her friend.

"I know, dearest friend. But Ashby does not think he deserves Garrett's offer of a manor house. He feels it's something that must be earned."

"So the fool would rather go to France and have both of us wallow in misery than swallow his pride?"

Madeleine laughed. "That about sums it up."

She brushed the tears from Marielle's cheek. "Oh, Marielle, I know he will come to his senses. He loves you, he truly does. We simply will wait him out. Be patient. He is a good man and well worth that wait."

ASHBY CANTERED ALONG the road, Monteville land on both sides of him. He had no interest in calling upon Marc de la Tresse, the man who now was Comte of Monteville and owner of everything in sight. Ashby wished he could find a way to punish such a wicked, despicable man. At least Marielle was safe, far from de la Tresse's grasp.

He made his way along to Chateau Branais. He would stop there first and find out from the Bouchards where Marielle's parents lived. He didn't know if the new comte had sent word to them about her disappearance or even checked to see if she'd fled to their care. Ashby wanted to assure them of their daughter's safety.

He also wondered if de la Tresse blamed Cadena and Robert for Marielle having gone missing. As far as he could ascertain, they were the only people Marielle had contact with in the area. Jean-Paul never allowed her to travel with him. She had lived almost as a cloistered nun within the walls of Monteville.

His mount was a suitable replacement for Lightning. He'd left the horse with John back in London. He didn't know how long he'd be in France, much less whether he would return to England to live, so he'd chosen the best horseflesh he'd seen upon his arrival. Raven was a good sixteen hands high and jet black, with a steady nature. His owner told Ashby that Raven was a dependable horse, not easily frightened by noise or the elements. He gave the horse a friendly pat as they cantered along.

He approached Chateau Branais from the north. When he reached its vineyards, he saw workers busy in the fields. He hadn't ridden five minutes when he caught sight of Pierre, who waved at him and trotted over to meet him.

"*Bonjour*, Ashby. We did not expect your return so soon. Is there trouble?" His face filled with worry.

Ashby shook hands with him. "No, Pierre. Things are fine with Garrett and Madeleine. I am back sooner than we planned. I was going to stop by and visit with your parents."

"They will be delighted. They missed you from the moment you left."

"Then I will ride directly to their house."

Pierre wiped his brow with a rag. "I will see you when we dine later. *Au revoir.*"

He made his way to the manor. A groom met

him, praising his choice of horseflesh. He'd planned to care for Raven himself but Cadena appeared.

"Ashby! What a delightful surprise. Please, come in. I am thrilled to see you." She took his arm and led him into the house. He could smell apple tarts the moment they stepped inside.

"I suppose you will have to put up with me at least until I have had some of those tarts. Apple is my favorite."

Cadena's eyes welled with tears, surprising him. "Come and sit." She called for soap and water to be brought and he washed the dust of the road from him.

"I am here again on business for Garrett," he told her as a servant assisted him with the water and towels, "but I also want to look in on Marielle's parents while I am here. I want to let them know she is safe. Was the Comte de la Tresse fit to be tied when he returned to find her gone? I hope you did not bear the brunt of his wrath. Did he suspect your involvement in her disappearance?"

Cadena's lips trembled. She looked over her shoulder as the servant exited the room and turned back to him. Her entire demeanor had undergone a sudden change.

"Oh, Ashby." Her voice was barely above a whisper. "It's horrible what that wicked man has done."

Every fiber of his being came to full alert at her words. "What has happened, Cadena?"

"Marc imprisoned Marielle's parents. He said they will rot in his dungeon unless Marielle returns to him."

CHAPTER NINETEEN

"WE LEARNED OF it just this morning," Cadena continued, tears welling in her eyes. "Marc visited here not an hour ago. I have yet to share the news with Pierre."

Ashby led her to a chair and knelt by her side. "Tell me everything, Cadena. Leave nothing out."

She composed herself, mopping her tears with the apron she wore. "It wasn't the first time he has been here since Marielle left. He came a month ago, right after he returned to Monteville from whatever business he had. He was frantic that Marielle disappeared without a word."

"Did he accuse you of aiding her?"

"Not at first. We sent word that she decided to stay overnight with us. That was the day you left France. Etienne came over the next afternoon, worried that she had not returned. He thought mayhap she had fallen ill. I assured him she left Chateau Branais early after morning mass. I mentioned how eager she was to visit her parents since it had been so long since she had seen them."

Cadena frowned. "I hated lying to him but what was I to say? He and Donatien turned the countryside upside-down looking for her. I think they feared just how great Marc's wrath would be when he returned."

Ashby asked, "And was it?"

"That was the amazing thing. When Marc arrived, he seemed quite calm about the whole affair. Usually, he swings between being sullen and irrational. He displayed no temper whatsoever. He did question me thoroughly."

She twisted her hands nervously. "I knew Robert would not be up to it. His is a transparent face. He wears all his feelings on it for the world to see. I sent him to our chamber when Marc came that day, telling him that Robert was resting.

"We thought all was well until this morning. We had not seen Marc again these last two weeks. Then suddenly, he turns up this morning. He asked to see Robert privately. Thank the Lord Almighty Robert was determined enough that I should sit in on this audience."

"What exactly did Marc say, Cadena? Try to remember as much as you can."

She reached into her apron pocket and extracted a piece of parchment. "Everything's written here."

He looked at her in confusion but took the parchment she offered.

"Read it. Once you have, come to our chamber. Robert has taken to his bed. He has not been strong since his illness last summer. This letter has done him in. He thinks so highly of Marielle and is so very worried."

She gave his shoulder a reassuring squeeze and rose from the chair. She carried herself with a dignity and grace that Ashby often saw echoed in Madeleine's bearing.

He took the chair she'd vacated and opened the scroll. The script was dark and disjointed. He could almost feel the cold anger pouring from it as he read.

Marielle –

Gautier and Blanche Matesse now reside in the dungeon of Monteville. They may rot in there until the Christ comes again, for all I care.

If you wish to gain their freedom, you will return at once to Monteville.

Their fate is in your hands . . .

Your loving fiancé,
Marc

Ashby tried to still the chills rippling through him. What kind of monster would toy with people's lives in such a way? He read the text again more slowly, hoping his translation of the French was accurate. The wording was simple, though. De la Tresse's message was clear. Marielle's parents would die if she did not return to France and marry her brother-in-law.

Despair gnawed at his soul. He'd played the gallant knight and rescued Marielle from Marc's clutches. Now Ashby would be the very one to escort her back and feed her to the jaws of the beast. Everything within him rebelled at the thought.

He decided at that moment to pay a call upon Marc de la Tresse.

RAVEN MUST HAVE caught his mood. The animal had been very even-tempered the entire journey to Chateau Branais but Ashby sensed a different horse altogether. Raven held his head higher. His step was quicker and more spirited. He liked the changes in the horse. It gave him hope that if he were able to spirit Marielle's parents away from Monteville, Raven would play a large part in that escape.

He was arriving unannounced, which he

thought wise. After speaking with Robert and Cadena, he decided to scope the lay of the land before taking action. He knew something of the castle's floor plan, thanks to his prior visit, yet he had no idea where access to the dungeon lay.

Ashby noticed during his prior visit that although Monteville had a thriving vineyard full of bustling workers, its knights were few. Several, with the men that had gone on the hunt being the exceptions, looked too well-fed and complacent. He wondered at the experience they had in defending their home, much less if they'd been used to warfare in general. He hadn't noticed any training exercises his entire stay. All this gave his spirit a sense of hope.

He covered the last hundred yards and waved to the gatekeeper. It was not the same one that had been on duty each time when he visited before. Before Ashby could call up a greeting and identify himself, the grim-faced watchman signaled for him to wait and the man disappeared from view. Another somber man took his place. The replacement eyed him carefully but made no move to address him, much less open the gate. It stirred Ashby's curiosity. His eyes searched the walls and noted several sentries stationed at consistent intervals. He'd not considered Monteville an especially well-defended property from his previous visit. That was no longer the case.

A good five minutes later, the first watchman returned, joined by a man Ashby did recognize. He spoke briefly to the man Ashby had seen first, the one with the surly expression that seemed permanently etched upon his features. He glared down at Ashby a hard moment before giving the signal. The gate opened.

Riding into the outer bailey, he immediately noticed the changes. Besides the additional guards along the wall-walk, the area bustled with activity. Ashby noted several groups of men involved in sword practice with full battle gear and shields in play. Two blacksmiths sat out in the open, fashioning mail coifs and hauberks with articulated shoulder plates. Two more made alavicas and ameures, their metal edges glimmering in the sunlight.

A beefy knight on horseback approached him. "Be you Ashby fitz Waryn?"

"I am he."

The man studied him a moment. "You were expected. Follow me." He took off at a steady canter. Ashby didn't like the fact that de la Tresse had anticipated his arrival. It didn't bode well. He set off after the rider.

They approached the stables and the guard slowed to a halt. He dismounted and tossed his reins to a stable lad that came running up quickly. Ashby recognized the boy from his previous visit.

"Good day, Jacques," he said pleasantly.

"Will you care for Raven while I visit your master?"

The boy looked hesitantly at the stout knight, who nodded back imperceptibly.

"Yes, my lord. It's a fine mount you have this time."

Ashby patted the horse. "Thank you. I plan to stay in France indefinitely and thought him a good investment."

He gave the reins to Jacques and turned to his escort. "May I see Monsieur de la Tresse now?"

"*Comte* de la Tresse." The knight's words were sharp and their meaning clear. Marc was definitely in charge of Monteville now in every sense of the word.

"Of course," Ashby replied smoothly. "If the comte is seeing visitors, I wish to be one of them."

Without replying, the knight turned quickly and started to the keep. Ashby followed, taking in all the new changes. His planned rescue mission, only half-formed in his mind, fell flat. This was not a two-man or even ten-man attempt. It would take a small army to storm Monteville and spirit away Marielle's parents.

He was led past the great hall and directed to a large room that must serve as Marc's study. It was not where Jean-Paul had conducted business. Ashby noted even this subtle change.

Marc de la Tresse awaited him behind a large

desk free of any papers.

"Fitz Waryn. Good of you to stop by." Marc looked at the escort. "That will be all, Gunther." He waited until the knight left before he spoke again.

"I find it . . . odd you have returned so soon to France. Especially when you know no Monteville land is for sale."

Ashby took the seat across from him without being invited. He enjoyed the angry flash that crossed Marc's face before he smoothed his features into a calm demeanor.

"I reported to Lord Montayne that the desired land was unavailable. Naturally, he was disappointed but I had searched the area near Chateau Branais for other possibilities."

"And?" Marc sat forward slightly, his fingers steepled, elbows on the desk.

"We will go ahead as planned. Lord Montayne wants to try a new vintage, one separate from what his people now produce at the chateau under the Bouchards. I am commissioned to find suitable land close to what he now owns. I will remain in France indefinitely to spearhead this project."

"Ah." Marc looked at him curiously. "You plan to live in France. Have you a wife that will accompany you? I do not remember you mentioning one on your recent visit."

Ashby knew Marc baited him so he replied

evenly, "I am not married nor have any desire to enter that state."

"A man for whom one woman will not do. Interesting." Marc poured some wine from a carafe and drank deeply. He did not offer his guest any. It amused Ashby that the new comte tried to assert his power in every word, every gesture.

"I remember you yourself are not married," he said. "Now that you are master of Monteville, will you choose a comtesse?"

Marc drained the cup of wine and sat back. "Of course, I am interested in providing Monteville with an heir. Something my brother could not do." He smiled. In that one smile, Ashby's blood froze.

"I plan to wed soon," Marc informed him, leisurely studying Ashby. "You know the bride. It is my dear brother Jean-Paul's widow. Marielle."

"I remember Marielle." Ashby wondered where this cat and mouse game headed. "She was a delightful hostess. Mayhap I can visit with her when we have finished our conversation here. I'm always up for a challenging game of chess."

Marc slammed a fist down. "Enough!" he roared. "Do you really think you fool me? I know you assisted Marielle in her pathetic attempt to escape," he sneered. "I traced you to Pauillac. You were seen together at the docks."

Ashby kept his composure though he longed

to lunge at the bastard and wipe the twisted smirk from his face.

The new Comte of Monteville laughed low. "What game do you think to play, fitz Waryn? Mayhap a gallant rescue attempt?" He studied Ashby carefully. "I think not. You see the changes I have made. Jean-Paul was a laggard when it came to defense. All he thought about was the grape. But I have rid Monteville of his broken-down knights and hired expert mercenaries in their place. I intend to produce not only the best-loved vintage in Bordeaux but I'll also own the most efficiently run castle. No one will dare breech these walls.

"I will also possess the most beautiful wife in all of France." Marc narrowed his eyes. "So give Marielle this message for me. Return. Or your family will pay in ways you cannot begin to imagine."

Ashby saw madness glimmer in the new comte's eyes. Even if Marielle did return and wed this man, he still might kill her for imagined indiscretions.

Yet how could he keep the news from her? That her parents had been imprisoned in the de la Tresse dungeons. That they would remain prisoners of the Comte de la Tresse until they died.

Unless Marielle came back and sacrificed herself for them.

She had not spoken of her parents with any kind of fondness—yet Ashby knew that she would feel responsible for them being imprisoned by Marc de la Tresse. He decided to try and glean any further information he could from the madman sitting before him.

"The comtesse has family?" he asked.

"She does," the comte said. "Parents who wished her to be gone, pushing her onto my dear brother." He paused, an evil smile spreading across his face. "Marielle's parents are now my guests at Monteville. In my dungeons. I have kept them as mere prisoners for the time being but if Marielle doesn't return soon, they will be subjected to brutal, excruciating agony."

Shock rippled through him. "You would torture them? All because Marielle has chosen to live away from Monteville?"

"She belongs to *me!*" roared de la Tresse, spittle flying from his mouth. "She always did. It was Jean-Paul's fault. She should have been mine."

The comte rose and began pacing, his words tumbling out as he raged. "Marielle is the most beautiful woman in France. I deserve her. I did without for so long. Jean-Paul and his wife barely acknowledged me. He thought me immature and lacking in common sense. He never realized that I grew to manhood and that I had needs. Desires. I should have run Monteville all along, not Jean-

Paul. He was an old fool."

Marielle had told Ashby of the jealousy that the younger de la Tresse had regarding his older brother. As the comte spoke, though, he seemed possessed by a deep-seated anger that must have festered for years. And somehow, Marielle had come to symbolize everything Marc de la Tresse wanted. If he possessed her, he would finally feel complete.

And Marielle would spend the rest of her life in misery, tied to this cruel monster, who thought to control her by threatening to torture her parents.

"You are the comte now," Ashby said, trying to soothe the man's temper. "You own land, rich and fertile, as far as the eye can see. Your estate produces magnificent wines. Why do even need Marielle? She was already wed for many years and did not produce an heir. You are young and handsome. You are a comte of France. You can have your pick of any woman. Find another. One sweet and young and eager to please you."

"I want Marielle," the comte said, coming to a halt before Ashby. "There is no other like her. I *will* have her. I will get sons off her. Jean-Paul was weak and old. He never produced any children with either wife. The fault lay in him. Marielle will lie with me thrice a day until her belly swells with my child."

Malevolence flared in his eyes. "You will give

her my message, fitz Waryn. You will implore her to return. Tell her she must—or I shall have her parents flayed. Their skin shredded. Ripped in layers from them until only their bones are exposed. Their screams will be heard throughout the entire length of France. And that is only the beginning." He paused. "You will do this, fitz Waryn. You will make sure she returns to me.

"Or I will do even worse to you."

Ashby wished to beat this arrogant man until he begged for mercy. He kept his fists by his sides, though, and his tongue from lashing out threats of his own. Somehow, some way, he would free Marielle's parents to prevent her from sacrificing her freedom for them.

As the comte glared at him, Ashby said, "I will return to England and deliver your message to Marielle. It is up to her whether or not she wishes to be escorted back to Monteville."

De la Tresse nodded sagely. "Oh, she will. She couldn't live with herself otherwise."

CHAPTER TWENTY

"**A**SHBY IS HOME!"

Lyssa came running into Marielle's chamber with a joyful look upon her face. Marielle's heart almost burst into song. He'd been gone barely long enough to make the journey to Bordeaux and back again to Stanbury.

Was Madeleine right?

Had he finally come to his senses after such a short time apart? Did he realize he needed her as much as she needed him?

Lyssa tugged on her hand. "Well, come on! We have to greet him. It's our way."

The girl chattered like a magpie as she pulled Marielle down the stairs. Marielle concentrated on the steps before her, not allowing herself the luxury of hope. Yet with every step she took, her heart cried out, *"He's home, he's here, my Ashby is back again."*

Madeleine met them at the bottom of the staircase, a knowing smile on her face. Lyssa dashed past her, leaving them alone for a moment.

Madeleine slipped an arm through hers. "I suppose I did not give him enough credit." She grinned. "He missed you much sooner than I would have expected. Our Ashby has made it back in record time."

The two women followed after Lyssa. They met Garrett coming from his study, a puzzled look on his face.

"Ash is home? What nonsense is this? I could hear Lyssa hollering it as she ran by."

Madeleine gave him a smug look. "Ashby must have forgotten something important," she said mysteriously and pulled Marielle along, Garrett bringing up the rear.

Marielle thought how seasick Ashby had been on the way back from France. That he'd gone through the voyage twice in so short a time gave her the confidence to meet him now.

They walked outside just as he rode up and sprang from his horse. He tossed the reins to a waiting groom and motioned for him to take Lightning.

That was when it hit her. Lightning was Ashby's pride and joy. He'd always taken meticulous care of the horse since she'd known him. An uneasiness filled her.

He started up the stairs, Lyssa tugging on his hand and babbling away. Immediately, Marielle saw the difference. She witnessed no joy in his step at having returned home to Stanbury, no carefree ease that he wore like a cloak. His shuttered eyes hid something from them. From her.

Something was terribly wrong.

He reached the top and greeted those awaiting him in a general manner. He avoided looking at her altogether.

Marielle knew then that he had not come home for her. Something far greater drove him back to England, not eagerness to declare his love for her and make her his bride.

Whatever it was, it was serious. His smiles for Lyssa did not continue to his eyes. That was something Marielle had always been drawn to in him. When Ashby smiled, his whole face lit up.

Today, his smile was as remote as a wintry day.

Garrett took the situation in hand. "I fear Ash is worn out from his travels. Lyssa? Would you go tend to Lightning? Make sure that the horse is properly cared for?"

The girl lit up with pleasure and pride, running from where they stood toward the stables without a word or backward glance.

"Shall we speak alone now, Ash?" Garrett continued.

Ashby looked at him with a pained expression. "Mayhap I should speak to Marielle alone." Then suddenly changing his mind, he added, "No. I think she would want you both present."

He looked at Madeleine. And finally at her. The pain in his eyes was all too real.

"Come. We shall go to Garrett's study." Madeleine took Marielle's arm as she spoke. "It will afford us the privacy we need."

The four walked without conversation and entered the small room, dwarfed by an oversized desk. Garrett's papers were strewn across it haphazardly. Ashby motioned for the women to sit. He stood awkwardly, almost like an unprepared boy ill at ease in front of his tutor.

Garrett closed the door and joined them.

Ashby finally directly his gaze at Marielle. "I thought to keep the news from you somehow but I cannot. You deserve to know the truth, though it will be painful."

She realized it must involve her parents since he'd promised her he would visit them and tell them she was safe.

"Are *Maman* and Papa ill? Has one of them died?" She stood and, without thinking, took his hand. "You can tell me, Ashby. They are very old. I am strong enough to hear such news."

His look of anguish sliced at her heart. "Please sit, Marielle."

"No," she replied. "Say what you must and

be done with it. I must hear whatever news you bring. Now."

He pulled a roll of parchment from his pouch. "Sit and read this."

Marielle gave him a quizzical look but did as he asked. She took the parchment and opened it. For a moment, her heart stopped when she recognized Marc's handwriting. She scanned the brief contents quickly and then, in disbelief, read it more slowly.

The page fell from her hands. "No," she cried hoarsely.

Ashby retrieved the letter and handed it to Garrett. Madeleine stood next to him and read the few lines. Marielle was conscious of Madeleine's gasp.

A deadly calm descended upon her. "I must go back. At once," she said. "I will pack now." She rose and walked from the room, her head held high. No tears came. What use would they be?

Marielle was now sentenced to a living death—a life spent as wife to a monster.

MARIELLE REFUSED TO see anyone that afternoon. She finally let Madeleine in for a few minutes. Ashby paced outside as they'd spoken. When

Madeleine opened the door, he rushed to meet her. She pulled the door closed behind her.

"She does not wish to see anyone, Ashby. She does want to leave on the morrow." Madeleine looked at him in sorrow. "Are you willing to escort her back to France?"

"I and no other," he proclaimed. "If I can do anything to remedy the situation, I shall."

"You mean to keep her from marrying Marc de la Tresse?"

Ashby set his jaw. "She is a strong woman, Madeleine. She will do as she sees fit. I will do whatever she asks of me."

He returned to his room and moped. Instead of going down to supper, he'd lain on his bed, searching for answers that would not come.

Now it was late. He knew he should try and get some rest but he doubted sleep would come. His mind was a swirling quagmire of second guesses.

A soft knock roused him from the bed. He sat up immediately, thinking it was Garrett wishing to speak with him. But when he opened the door, Marielle stood before him. She'd never looked lovelier. Those amethyst eyes burned brightly in her pale face.

"May I come in?" she asked softly.

He stood aside for her to enter and then closed the door.

As he faced her, all the intense longings for

her rushed through him. Why hadn't he taken Garrett up on his generous offer of a manor? Mayhap then he might have felt worthy enough to pursue this beautiful woman that stood before him.

Ashby placed his hands upon her shoulders. "I love you," he admitted softly. "The reasons why those words never came seem so pitiful now."

Marielle tensed. "It is too late for us, Ashby."

"Is it?" he asked, clinging to hope as Pandora surely had.

"Yes. We were never meant to be."

That sliver of hope pushed him to say, "Then why are you here?"

She started to answer but no words came. Marielle looked up at him helplessly. "Because tonight is all we will ever have."

She lay her cheek against his chest and wrapped her arms about his waist. He enveloped her, holding her gently against him. Her silent tears soaked his tunic. To comfort her, he kissed the top of her head, then he lifted her chin with a finger and gently touched his mouth to hers.

Passion ignited between them. The kiss stoked the fire that had lain dormant within them for close to two months. All the desire built up inside of him spilled forth from his mouth into hers.

She tasted as before, only sweeter now. He

wanted her more than he had wanted any other woman at any other time. Yet she was not his for the taking. Maybe she never had been.

Marielle sensed Ashby pulling away from her. She'd not come here for one kiss. No, what she wanted—needed—was one night to call her own. One night of rich passion and beautiful lovemaking that would be her own treasure. One night that she would pull from her memory again and again over the long years of hell to come. One night that Marc could never take away.

If she couldn't have Ashby, she would at least make a magical memory with him. Here. Now.

She must have this one night.

She slipped her arms around his neck and pulled him back to her, even as he tried to break the kiss. She pressed her body against his. He responded immediately.

Marielle put everything of herself into the kiss. She sensually ran her tongue along his lips until they parted and she gained entrance into Heaven. His tongue feverishly answered her own mating call. His hands slid along her back and down to her buttocks, drawing her closer.

"Love me," she whispered into his mouth.

He swept her into his arms, never breaking the kiss, and carried her to his bed. He lowered her to it slowly and then covered her body with his. She reveled in his weight against her, his mouth on hers, his hands running through her hair and down to her breasts. Somehow he'd untied her laces and pushed her clothing aside, fixing his mouth on her breast.

Marielle groaned aloud, the pleasure was so great. Heat built throughout her until she thought she'd been set on fire. Still, tingling bits of pleasure rippled up and down every part of her. Ashby lifted her clothes from her then and tossed them to the floor. His hands were everywhere, loving, worshipping every inch of her body, strong, firm, yet gentle and giving at the same time.

He parted her thighs and dropped a hand between them. Marielle felt a moistness there for the first time as Ashby slipped a finger inside her. She cried out her joy but it was lost in his mouth. His tongue and his fingers mimicked each other, both giving her the most exquisite pleasure imaginable.

Then she erupted in waves of happiness, a dizzying joy that had her head spinning. She lost track as wave after wave of intense pleasure rippled through her. Then it ended. She lay dazed, unsure of what had just occurred. He moved away from her but she was too weak to reach out for him. She whimpered a cry instead.

He stroked her cheek. "Just a moment, my love." He rejoined her almost immediately, now naked as she was, his heated body pressed against hers.

"Love me," she cried again, and he did. He entered her slowly, filling her until she cried out in ecstasy.

"Oh, Ashby. Ashby."

Never had she been loved as she was now. With a slow rhythm, he moved against her again and again, as something once more built inside of her, that something which she'd never known existed until this man's touch. The anticipation gathered within her as he moved with an agonizing slowness.

"More," she called to him. "More."

His lips caressed her throat and nibbled at her ear playfully. "You think you want more?"

She nodded, not trusting the words to come.

"Then you shall have what you desire."

He increased his movements, her hips meeting his every thrust. The pressure mounted. Then without warning, stars exploded, blinding her. Ashby kissed her again and again, his tongue stroking hers, murmuring words she couldn't understand.

He kissed her deeply, his breathing ragged as he stilled. Marielle felt a connection to him like none ever before. He fell to his side and brought her against him. She could feel the pounding of his heart against her cheek. It was her moment of greatest bliss.

She could stay like this forever.

"I love you," she whispered. The bliss turned

to bittersweet sorrow. She knew she would never be able to share this again with him. She began to pull away but he held her tightly against him.

"No. Stay," he begged. "Stay with me . . . always."

"It's not possible," she said simply. It was like plunging a knife into both of their hearts. "I must go now."

"Go?" His eyes met hers. The corner of his beautiful mouth turned up in a ghost of a smile. "You are not going anywhere, my love. We have only just begun."

CHAPTER TWENTY-ONE

MARIELLE AWOKE IN Ashby's arms. The candle had only recently extinguished itself. She could smell the faint smoke drifting across the bed.

She opened her eyes to the darkness. In all the nights to come, though, the darkness would be no more. Ashby had seen to that. Marielle knew she would take to bed with her each evening the recollections of this one night. His presence would always be with her. She would feel his arms about her. Recall the memory of his loving touch. Savor the richness of each kiss. She would use her heart as the key to unlock these memories and thus remember the precious hours forever.

He stirred in his sleep and held her more tightly as if he knew she was about to leave him. She could now make out his jaw line in the shadows and pressed her lips just below it against his throat. The ache in her heart was a physical one, its very heaviness causing her pain with each breath.

How would she live without him?

Marielle lifted her hand and gently moved Ashby's arm. It stayed along his side. Now was the tricky part. Their legs were entangled as they faced each other. She eased one leg up and began to pull away from him.

Suddenly, her back was against the bed. Ashby loomed over her, pinning her wrists down. He playfully nipped at her throat then ran his tongue along the curve of her shoulder. Marielle tried to rise but he was having none of it.

"I must go," she protested.

"Not yet, sweetheart." To prove his point, his mouth came down on hers in an exquisite, demanding kiss that caused him to harden again. He slipped inside her one last time. She reveled in each possessive thrust as he branded her as his. His alone. Forever and always. Minutes later, he'd left her weak and shaken.

Marielle's mouth quivered from need as he pulled away, his breathing harsh. She reached up and pushed his damp hair from his brow. He captured her hand and pressed a fervent kiss to each fingertip. No regret filled her. Only pure love for a man she would never have again.

"I must go," she said again.

He brushed a hand through her hair. "I

know," he whispered. He rose from the bed and took her hands in his. It was as if she floated up and into his arms. Ashby held her close in a loving embrace. Then he pressed a last, soft kiss against her lips. That tender kiss alone had been worth her coming to his room. Marielle wished it could go on forever but she must face what the dawn would bring.

She broke the kiss with reluctance. "Can you help me find my garments? The candle has gone out."

She heard him rustling about before he slowly began to dress her. She hadn't a clue how he knew where to place the clothing. He'd obviously had much practice with dressing—and undressing—women in the dark. It caused her a small moment of hurt, but she pushed it aside. She would concentrate on the feel of his callused hands gliding along her skin, his strong fingers tying and smoothing, the stolen kisses between each layer he placed upon her.

Finally, she knew she was presentable in case anyone saw her in the corridor. She turned to go, no words coming from her. It was as if words would ruin anything at this point.

Marielle lay her hand upon the door handle, only to find Ashby's fingers close over hers.

"Don't go."

The anguish in his voice tore at her heart, the raw need that she herself experienced.

Ashby took her shoulders and turned her to

face him. He bent and brushed his lips against hers then placed his forehead against hers.

When he spoke, his voice was low, but she caught every word.

"Tell me to go for the priest now. Say you will marry me before we leave England."

"But Marc—"

"Marc be damned," he hissed. "What can he do if you are already wed to me?"

Marielle knew exactly what he would do. She had a good idea that Ashby did, too, else he wouldn't sound so full of despair. Still, she knew the words must come.

"He would kill them," she said dully. "He would claim they were his guests and he would leave them in that dank, rat-infested dungeon until they perished."

She lifted her hand to cup his cheek. "The cost of our happiness would be their deaths. Neither of us wishes that. It would taint everything we did or said."

"I cannot ask you to live like that," he said softly. "But if you won't wed me, we must first try something else before you hand yourself over to be devoured by that monster."

Marielle shook her head. "What? There is nothing else we can do, Ashby. We have shared this time together. It will have to be enough. I know what must be done. I am the only one who can free my parents."

"I can't see you relinquish your freedom and

be enslaved by that monster."

His hand smoothed her hair. "What if we went to the magistrate together and explained the situation? We could tell him—"

"No. It doesn't work that way. Magistrates should work for justice and the people but they understand the way of things. None of them would ever go against a comte's wishes. It would mean their head on a platter—and it still wouldn't change anything."

Desperation filled his eyes. "Then we petition the government. We will seek an audience with the king himself."

She shook her head sadly. "The king wouldn't care about an old couple rotting away in a comte's dungeons. To even gain an audience with the king might take years. My parents don't have that kind of time. Marc is not a patient man."

Ashby gripped her shoulders. "Then we pay off someone. There is always a government official who can be bribed. Or we go to the bishop. No, a cardinal. Or even the Pope. Surely, the Church would intervene in such an affair," he pleaded.

She captured his face with her hands and gazed into his eyes. "You speak of things you know would never come to pass. I have accepted my fate, Ashby. You, too, must accept what I must do. You are making it harder on me."

Regret filled his eyes. "I am so sorry, Marielle. I have never felt so utterly useless. So devoid of hope."

Her thumbs caressed his cheeks. "We shared this night, my love. It will be what I cling to always," she told him.

"Know that I will always love you." He pressed his lips to hers as his pledge. "Now—and forever."

***

MARIELLE DRIFTED THROUGH morning mass, her own fervent prayers crowding out the priest's words. She would break her fast and then be ready to leave Stanbury, never to return. As the household left the service, Garrett stopped her.

"A word, Marielle?"

She nodded and followed him to his study. He closed the door and studied her a moment. Marielle saw in him a strength she hadn't observed before, probably because she'd been blinded to everything except Ashby. She knew in that small space of time why Madeleine was so drawn to Garrett and why Ashby valued him as a friend. He had an intense energy vibrating about him that immediately made her willing to do whatever he would now ask of her. Garrett Stanbridge, the Earl of Montayne, was not a man who would take anything lightly. She knew what he next said would be very important to her.

"I won't pretty this up and tell you that Madeleine longs to see her parents and that this is a good time for it. Frankly, it's not. She told me about the babe. Traipsing off to France is the last thing we should do. Still," he added, "we do not want you to face Marc de la Tresse alone. I have met him in the past, and he's the embodiment of pure evil. We would ask that we be allowed to accompany you and Ash to Bordeaux. Mayhap I might intervene in some way, being his neighbor, so to speak."

He sat behind the desk and rubbed his eyes wearily, as if he'd stayed up all night trying to solve her problems.

"I would do anything to see Ash happy," Garrett explained. "I fear he never will be without you. If Madeleine or I can make a difference in this situation with your parents, then we would like to accompany you and Ash to France. With your permission, of course."

His words moved Marielle, touching the bleakness surrounding her heart. "I thank you for your kind offer, Garrett. I doubt you could ever change Marc's mind but I think it would do Ashby a world of good to have you present. I fear he will need all your strength and good judgment in what lies ahead."

Garrett smiled wearily at her. "You don't think he might do something rash, do you? Not our Ash."

He stood and took her elbow. "Come. Let us break our fast and make haste to London. Madeleine has been packed since last night as it is. Not even the Second Coming of the Christ would stop her from joining you on this journey."

He led her into the great hall. Marielle saw Madeleine spot them, a questioning look on her face. Marielle turned to Garrett and caught him nodding at his wife. Immediately, Madeleine busied herself, gathering Lyssa and Cynric around her.

As they joined her, Marielle heard Madeleine's last words to her children. "So you shall see Chateau Branais sooner than we planned."

Garrett frowned and stepped forward. "But I thought—"

"You know, Garrett, it will be Christmastime while we are there. I know the children would love to spend it with their *grandmere et grandpere*, as well as their parents." She flashed him a brilliant smile.

Garrett turned to Marielle. "You see, Marielle, this is how marriage works. We discuss plans. I tell my wife my wishes. I assume things are in order, then she springs some lovely surprise on me. A surprise that attests to her iron will, which I am wise enough to bow to."

Madeleine linked an arm through her husband's. "You know we would both miss the children dearly, especially at such a festive time.

And *Maman* will be thrilled to have the extra company. She will take wonderful care of them while we . . . resolve . . . this . . . other matter."

Marielle wished things could be untangled so easily but she knew they would not. Still, it would be nice to have the Lord and Lady Montayne there, not only for herself but for Ashby's sake.

At that moment, Ashby joined them. Lyssa dropped Cynric's hands and stopped her dance of joy, only to take Ashby's hands in hers and dance away with him. She must have informed him they were all going to France, for he shot a puzzled look in their direction. Garrett shrugged helplessly, while Madeleine winked at him. Marielle had dreaded the trip to Bordeaux. Thank goodness, now, it would be bearable.

Ashby ended his dance with Lyssa and came to her. "Is it your wish that the entire family come to France with us?"

Marielle made light of it. "I suppose Lyssa is our secret weapon. We simply turn her loose upon Marc and she will talk him into submission."

Ashby chuckled. "I had not thought of that. It's an excellent plan. I had thought to throw him upon the rack or merely draw and quarter him. He might beg for mercy after a few hours with Lyssa's incessant babbling."

Marielle laughed. For a brief moment, her spirits lifted.

CHAPTER TWENTY-TWO

"WE ARE CLOSE to the waterfront," Ashby remarked. "I can smell it in the wind."

Garrett pulled his cloak about him tightly. "Then your nose is better than mine. I do know it's London by the dank chill. I have never understood why this city's cold oozes into my bones. Stanbury is never like this."

"That's because Stanbury is perfect," Ashby quipped. He knew what Garrett meant, though. The country air always smelled fresh and invigorating, no matter what time of year. Even when the winter season invaded London, vile smells of all sorts seemed to permeate the buildings of every street.

"At least the trip has given us a taste of Maude's cooking," Garrett returned.

"Have you ever thought to bring her to Stanbury?"

Garrett grinned. "Never. Because sometimes it's only the thought of Maude's cooking that can get me to come to this hellhole." He shrugged. "Besides, Maude spent many a year there when we were growing into strapping lads. She actually prefers London. Says she gets bored in the country."

They rode in silence for a few minutes, winding their way through the hawkers in the fish market stalls. As they reached the edge of the waterfront, Garrett pulled Ebony up.

"We need to see Raleigh first."

Ashby remembered him as the harbormaster. "I hope the man is not in a drunken stupor."

Garrett chuckled. "You may be right in that but Raleigh's a good man. No matter how down in his cups he goes, he always rises back up. Not much gets by Raleigh, least of all in this harbor."

They tied their horses nearby and entered the office of the harbormaster. Raleigh sat behind a massive desk, books and papers scattered across it in disarray.

"Why, look who's here. If it isn't Lord Montayne," boomed Raleigh.

Ashby noted how red the man's eyes were. He had the look of a drunk, one of many years, at that. Still, Garrett had done business with him for some time now and Ryker before him.

Raleigh stood. "I sees you brought your friend." He screwed up his face and studied

Ashby with care.

"Fitz Waryn," Ashby supplied.

"Ah, I remember you. A name may escape me, but a face never does. Not yours, nor anyone's." He turned and smiled at Garrett. "Especially not your pretty wife's face. How is Lady Montayne doing?"

"Tolerably well. She's with child. It's early yet. We are off to visit her parents in Bordeaux."

Raleigh's eyes gleamed. "And the little ones?"

"The entire family is coming, Raleigh. That's why I needed see you. We must secure passage to Bordeaux for four adults and the two children. None of my ships is available now, much less suitable for such a journey."

Raleigh nodded. "I hear business is good for you. Well, let me see what I can do." He began pushing papers around, tossing them one way and another. He scratched his head, lost in thought, then looked up.

"Give me half an hour, my lord, to find what you need. Mayhap you'd like to pass the time getting a drink. I can recommend a place or two."

Garrett held up a hand. "That's all right, Raleigh. I think mayhap we shall wait outside for you to work your magic."

Ashby turned and followed Garrett out the door. He sensed his friend's unease in this place and remembered that it was here Garrett found Madeleine, close at death's door in a nearby tawdry inn. Her husband had not only beaten her beyond recognition but Henri de Picassaret attacked Garrett with a poisoned dirk. Garrett turned the knife on the man and saved not only himself but Madeleine from her hellish marriage. Ashby doubted Garrett had since returned to London without the lingering shadows of those memories.

His friend interrupted his thoughts. "We have not had much time alone, Ash. We need to discuss whatever possibilities we can muster in order to help save Marielle's parents."

"It's an awkward place to be in, Garrett. England and France are at each other's throats. I'll not see you send knights to Bordeaux and create an incident that could escalate things between the two countries."

Garrett gave him a sad look. "Not even for a beautiful lady in distress? I believe it was Helen of Troy whose face launched a thousand ships—and a lengthy war."

Ashby shrugged. "I was never much for history. You know that. Besides, I would swear Marielle possesses more beauty in her smile than that troublesome Helen ever did in face and figure." He hitched his leg up against a crate. "I refuse to drag you and your family into my problems, Garrett. I must solve this on my own."

Garrett lay a hand upon his shoulder. "We *are* your family, Ash. Even if I had no desire to lift a finger, Madeleine would have us smack into the thick of things. She cares for Marielle a great deal." He shrugged. "If the two people who mean the most to me need us to save this girl and her parents then, by the Christ, we will."

Despondency flooded Ashby. "But how? We cannot take your knights with us. Even if we could, Marielle must not know or even suspect something is afoot. She could unwittingly tip our hand to Marc."

Garrett turned pensive. "We could hire from the waterfront once we dock in Pauillac. The men we find there might be rough around the edges but certainly fierce enough to fight. I also have a ship due there in less than a week after we arrive. It's my own crew, Ash. That kind of loyalty cannot be bought."

He shook his head. "But they're sailors, Garrett, not trained knights. You haven't seen the situation. It would take weeks—nay, months—to have a sea crew in true fighting form."

Garrett snapped his fingers, his excitement visible. "Then we hire mercenaries—French, German—whomever we can find—to help us make a stand."

Ashby frowned and shook his head again.

Garrett exploded. "It's the only plan I have at the moment, Ashby fitz Waryn!" He threw his hands into the air. "Why you chose to fall in love with a woman that brings a cartload of problems with her is beyond my realm. That is your way, I suppose. You have always been the most difficult, most conceited, most arrogant—"

"Enough!" Ashby cried, laughter bubbling over. "Now there's the blackest man in England speaking. The one I know and love. The savage beast whom the sweet French maid tamed has once again burst his bonds. Why, my friend, I do think you could march up to the French king at this moment and demand that he lop off the head of Marc de la Tresse."

Ashby grew solemn. "I am afraid that's what it would take, a royal edict and no less—for this situation to be resolved."

Garrett calmed immediately. Ashby could almost see his friend's thoughts whirling, a maelstrom waiting to collide as a new plan formed.

"The French king . . . I wonder if we could involve him in some way," Garrett mused.

Ashby seized upon a thought. "It is rumored that he does love your wines. But would he help an Englishman? Against one of his own countryman?"

"Hah!" Garrett declared. "I *know* someone close to the French king. I will send a missive to him and ask for an answer to be awaiting us at Chateau Branais." He sobered and said, "All isn't lost until their vows are sealed. There's time yet. Have faith, my friend."

Ashby returned the somber stare. "Faith is all I have left."

"LET ME TAKE the children, Madeleine. I have much to show them."

Marielle watched Lyssa and Cynric head off with Maude. She was glad for a moment of quiet. Her jumbled thoughts had left her uneasy. She hadn't had time to try and settle them since they'd set out from Stanbury for London.

"Maude is perceptive," Madeleine said. "She knew we needed a moment alone." She took Marielle's hand. "How are you? That letter was a horrible business. I know how it affected you. You have hardly eaten or slept."

Marielle flushed guiltily. "A great deal of my anguish can be laid at Marc's doorstep yet there are other things that have had me out of sorts, too."

Madeleine's eyebrows raised. "Anything you wish to share with me?"

She gripped her friend's hand. "It should probably stay a secret but I must tell someone, else I'll go mad." She bit her lip. "The most beautiful thing that ever was has happened to me."

Madeleine squeezed her hand. "You have

coupled with Ashby?"

She nodded. "All my years with Jean-Paul. What a waste. I felt more alive in one night with Ashby than I have in my entire existence."

"Then how can you go to Marc so willingly?"

Her eyes brimmed with unshed tears. "I owe my parents. How can I not do what is within my power to set them free? I am in debt to them more than most."

She rubbed her eyes wearily. "I have not spoken of this in nigh on twenty years." Marielle heard the tremor in her voice and swallowed, trying to push the pain aside.

"I cost them the life of their favorite child."

Marielle sensed Madeleine's sudden stillness, grateful her friend didn't rush at her with a dozen questions. The only look she saw in her friend's eyes was one of sympathy, not judgment.

"I was one of twin girls," she explained. "Arielle and I were but five years of age. She was shy, a timid beauty whom my parents doted upon. Yet for some reason, Arielle wanted to be more like me—her loud, rambunctious sister. I was always getting us into trouble."

She sighed and shook her head. "I dared her all the time. Taunted her if she would not take up the challenge I issued her. I threatened to leave her behind and have fun without her."

"What did you encourage her to do?"

Marielle shrugged. "Mostly silly things. Hide

things from our brothers and sisters. Switch a rug order at my father's shop. Steal a Communion wafer when no one was looking. All sorts of mischief. Once, I dared her to play tadpole in a stream. Arielle almost drowned in the strong current. If not for my eldest brother, she would have been lost that day."

She fell silent, remembering the last day. She could still hear the song of the lark in her ears. Feel the sun's warmth upon her back. See the petrified look frozen on her sister's face.

"I demanded she climb a tree. A very tall one. Arielle was terrified of heights but she ventured up anyway. She went so high that she was scared to come down again. I called her a baby. I threatened and cajoled her. Nothing worked.

"Finally, as it grew dark, I went for help. When I returned with my brother, Arielle lay at the foot of the trunk. I know not if she slipped or actually tried to follow me after I left. Whatever occurred, she broke her neck in that fall."

Madeleine wrapped an arm about her shoulder. Her hand stroked Marielle's hair. She found comfort in the simple gesture.

"I never forgot how she looked, nor the expression on my father's face when we brought her home. Punishment was swift. My father beat me senseless and then I was sent to Sisters of Merciful Heart Convent. My parents never spoke a word to me."

Marielle shuddered. "All the nuns knew why I was left with them. They warned the children there. All the girls shunned me. The only soul who ever showed me any kindness was a visiting priest, a brother to the abbess. Father Julien always gave me a thoughtful word. The others ignored me, pious sisters and children alike, but Father Julien spoke with compassion and warmth. He would find me wherever I was and we would have long talks about all sorts of things. I so looked forward to his visits. They stopped after five years."

"Did you ever see him again?"

"No. I did learn after my marriage that he had risen through the ranks over the years and had been named a cardinal. They say it's Cardinal Corot who now has the king's ear."

Madeleine stood abruptly. "He's the one to ask for help!"

She shook her head. "No. He would not remember a small, troublesome girl from so many years ago."

"I believe you're wrong about that, Marielle. A merciful man such as this priest would not forget you." Madeleine smiled broadly.

"Besides, Garrett knows him."

CHAPTER TWENTY-THREE

ASHBY SWUNG THE lantern from the cart and reached a hand up to Marielle. She took it and climbed down. Garrett followed, Lyssa asleep in his arms. Ashby handed the light to Marielle and reached his arms up. Madeleine responded by lowering a sleeping Cynric to him.

They arrived very late at Chateau Branais. Garrett had sent word ahead. They didn't know if Marc had spies at Pauillac where they docked but they hoped they might have a day to themselves before he was made aware of their presence. Garrett insisted they go several miles out of their way so as to avoid Monteville entirely. They'd seen no one along this secondary road. The chateau mirrored the same quietness.

Ashby thanked the Blessed Christ again that the journey over had not been nearly as bad as his previous trips at sea. He lost the contents of his stomach once they'd left the protection of the Thames but he recovered very quickly. Garrett told him the size of the ship had quite a bit to do with his seasickness. Ashby adjusted to the rolling motion much more easily on such a large vessel.

He looked to the sky. Dawn would arrive in just over an hour. He joined the others as they made their way up the steps of the chateau.

"We saw no one on the roads. That's a good sign," Garrett said quietly. Ashby saw him turn to Madeleine. "It reminds me of another time," he said to his wife, the look of love in his eyes.

Marielle shot a questioning look at Ashby. He didn't answer, as the door opened and the Bouchards slipped out, beaming smiles upon their faces.

"Oh, Madeleine." Cadena looked from one sleeping child to the other. "They are so beautiful," she whispered as Robert smiled at his grandchildren.

"And very tired, *Maman*. Let us get them abed." She brushed a kiss upon her father's cheek and took his arm to lead him back in. Garrett and Ashby took the children to a waiting chamber and placed them upon the bed.

Cadena followed them and said, "I shall stay with them. I would not want them to awake alone in unfamiliar surroundings."

The two men returned to the others. Garrett insisted Madeleine lie down as well.

"I will wake you in a few hours, my love, but now you need your rest. I insist."

She didn't protest, which Ashby took to mean she was exhausted. Garrett returned a few minutes later.

"Bread and wine awaits you," Robert indicated. "Come. Let us sit."

He led them into a small dining room. Ashby's mouth watered at the smell of hot bread. They sat, Robert pouring them all wine. After they settled in, he spoke.

"No word has come from the cardinal yet, Garrett. I know your message said it should be forthcoming."

"If none comes by the morrow, I will go and see Marc the day after," Marielle said, her voice surprisingly firm.

"We will all go together," Ashby told her. "You shall not go into that lion's den alone."

THEY SPENT A quiet day with the Bouchards yet Marielle sensed the charged current under the surface of polite talk. When the next day came with still no word, she set out with Ashby and both Lord and Lady Montayne accompanied her.

As they drew close to Monteville, Marielle's fear became physical. She clasped her trembling hands in her lap, willing them to be still. Her shoulders sagged. Her teeth began to chatter. She locked her jaw hard against the movement. She refused to let Marc de la Tresse see her quake in his presence.

She felt the stares of the workers in the vineyards as they rode by on their way toward the castle. The ripples of activity ceased as they passed. Marielle forced her eyes to the road ahead. What she saw surprised her.

The heightened security immediately leaped out at her. Activity buzzed upon the wall-walk. Jean-Paul always had men posted along it but it was a mere skeleton's crew compared to the numbers she now saw. Her fantasies of Ashby rescuing her parents and helping them all escape Marc's clutches died quickly.

It seemed odd to be stopped at the entrance to Monteville. She had not realized she would have to ask for permission to enter her former home. She'd been away just two months and yet it seemed like a lifetime ago that she'd been a part of daily life here.

Her party of four found themselves escorted by armed guards as they passed through the outer and inner baileys and into the castle itself. As they made their way down the corridor, Marielle remembered the long days of working at her tapestries. The stolen hours with her treasured books. She looked around for Jean-Paul, knowing he was no longer there, but she couldn't help it.

A fire roared in the grate of the great hall, its shadows dancing along the walls, as they were led in and seated. Those walls were ringed with men, soldiers of Marc's. They swarmed everywhere throughout the castle. Marielle wondered why so many men were necessary.

They waited almost half an hour in silence before Marc sailed through the doors and came to stand before them.

"Ah, greetings to all. I am glad to see my English neighbor again." He inclined his head to Garrett, who wore a wary expression on his face.

"This must be Lady Montayne. I know your parents." He swept a quick kiss across Madeleine's knuckles. Her features remained bland and indifferent.

"Fitz Waryn." Marc's tone changed slightly as he acknowledged Ashby. He looked cautiously at Ashby, who returned his alert stare.

Finally, he turned to her. "Marielle. It does me good to see you again." He crossed to her and lay his hands upon her shoulders, grazing cool lips against her cheek. She fought recoiling from his touch and remained still.

"Marc." She was pleased her voice was even as he linked her arm through his.

Marc turned and gestured to his visitors. "I thank you for escorting my fiancée home safely. I must insist you all stay for our upcoming wedding."

He gazed at her steadily. "Several of your relatives have already arrived for the festivities. I believe three of your siblings have been visiting, along with your parents."

She stiffened against him. He sank his fingers deep into her upper arm but he'd already driven his point home.

"And their families?" she asked, trying not to faint.

Marc smiled genially. "They were unable to make it, I am afraid. Still, all the Matesses will be so happy to know you are home again and ready to wed me." His eyes held an amused light, as if only he were in on a secret. "They are . . . eager to return to their own kin."

"Might I see them? And my parents?"

"Of course. They will be thrilled." He turned to his guests. "Please, be seated, *mes amis*." He snapped a finger. "Wine for my guests. We will return shortly."

Marc turned to her. "I will escort you to your family."

Ashby rose to protest their leaving alone but Marielle gave him a pleading look, asking him with her eyes to cause no trouble.

They left the great hall leisurely. Once they'd exited, Marc sped up, dragging her along, causing her to stumble. The genial smile upon his lips quickly faded and he no longer kept up a pretense before visitors. He railed quietly at her as they moved along the corridors and down the stairs, deep into the bowels of Monteville.

"You little witch," he hissed. "How dare you run off with a lover?"

"You think Ashby was my lover?" Marielle asked defiantly. "That is merely one sign how poor your judgment is, Marc."

His fingers dug more sharply into her. "Watch your tongue," he warned. "And no more lies. If the fool was not your lover before you left France, surely he has been paid in full by now!"

"You think I bartered my body for freedom?"

Marc chuckled low. "It does not matter. You have returned. You are mine." His eyes gleamed at her. "You will *always* be mine."

They reached the lowest part of Monteville. Marielle had been to the dungeons only once, at Jean-Paul's insistence. He'd proudly shown her every inch of Monteville when she arrived as a young bride. She still remembered the dank smells, the dim lighting, and rats that freely roamed. She vowed never to return here.

Until now.

A mixture of musty odors and rotting decay filled the air. What lay dead, she didn't know— and wouldn't dare venture a guess. Marielle fought the panic that welled inside her, the racing heart and screaming mind that willed her feet to flee from such a godforsaken place.

They passed several guards, all men of good size and alert features. Marc had paid a pretty penny to hire such soldiers.

He paused at one cell and gestured for a light. A knight brought a torch from its sconce. Its light illuminated the small space. Marielle caught sight of two people hovering together in the damp chill. They raised sunken eyes to her. Eyes with no life.

Suddenly, a low moan permeated the dungeon. It was almost animal in nature, as if wounded. It came from the shell that was her mother.

"Blanche, quit that noise," Marc commanded. "My men tire of it."

Her mother collapsed onto the floor, muttering words Marielle couldn't catch. Her father came to face her, his bony fingers twisting around the bars of his cell. The accusatory look in his eyes nearly did her in.

"Papa," she began.

"Get me out!" he roared. "You careless, thoughtless, ungrateful child. Look at your mother. Look at what you have done to her. To us all."

Gautier continued to rant at her. "You were always a wild child. Unlike Arielle and the rest of our children. We couldn't understand why God punished us with such an unruly daughter."

"You are spawned from the Devil himself," a

voice called out.

Marielle turned and saw one of her brothers and two of her sisters imprisoned in the next cell.

Her brother screamed obscenities at her, as her sisters joined in.

"You never cared for any of us," one sister accused. "You lived in your own world. You barely acknowledged us."

"You were always a troublemaker," the other one said. "Causing mischief left and right, making more work for all the rest of us. And look at us now. Taken from our families. Locked away and starved because *you* refuse to wed a comte. What woman in her right mind wouldn't trade places with you?" she shrieked. "You married one aristocrat and can wed another—and yet you refuse?"

The accusations continued for some minutes, her brother and father joining in again, their words ugly and bitter, blending into a cacophony of anger, filling the dungeon. They all blamed her for their lot. Not Marc. They screamed. Begged. Pleaded with her for their release.

Marielle stood there, dumbfounded. Her siblings were the ones who had barely acknowledged her presence, being so much older than she and Arielle. She had only been a small child and certainly not guilty of the blame they laid at her feet. What she couldn't fathom was that all their bitterness was directed toward her. Marc was the one who had taken them from the lives they had known. He had forced them to become prisoners in this dank dungeon. Yet their rage was only focused upon her.

She could take no more. Their conditions were beyond awful. Despite not being responsible for their confinement, guilt flooded her. She rushed to assure them of her good intentions, despite the hurt and rejection their cruel words brought her.

"Hush, my family. Hush. You will be free. I will see to it. I will do whatever it takes but I promise you will leave this place of doom." She looked pleadingly at Marc.

"Yes, I can see your family leaving . . . and never wanting to come back. Of course, Blanche and Gautier will make their permanent home with us. Their presence will assure me of your good behavior."

"Here?" Marielle's voice cracked. Surely he wouldn't hold them in this black cavern.

"That depends upon you, Marielle. If all goes well, they may take rooms in the east wing. If not . . ." His voice faded, the threat obvious.

She touched his sleeve as he turned to go. "Can they be freed now? All of them? Please." She hated pleading but she would do anything to remove her family from such vile circumstances.

"No." The word rang loudly and clearly throughout the dungeon, echoing emptily. "Once the wedding ceremony has been performed, I guarantee their safe passage."

He walked away, Marielle following, the cries of her relatives tormenting her soul as they ascended the stairs. Waiting for the cardinal's return message was no longer an option. She knew what must be done.

She would marry Marc de la Tresse as soon as possible.

CHAPTER TWENTY-FOUR

ASHBY FIDDLED WITH a loose string at the hem of his tunic. A casual observer would think him totally preoccupied, but that was far from the truth. He studied the great hall—its size, the number of soldiers in it, the various entryways. He glanced briefly at Garrett, who was in quiet conversation with Madeleine.

Suddenly, he sensed Marielle's approach. He turned as she and Marc entered the room. Her eyes briefly met his. They were dull. Lifeless. As if she'd already resigned herself to the anticipated marriage. Ashby wondered just how wretched the conditions were in Monteville's dungeon to cause the spirit to go out from her so quickly, much less the kind of reception she'd received from her imprisoned kin.

Marc immediately came to the center where they were gathered, Marielle trailing behind him.

As she approached, Ashby saw she was visibly shaken. He longed to punish Marc de la Tresse for causing the woman he loved such grief. Running a sword through him seemed too generous.

The new Comte of Monteville signaled for more wine to be poured then he raised it for a toast.

"Shall we drink to my bride?" He gave Marielle a mocking smile. "I feel certain she is as eager as I to seal our union." He slipped an arm about Marielle's waist. Ashby flinched at the motion.

"I have called for our priest." Marc looked about the room. "I would have thought him here by now." He gave Marielle a squeeze, pulling her closer to his side. "We can adjourn to the chapel for the wedding mass. I will have the old fool meet us there."

Madeleine spoke up, a charming smile lighting her features. "Oh, I think it's lovely you want to show off your chapel to us. I'm sure it's a fine setting for all your guests that gather for the wedding. It's fortunate Marielle has so much time to prepare for the ceremony."

Ashby noted the puzzled expression on Marc's face and looked back at Madeleine. His friend was up to something. He wished he knew what.

Their host motioned to a servant who scurried over. Marc took a sheaf of papers from him.

He set them down on a nearby trestle table.

"The contracts for the betrothal are drawn." He gave Marielle a smirk. "No dowry will be required of you, my dearest. You have provided your friends as witnesses. That will be all I ask of you."

Marc pulled a large, gold ring from his pocket, holding it up for inspection. "This will do for now, Marielle."

Ashby recognized the heavy, gold ring as the one Marielle had worn during her marriage to Jean-Paul. She must have left it behind when she escaped from Monteville. How spiteful of Marc to use the very ring his brother had gifted Marielle with.

"Once the betrothal contracts have been signed, I see no reason for us to wait. Do you, Marielle? We could be married today, here with your friends to share in your joy."

Ashby watched as Marielle closed her eyes for a moment, as if to gather her courage for what would take place next.

"Oh, really? You must not have known, Comte. No one can marry during Advent—or the twelve days of Christmas. You'll have to wait until after Epiphany before your priest can speak the nuptial mass."

All attention in the room immediately swung to Madeleine. She smiled sweetly at her husband. "Remember, Garrett, how you were mad to marry before Christmas and how we had to wait?"

Understanding dawned upon Garrett's face. Ashby, too, recalled how Stanbury's priest refused to marry the couple. Madeleine had looked for an excuse not to marry Garrett since she was already married to Henri de Picassaret at the time. The respite gave her time to slip away to London, Garrett hot on her heels.

Ashby watched Garrett slip his wife's arm into the crook of his elbow.

"She is right, you know. I had totally forgotten about the Church's law," replied Garrett. "Well, Marc, this will give Marielle time to plan a proper wedding. You can have guests come from far and wide since it will be weeks before your vows can be spoken."

At that moment, Monteville's priest entered the great hall. He shuffled to where everyone gathered near the fire. Ashby wondered how he put one foot in front of the other. The man looked three times older than anyone present. The grayish pallor of his skin made him look as if he already had one foot in the grave.

Marc bent and spoke in the cleric's ear. Ashby saw him begin to shake his head. Whatever the priest said angered Marc a great deal. Ashby assumed he confirmed what Madeleine had revealed.

The priest left the room, all eyes watching

him and then returning to Marc. His face had gone bright scarlet with rage.

"Then I will get a special dispensation!" he proclaimed.

Garrett interrupted further thought. "I know all about that. A special dispensation must go from your bishop to the cardinal to Rome itself. By then, with the time it would take to wait for a reply, you could be married without it." Garrett smiled broadly. "But what's another month? You will have the rest of your life to spend with Marielle."

Ashby expelled the breath he'd held, his gaze finding Marielle. Her mouth trembled slightly. He knew she was trying not to give up hope. At least this bought them some time to try and extricate her—and her family—from the situation.

Marc looked ready to explode. He'd now grown purple in the face. A servant rushed to him, fussing over him. Marc pushed the man aside. Instead, he went and filled a goblet with wine, which he downed with remarkable speed. He poured another and drank it, too.

Ashby noted Etienne, the Monteville steward, hurried to Marc's side. He got Marc's attention and whispered something low, which Ashby didn't catch. Immediately, Marc's color went from dark to almost ghostly white. Whatever news Etienne had shared must be monumental.

Marc reached up and took a scroll from the steward. He sat in the nearest chair and broke the seal, unrolling it along the table. Ashby instinctively moved closer, wanting to know what caused Marc such distress.

The parchment was thick, of very good quality, and the wax seal abnormally large. It could only mean one thing.

The King of France had sent a message to Marc de la Tresse.

Ashby watched Marc's lips move silently as he read the text. He rose quickly and looked flustered. Nervous. Ashby wondered what the king wanted.

Marc grabbed the scroll, holding it to his chest. He looked about and motioned for Donatien and Etienne to follow him. As he left, he seemed to remember his guests. He paused in the doorway.

"Please stay a bit. I will have refreshments brought to you. I have matters that must be attended to at once." He turned and quickly exited the room.

The four quickly closed ranks into a small circle. Ashby touched Madeleine's elbow and gave it a squeeze.

"Congratulations on remembering about no marriages during Advent. You really threw him off course."

Madeleine beamed. She slipped her hand into Garrett's. "It suddenly came to me and I knew it was the only way to put him off."

She looked across at Marielle. "I am not the person I was then, Marielle. I ran away from an abusive husband. Fate led me to Garrett and I fell hard for him." She looked up at her husband, love shining in her eyes. "He wanted to marry me but I was not free to do so. Waiting due to Advent gave me time to flee."

Madeleine reached out a hand to take Marielle's. "Time is on our side now. Mayhap Cardinal Corot will send word to us in the meantime and help you out of this complicated situation."

Marielle's eyes were bright with unshed tears. "Are you certain he will reply to you?" she asked Garrett.

He nodded. "I rescued the cardinal from a perilous situation. I was on my way home to England when I came across highwaymen in the road. They had forced the cardinal and his manservant from their horses. In his royal robes, there was no mistaking who he was. The thieves thought to help themselves to his ring and other treasures he carried with him. I made sure it never happened."

Garrett's last words caused a chill to course through Ashby. He knew exactly how ruthless his friend could be when seeing someone wronged. He had no doubt the cardinal remembered

Garrett's actions and would return a favor to his rescuer.

He was itching with curiosity, though, about Marc's situation. He thought quickly what he might do and excused himself. A guard at the door stopped him.

Ashby moved closer to the man and said quietly, "I am in sudden need of the garderobe. Quick, where may I find it?"

The soldier whispered brief instructions and let him pass. Ashby found himself in the hallway alone. He moved quickly along the corridor, heading toward the room Marc conducted business from on his last visit.

He reached it and found the door slightly ajar. Voices came from within. Ashby leaned close to listen.

"Brideau is a lunatic if he thinks I cheated him!"

Ashby recognized Marc's panicked voice and smiled.

"Then explain your case to the king. He is said to be an understanding man." That was Donatien.

"But Brideau has the king's ear. If he says he has been deceived, he will be believed. No, I have been summoned to pay the piper. Donatien, you and Etienne must help me spin a credible tale."

Ashby had heard enough. He hurried back to the great hall and pulled Garrett away from the women, sharing what he'd just learned.

"This summons from the king is a good sign," Garrett murmured. "I wonder if Cardinal Corot is behind it."

"I doubt it. Marc seemed too upset. I would wager my Lightning that he double-crossed this Brideau fellow. He's in a panic, Garrett."

"Which can still work to our advantage."

Marc returned, having regained some of his composure. He thanked them for coming.

"I am so glad you are here with Marielle, as I have been called away on business for the king." He clasped Marielle's wrist in his hand. "Would you like for your friends to keep you company while I am away, my dear?"

Madeleine spoke up quickly. "My children need me, Comte. I am afraid we must decline—"

"Then send for them, my lady." The comte's eyes gleamed. "Monteville has plenty of room for you all."

She looked Marc squarely in the eyes. "They shall not spend one night under this roof."

He shrugged. "So be it. You will remain here. As my guests. Without these children." He snapped his fingers. "Guards. Escort these fine gentlemen below. They will be sharing quarters with our other visitors."

Ashby stepped quickly forward to challenge Marc. Armed knights drew weapons at once, blocking his way. The steel of their swords gleamed menacingly in the light.

Marc smiled. "I bid you enjoy my hospitality. And if either of you cause my men trouble of any kind, we will add both ladies to your company."

Ashby knew there was no escape. He and Garrett were outnumbered by more than twenty armed men. He knew, too, that Garrett would not risk anything happening to Madeleine, especially in her delicate condition. He cursed silently, berating himself for dragging his friends into such turmoil. Then a thought occurred to him.

"Give her your ring," he hissed at Garrett.

Garrett immediately withdrew the ring from his finger without question. A circle of men now surrounded them. Marc had left the room.

Garrett held the ring up. "May I give this to my wife? She may wish to send word to her parents that we have extended our stay." He glared at the commander with eyes of steel. "They will need the seal from my signet ring to make any such message believable."

The knight in charge pondered Garrett's words and then reached for the ring. He took it and handed it to Madeleine. Then the guard motioned for Garrett and Ashby to leave the room.

Ashby turned back for what might be his last glance at Marielle.

CHAPTER TWENTY-FIVE

MARIELLE WATCHED ASHBY and Garrett being led from the room. Why could she not be a man? Then she would have the strength and the courage to stop these events that now spun out of control. A numbness spread throughout her body. She sank into a nearby chair.

Madeleine sat down next to her and called for parchment. "I must write to my parents so they will not worry about us," she said sweetly to the captain of the guard. "They will be delighted that Marielle has returned and is soon to wed the comte."

Marielle admired Madeleine's spirit. Even in such adverse conditions, she kept her head about her. She lay a hand over Madeleine's and gave it a squeeze, hoping she might draw comfort and strength.

"I am writing directly to Cardinal Corot," Madeleine whispered. "I doubt they will break the seal before they take it to the chateau. Papa will know immediately what has occurred. He will send it posthaste to the cardinal himself."

Madeleine smiled reassuringly at her as the inkwell was set in front of them, along with paper and sealing wax. Madeleine wrote smoothly and quickly, smiling all the while. She finished her note and folded it, dropping the hot wax onto it and pressing Garrett's ring into it to make a deep impression.

"Please see that this goes to Chateau Branais," she asked the closest soldier. He accepted the letter and withdrew from them.

As Madeleine had written, Marielle racked her mind for a way out. Part of her simply wanted to accept the circumstances and marry Marc the day after Epiphany. That way her friends—along with Ashby—would be free of her. Yet another part rebelled against such a notion of a lifetime of misery. A life with Marc de la Tresse.

She'd tasted love in all its sweet glory. Both her body and soul had entwined with Ashby fitz Waryn's. She refused to give in. She must find a way to see them reunited for all time.

Marielle knew how Ashby admired Madeleine and she, too, had come to love and respect this women as her dearest friend. Why couldn't she be calm and reasonable in such a crisis?

Despondency filled her, blackening her mood when she'd thought it could grow no darker. Suddenly, an idea sprang forth, as if a bolt of lightning hit her. She knew exactly how to escape from Monteville and into the arms of safety.

She rose as regally as possible and addressed the captain. "May I assume my usual duties, sir?"

The man frowned at her. "What need you do, my lady?"

"I know it is close to the noon meal. I would go and supervise in the kitchen as always. Madeleine?"

Her friend stood. "How may I be of service, Marielle?"

"If you would be so good as to have the trestle tables taken down? The vineyard workers will be arriving shortly. Mayhap these good soldiers could see to your bidding?"

She nodded at Madeleine briefly, trying to convey with her eyes that she knew what she was doing. *Trust me*, she willed.

"Very good, Comtesse." Madeleine turned and motioned a few men over, assuming the task.

Marielle immediately went to the far end of the great hall and into the kitchen. Stew bubbled in several pots. She could also smell the baking bread that would accompany the meal. She slipped from the room and rounded the corner to the storeroom. Marc may have taken precautions throughout Monteville but he'd ignored locking the storeroom.

She quickly entered the room and went to the far left where the herbs and spices were gathered. Beyond that in a tiny alcove were jars and vials of medicinal herbs, exactly what she required. She moved quickly, pocketing what she needed before returning to the great hall.

The tables were set up and the first of the hungry workers began to stream in. Marielle stopped a kitchen servant, a young girl of not more than ten and two. Marielle thought her name was Jeannette.

"Who takes the meal to the guards below and their prisoners in the dungeon? Or do those men come to the hall for their repast?"

The girl replied shyly, "I have done it before, my lady. Usually they are given bread and cheese at midday. They are to stay there until the evening meal is served before they are relieved. Would you like me to do so again today?"

"Yes, child, but let us wait until after these good people above have been served."

The servant curtsied and continued on her way. Marielle hadn't counted the number of guards she'd seen while visiting her parents. It would be better to take a pot down with wooden bowls and serve up the meal that way.

She found Madeleine and the two women took their places. Sharing a trencher made their quiet conversation a bit easier, especially since the hall was filled with boisterous laughter and a hundred workers speaking at once.

"I have a plan. I will need your help. Whatever happens, do not let anyone but the guards eat from the stew. You will help me serve them after the meal has been completed."

Madeleine nodded and broke off a piece of bread, chewing it thoughtfully. "I knew you would think of something."

"Nothing is accomplished yet but we will certainly give it our best effort. Now, eat up. You will need your strength."

They finished in silence. Marielle's nerves were taut. She noticed the captain watching her with interest. Marc must have commanded the man to keep an eye on her. She would have to be careful and not give anything away.

The laborers finished with dinner and rose as a group to return to the vineyards. The castle's servants began clearing dishes. It was time to set her plan into motion.

Marielle approached the captain. "Sir, I would ask that I be allowed to take my family something to eat now that the meal has been completed." She caught the eye of the girl she'd spoken to already and waved her over.

As she arrived, Marielle said, "Jeannette often takes the guards below their bread and cheese. I would simply ask to accompany her and see that they and my family are cared for properly. Surely you can grant me such a request?"

Marielle smiled at him shyly, her head bent down while she looked up through thick lashes. "I would be ever so grateful."

"You may," he said gruffly. "But I will escort you myself."

"Then let me get the food we shall need. I thank you for your kindness, sir."

She and Jeannette returned to the far end of the great hall and crossed into the kitchen. Fortunately, Madeleine fell into step behind them. She began talking to Jeannette, smartly distracting the girl as they reached the serving area. Marielle had not told Madeleine exactly what she would do but Madeleine knew it involved the food. Her friend held the girl's attention as Marielle bent before a container of stew still on the fire.

With a quick glance around, she removed a vial from her pocket and poured it in, then another one. She reached for a wooden spoon and stirred the stew well before gathering several bowls and spoons.

By this time, Jeannette and Madeleine had gathered a basket of bread and a few rounds of cheese. Marielle nodded slightly at Madeleine, letting her know the first step had been taken.

"The captain said he would escort us. I shall summon him." Marielle began walking that way, only to be met by the man himself, looking about warily.

"Would you be so good as to lift a pot for me?" she asked. She wrapped a cloth around its handle. "Now careful, for it's very hot."

The solider looked uncertain. "The men usually get bread and cheese now."

"Oh, we have that, as well." She indicated Madeleine and Jeannette. "I know they would appreciate a hot meal, though. The dungeon is such a cold, dismal place. And if they are allowed to return above to sup at eventide, they will not receive anything hot at day's end."

Marielle tried to look her most appealing. "Please? I would also see my parents get something warm in their bellies. They are old and feeble. Surely you would not begrudge them a simple fish stew?"

"No, I suppose not. Come." He took the heavy pot and lifted it easily as he led them to the dungeon. Marielle quieted her fears, praying desperately that her scheme would not fail.

The guards looked surprised to see not only their captain but the steaming pot he carried. A stomach gurgled loudly as the men caught a whiff of the cooked fish. They laughed companionably and took the wooden bowls and spoons from her.

"Set the pot here, Captain," Marielle instructed him. "Let's be sure all your men are fed properly and then we'll see if there's enough for the others."

The men quickly encircled her like flies as she dished up hearty portions to all. Marielle caught sight of her father in the dim light, a sour look upon his face as he watched his daughter feed his jailers. He turned from her, disgust evident by his very posture.

By the time she finished, very little was left in the iron pot.

"Less than a serving remaining, my lady," the captain noted.

"Well, we brought plenty of bread and cheese. May I distribute that to my family?"

He nodded. Marielle wanted to make sure the guards got most of the stew into their bellies before she ever offered them more. She didn't want the meal diluted by anything else.

She took the bread from the basket Jeannette had brought, breaking it so that it fit between the bars of the cell. Her father still had his back to her but her mother rushed at her and swiped the bread from her very fingers, greedily tearing into it. She was dressed in rags and Marielle could see how thin she'd grown. Marc must have slowly starved them. The thought sickened her but quickened her resolve to see that they escaped from Monteville.

"Here. Give this to Papa." Her mother greedily took the offered bread and held it close. Marielle wondered if her father would receive any or not.

She took some to her siblings, all the while listening to their disparaging remarks. It was obvious they longed for something warm to eat and felt betrayed that she'd given it to the guards. Yet she couldn't whisper an explanation or warn them not to eat any if a guard offered any remaining to them.

Marielle last went to Ashby and Garrett's cell. As she passed the bread to them, Ashby briefly stroked her finger. The tender gesture almost undid her. Her knees buckled. She locked them to keep from falling. He must have realized how fragile she was for he gave her a rakish smile and winked at her.

It was what she needed to bolster her spirits. Marielle turned back to the others. Jeannette and Madeleine had distributed the cheese to the prisoners. They looked to her for further instructions.

"We may go now, Captain. I will leave the remaining bread and cheese for the men to partake of after they have finished their stew." She inclined her head slightly to him. "I thank you for your generosity."

He nodded to her and led them out of the bowels of the earth again. Marielle sucked in the sweet air as they reached the top and then turned to flash Madeleine a look.

"Oh, Madeleine, are you all right? You are so pale."

Madeleine's instincts from her play-acting days with the mummer's troupe must have kicked in for Marielle witnessed an immediate change in her. Madeleine's posture stooped. Her mouth grew slack. A hand weakly fluttered to wave in front of her, as if to stir the air.

She slipped an arm about Madeleine's waist and looked to the captain.

"Might I take Lady Montayne to rest in my chamber? I do not know if rooms have been prepared for her yet."

Madeleine gave a slight moan and started crumpling to the floor. The captain came to her rescue and helped her to stand.

"Thank you," Madeleine whispered. "I am with child and find myself growing weak at the oddest moments. If I could only lie down . . ." Her voice faded.

Marielle interjected, "You usually nap at this time of day, dearest. For several hours?"

Madeleine picked up on the cue. "I would like to but only if it will not inconvenience you, Marielle."

She brushed a stray strand of hair from Madeleine's cheek. "I insist upon staying with you. It wouldn't do for you to awaken in a strange place."

They made their way to Marielle's former chamber, the captain trailing helplessly behind. When they arrived at the door, Marielle paused.

"Would you see that no one disturbs us, sir? I, too, feel a bit of rest would help me after our long journey from England has now ended."

Jeannette had followed them upstairs. Marielle looked to her now. "Pass along the word, Jeannette. We are not to be disturbed."

"Yes, Comtesse."

The two women entered the chamber and closed the door. They walked over to sit on the bed and threw their arms around one another.

"Oh, Madeleine, you are too good for words."

Her friend grinned impishly. "Farley always said I had a bit of talent. He preferred using me as a troubadour but there were a few times I filled in on stage with the other mummers. Did I look sufficiently frail and faint?"

"Oh, yes. I think you could have fooled even Garrett."

A shadow crossed Madeleine's face. "Oh, Marielle, pray tell me how we are to get them out of such a sorry place. I cringe thinking of my Garrett there for even a few hours."

Marielle sketched out her basic idea to Madeleine, who nodded enthusiastically as she described each step.

"I do think it will work." Madeleine hugged her tightly. "You are brilliant, Marielle Matesse."

"Then we should give it another half-hour. Only then can we make our move."

CHAPTER TWENTY-SIX

MARIELLE CAUTIOUSLY OPENED the door and looked outside. She saw no one in the corridor. It was a perfect time of day for them to try to sneak back down to the dungeons. The castle servants would have tidied all of the upper chambers by now. Some might be involved in baking tarts. Others would be working on mending. A few might even have tasks outside to complete. Donatien would be in the fields supervising the workers. Etienne would be buried in the accounts.

She sent a plea to the Christ Himself and motioned for Madeleine to follow her. The two women walked single file down the corridor. Marielle had explained their route beforehand and Madeleine simply followed in her steps.

They reached the door that would take them to the stone staircase, where they would descend into the vaults below. Marielle took a waiting torch from the wall to light their way as they moved down the hundreds of steps to their destination. She heard no voices, only the scurrying rats and dripping water as they moved farther into the bowels of the earth.

When they reached the bottom of the staircase, Marielle turned to Madeleine, who gave her a reassuring nod. She stepped out into the narrow passageway that led to the dungeon's cells. Her lips moved in a feverish prayer, begging God to have let the herbs work.

They had.

Contented smiles played upon most of the eight men's lips as they slumbered peacefully, their bellies full of a hot meal dosed with what she prayed would keep them asleep for several hours. Most slumped against the wall. One even rested his head on another's shoulder. Another one had pillowed his hands beneath his head.

Marielle and Madeleine tiptoed past the sleeping guards and the cells containing her parents and siblings. They came to the last cell on the right. Ashby and Garrett awaited them, determination on both their faces.

"The one with the red beard has the keys," Ashby said quietly. "He is left-handed, so look in that pocket first."

Marielle moved to the sleeping soldier and bent beside him.

"What are you doing?" Her father's voice thundered through the enclosed space.

Marielle held a finger to her lips. When she saw he would speak more, she rushed to his cell.

"Please, Papa," she said softly. "I am trying to free you. You must be quiet."

Gautier mumbled something, his fingers locking around the bars that held him.

Her mother began that strange keening again.

"Hush!" she commanded to Blanche in a loud whisper. "Hush—or I will leave you here." She regretted such harsh words but hoped that they would quiet her mother.

Marielle turned to see Madeleine removing the keys from the guard's pocket. She quickly went to Garrett and Ashby's cell and released them. The four gathered in a tight circle, the men looking expectantly at her.

Marielle calmed her frayed nerves and spoke. "There are a series of passages below Monteville. They haven't been used in years. They buried the dead in these catacombs for many years. It's been a good two hundred years since they were used.

"Jean-Paul told me about them. I have never been in them but I know where they start. Jean-Paul said that no one knew they existed, only the Comte of Monteville. Not even Marc knows about them. The knowledge is passed from one comte to the next—and to his comtesse—in case he is killed in battle. They are to be used for safe passage in only the direst of circumstances."

"Where do they lead?"

Marielle looked at Ashby, her throat tight, knowing what a predicament she'd gotten him into. Wanting to make things up to him.

"They run for almost two miles. They end at Blessed Heart, where the comte and his family would find sanctuary from their enemies."

Ashby took her hand in his and entwined his fingers with hers. "How long will they sleep?"

"I cannot be sure. It could be for a few hours. Maybe longer. It's hard to judge. I have only given the sleeping draught to one person in a single cup. I know not how long it will remain in effect, having dumped the herbs into their stew."

Ashby looked to Garrett. "Think we should risk moving them into the cells? If they awaken sooner than later, they would be trapped with no way out. Even their screams would not be heard from above."

Garrett pondered the question. "It's a risk to move them. If even one awakens, he could sound the alarm."

Ashby nodded. "Then let them sleep peacefully. Even if the potion wears off, they may sleep naturally until their relief shows up. I don't think it worth the time it would buy us in the long run."

"You are right," Garrett agreed. "They may

also be able to trace us if the passageway is as undisturbed as Marielle suggests. Our tracks will undoubtedly stir the dust. Eventually, they will realize we found our way out from below. We must move quickly." He grasped the torch Marielle held and she passed it willingly to him.

Ashby took the keys Madeleine held and used them to open the cell door to free Marielle's parents. Gautier took three strides out and slapped Marielle hard, causing her head to snap back.

"The Devil is in you," he uttered. "You killed your sister and now almost your family. You have been nothing but trouble since the day you were born. Everything is all your fault."

Marielle fought the stars that blazed brilliantly for a moment, though her father's words wounded her far more. She blinked hard, fighting off the woozy feeling his blow had caused. When she could once again focus, she saw her father up against the wall, Ashby only inches from his face.

"She is risking her life for you, old man," he growled low. "She came back to make a marriage with a monster, all to see to your freedom. How dare you treat her so shabbily."

Marielle heard the controlled anger in his voice. Her heart sang as he championed her to her unforgiving father. She took a step to him and placed a hand upon his arm.

"Cease, Ashby. Show him leniency."

"When he has shown you none?" Ashby countered.

Marielle shook her head. "It doesn't matter what he thinks of me." She turned to Gautier. "Come now, Father, if you want to shake the dust from this place. Do whatever they say. Soon, you will be back to your money-counting and hard-hearted ways. I promise I will never set foot in your sight again."

She turned away, only to face her brother and two sisters. Both Minette and Marie's eyes blazed with hatred, while Gustave did nothing to hide his disgust. All her life, her father's loathing had shone in every glance he tossed her way. To see the same enmity in the eyes of her siblings wrenched her heart.

Marielle took a calming breath. "The same goes for you, as well. I am sorry Marc dragged you into this shameful mess. You need never see me nor hear from me again once you are free."

She motioned to her brother. "See to *Maman*, Gustave." She turned and lifted a nearby torch from the wall. "Let us take the two remaining torches and go."

Ashby and Marielle reached for the torches and set out. The group of prisoners huddled together and followed them. She looked back to see the pitch darkness they left behind. She hoped it would help the guards to slumber even longer.

They walked about three minutes and came

to a fork. Marielle thought a moment. She remembered there would be three decisions to be made. Left, right, then left. After that would be a long, straight path until they reached the church.

"Follow me," she urged.

Marielle tried not to think about her surroundings. The decaying smell. The occasional flash of bones that gleamed in the torchlight. The feel of the rats sweeping across her feet. She put it all from her mind. What mattered was freedom. For her family and for her friends. She couldn't bear it if Madeleine and Garrett never saw their children again. Even her parents didn't deserve what Marc had put them through these last few weeks. Once they reached the safety of the church, though, they would gain sanctuary.

With their arrival at Blessed Heart, even she would be free. Marc wouldn't dare breach the walls of a sanctified place. Not that he could, for even now he rode to the king to answer his summons.

No, this would give her time to do what she should have done from the beginning—make her way back to Libourne and enter the convent of Sisters of Merciful Heart. She should never have followed her heart and reached out to Ashby for help. She was cursed. Anyone she cared for only suffered pain. Arielle died because of her thoughtlessness and now her friends and family and the man she loved were in danger that could easily lead to death.

She would stand strong and travel to the nuns and find the refuge that Sisters of Merciful Heart would offer. She would not risk Ashby's safety nor her friends' lives again. She would insist they return to England at once. Marielle knew how driven Marc was. He would come after her when he returned to Monteville. She planned to be far from his grasp when he did. Sisters of Merciful Heart offered the only safe haven. She would learn to be content within its walls. She would have solitude.

And her memories of one glorious night.

The torch grew heavy in her hand. Despite the chill in the hidden passageway, beads of sweat broke out across her forehead. It seemed they had walked forever. All sense of time and place were lost journeying underground.

Suddenly, they came to an abrupt end. Ashby stopped and waved a hand to halt the party of bedraggled travelers.

"The pathway has stopped. A ladder leads upward. I will ascend it and see where we are coming out."

He shifted the torch in his hand and began up the ladder. He reached the top and lifted up a trap door, disappearing almost from view. Only a faint glow of the torch showed him still to be far above them.

Moments later, he came quickly down. "I

think it best if Marielle comes with me. She will be known here. We need to find the authority in charge and plead our case for sanctuary."

He looked to Garrett. "You will remain here?"

Garrett nodded. "We shall be safe for some time. Even if the guards awoke now, they would have quite a while before they caught up with us. Go."

Ashby handed his torch to her father and said, "The way up opened into a confessional. Best we not catch such a narrow place on fire. I don't think any priest would be too forgiving in that circumstance."

Gautier's thin lips held not a trace of a smile, despite the fact that he and his family had escaped their grim prison. He took the light from Ashby and remained mute.

Ashby turned to her. "Follow me closely, Marielle. There's nothing to be frightened of." He gave her a smile and walked to the ladder.

She let him climb several rungs before starting up after him. She was thankful she had no fear of heights as she ascended up the ladder.

A faint light came from above. Ashby blocked it for a moment and then reached out a hand to her. She took it and he helped her the last few feet.

The confessional booth was very small. He guided her to its edge and closed the trap door.

"We would not want a priest to walk in and fall through."

Even in the dimness, she caught the humor in his eyes. A nervous giggle squeaked from her lips.

"Hush, Marielle," Ashby commanded.

She tried but all she'd been through that day seemed to catch up with her. The laughter threatened to bubble out from her. She knew it for hysterics but had no control over it.

Ashby grabbed her shoulders and pulled her to him. His mouth came down over hers hard and he wrapped his arms around her, crushing her to him.

Suddenly, a very different feeling flooded her. A hot, liquid warmth ran the length of her spine, flooding out to her limbs. She felt herself go weak, collapsing against him. He pulled her even closer to him, his mouth now running along her jaw and down her throat.

"Oh, Ashby," she murmured.

Her words seemed to set him in motion. His hands pushed into her hair, kneading her scalp, running down to her shoulders, along her back. His lips scalded her everywhere they touched, causing shivers both hot and cold to run through her. She gave up into his kiss, surrendering as never before.

"My Marielle," Ashby whispered against her lips, her cheeks, into her hair, over and over, her name pouring forth. "Oh, God. When I thought I had lost you . . ."

His held her next to him, tenderly, his heart beating fast against her breasts.

"This will soon be over, love. Then we can be together." His mouth seized hers again, the kiss full of promise and passion.

Through her haze, she fought the feelings he stirred within her. It was cruel misfortune that he now seemed to be willing to give up his foolish notion of not being good enough to woo her, just as she decided she must put aside her desire for him. No, she loved him far too much to endanger him further. She must see to his safety and her friends and family, as well. She would see Ashby returned safely to England, far from Marc's madness, while she cloistered herself away from the world.

Before she could answer him and tell him what must be, a loud cry rang through the church. Marielle stiffened in Ashby's arms.

It was Marc's voice.

CHAPTER TWENTY-SEVEN

"WHERE THE DEVIL is someone? I need help. Now! A horse . . . a weapon . . . anything!"

An icy wave rushed through Marielle. The words she heard were in the distance but they definitely came from inside the church. Had she become that confused by Ashby's kiss? Why would she imagine Marc here, of all places? They were free of him. He'd left Monteville at the king's summons. It would be days, maybe weeks, before he returned. She would be safe by then. Ashby and their friends would be far away in England. No, it couldn't be Marc.

Ashby's mouth lifted from hers. He replaced it with a finger, urging her silence. Marielle found herself trembling in fear and frustration.

"Do not move." Ashby's whisper was so faint, she hoped she'd heard him correctly. His warmth faded as he stepped a foot away from her. She longed to call out to him to bring it back.

He cracked the confessional door open a few inches. It was Marc de la Tresse, all right, looking as if he'd been in a fight—and lost. His clothes were ripped. His hair was askew, full of leaves and twigs. One eye was swollen completely shut. He wiped at his forehead with a dirty sleeve. Ashby saw the ragged cut jutting above his eyebrow. Blood dripped down his face from it.

What in Christ's name had happened to him?

Marc limped up the aisle of the church, his face contorted with rage. He passed beyond the confessional and continued toward the altar. Ashby knew of only one way to discover the truth.

Cracking the door ajar, Ashby called out in a deep voice, "Come here, my brother. Confess your sins. God will surely give you the help you seek."

He waited until Marc began to turn around and then slowly closed the door, hoping the comte would take the bait. If he'd played his cards right, Marc would have seen at what door assistance awaited. Ashby offered a prayer of forgiveness for what he was about to do and lowered himself to the seat in the booth.

He heard staccato steps approach the confessional. For some unknown reason, Ashby slid the lock into place at the last minute. Seconds later the handle turned but Marc was unable to open the door.

"Damn you!" he roared. "Unlock this door, you sniveling coward." He rattled the door as he spoke.

Ashby thanked the Church for building such sturdy booths as a muffled gasp came out of Marielle. He willed her to be quiet as he pushed her to the floor. If he could convince Marc to enter the next compartment, he did not want her silhouette to give the game away. Ashby reached for her hand and found it, cold and trembling. He drew it into his own and gave it a squeeze.

"I'm no coward, good sir, but a simple man of God. Come. Enter the confessional and unburden your sins."

"I've no time for confession, Father. Men hunt me even as we speak, men who will cut me down without a second thought. I need help, not advice on how many *Hail Marys* I should complete."

"You have come to a house of refuge. God will not turn away from you in your time of need, my son. Come. Speak with me of your sins. What is a few minutes when you have sanctuary from any enemy within these stone walls?"

He could sense Marc's hesitation even through the locked door. Then before he offered any further words of encouragement, he heard the adjacent stall open. Ashby turned his attention to the panel beside him and opened it in one swift motion. Through the latticework, he saw the dim image of another man seated on the other side.

"Bless me, Father, for I have sinned." De la Tresse's words came out in a weary sigh as the nobleman fell into the familiar ritual.

Ashby took a deep breath and replied, "God is all-forgiving, my son. Pray tell me what troubles you so today."

Silence echoed loudly. He had almost given up hope when Marc began to speak. Instead of remorse, Ashby heard the bitterness in his words.

"None of this was meant to happen, Father. I have lost everything. Everything."

Marc suddenly struck at the partition separating them, his anger radiating through it. It shook a moment but held. Ashby said his own swift prayer of thanks before slipping back into his role of priest.

"Have you injured these men? The ones who wish you harm?"

A cruel laugh sounded from the other booth. "Greed and pride have been my favored companions, Father. Of course, I have wounded them. I went after what I wanted—and now it will bring about my death."

Ashby gently encouraged him. "If you fear death is imminent, my child, you must cleanse your conscience and soul before you go to meet your maker."

Marc snorted. "I fear nothing. Not even your God. Would a just and willing God have taken my parents from me at so tender an age and set a pompous ass as my brother over me all those years? Jean-Paul claimed he loved me but I never saw any sign of that love.

"Did he let me grow as a man? Achieve on my own? No, I was forever his slave, performing the tasks he refused to do. I had not a crumb of bread I could call my own, so great was my poverty. No respect from even the lowest servant. No friends to call my own. Every waking hour was spent in service to my brother, the powerful comte. And when I told him of a beautiful young girl I had seen in a merchant's shop in Libourne, he immediately offered for her."

Marc's hand slammed against the intricate latticework again. "He made her his wife and flaunted it front of me for years. *I had wanted her.* She had a freshness and innocence about her. I knew I could bear all else if I had her by my side."

Marielle's grip tightened on his hand. Ashby gave her shoulder a reassuring squeeze.

"Oh, stand in judgment of me if you will. I care not." Marc sighed wearily. "All is lost."

"It's not my right to judge but merely advise you."

Marc laughed. Ashby noted the rising hysteria in his voice. The nobleman was close to the breaking point.

"As if your advice would change things. My evils are legion, Father. I am doomed, by either your God or the king himself. I have no more need to admit my sins to you. Know only that I have broken every commandment there is. I have lied and cheated and sabotaged my fellow nobles and vineyard competitors. I have coveted all my brother had and killed him to gain it.

"Even now, his widow's family is imprisoned in my dungeons, in order to force her into marriage with me. Now that, too, will only be a shattered dream. I received a summons from the king today and rode out with my men, sure that he would confront me with infecting Brideau's wines. Instead, Brideau and his knights awaited me several miles down the road. For all I know, it was Brideau himself who sent the missive luring me from Monteville. When we were far enough along the road, he attacked."

"And you escaped?" Ashby asked.

Marc sighed. "After a fight for my life. Twenty men accompanied me, Father. I doubt even two survived the slaughter. I have nowhere to turn and will have no life with my Marielle now. I have crawled like a mongrel into Blessed Heart and have spilled my story to you for naught. I care not to be absolved from my sins, Father. They are mine. I wear them as a badge of all I have survived. I have kept my end of this unholy bargain and confessed to you all my misdeeds. I now seek your aid. I need a horse and a sword to ride to Monteville."

"We keep no weapons in the house of Our Lord."

"Then a horse, damn you." Marc's impatience spilled forth.

A vicious sneeze erupted. Marielle had fought the urge for several minutes but the musty confessional was full of dust on its floor. The priests in residence must not take the time to sweep the booths but once a year.

She muffled it as best she could, but her usual, high hiccup squeaked out afterward.

"Marielle?"

She heard the surprise in Marc's voice and cringed. He had ridiculed her for years over that very sneeze. Now it would mean their downfall.

"That damnable sneeze!" Marc roared. "I would know it anywhere."

"Stay here," Ashby commanded her.

Marielle heard the lock being thrown and clutched his leg.

"Nay, you mustn't," she begged.

He opened the door, casting a ray of light inside the confessional. "The time has come for you to longer worry about Marc de la Tresse."

Marielle heard Marc scrambling from the neighboring confessional as Ashby stepped out into the church. The door crashed open and Marc flew by, smashing into Ashby, carrying them both to the floor. Marielle watched in horror as Marc's fingers wrapped tightly about Ashby's throat.

"You protect her even now," Marc ground out, his fingers stark white as he lifted Ashby by the throat and slammed his head against the intricate tiles.

The explosion in his head lit a fire within Ashby. Marc had caught him off-guard but instead of overpowering his enemy, Marc's actions gave Ashby new life. His hands, locked around Marc's wrists in an effort to force the Frenchman to relinquish his grasp, now tore his foe's hands away from their target. The multitude of stars that danced before his eyes still blinded Ashby but he knocked the nobleman back and flung himself upon him.

They rolled several times across the floor until they hit a column, halting their movement. Ashby yanked at Marc's tunic and thrust him back against the pillar, satisfied to hear the groan that followed.

Marielle froze in horror, still crouched on the confessional floor. She watched their death struggle, horrified at its intensity. She longed to intervene but did not want to cause Ashby to lose his focus.

Marc threw a wild punch that connected with Ashby's jaw and then soundly struck his fists against both of Ashby's ears. The look of pain upon her beloved's face caused tears to spring to her eyes. Marc pushed at Ashby and kicked him away. Ashby rolled and staggered to his feet, grim determination upon his face.

Ashby rushed his opponent, butting his head into Marc's stomach and ramming him into a pillar. Marielle heard a nasty crack and saw the agony etched on Marc's face. He gasped for air as Ashby landed several solid punches in Marc's kidneys, causing him to slide to the ground. He fell onto his side, wheezing. It looked as if all the fight had gone from him. The cut over his eye bled freshly again, pouring down the right side of his face. His one good eye had begun to swell.

Ashby kept one eye on Marc as he moved toward Marielle. She scrambled from the confessional to meet him, flinging her arms about his waist. She clung to him, her body shaking. He stroked her hair, inhaling her scent, marveling at how perfectly she fit against him. It was as if she were made for him alone. He tilted her chin up and brushed a tender kiss upon her lips.

"God's teeth, man. I thought the rats would drive us to madness before Marielle moved and I could open the trap door."

Ashby lifted his head to see Garrett exiting the confessional, shaking the dust from him.

His friend surveyed the scene. "Looks like I missed out on all the fun."

Marc staggered to his feet as Garrett spoke. He swayed once before falling back to his knees. Ashby released Marielle.

"Go help the others," he told her.

He watched her move shakily toward the booth and turned to Garrett. "Ran into a bit of a problem."

"I could only make out a few muffled phrases. The trap door was too thick for me to hear all." Garrett grinned. "I gather I am speaking to *Father* Ashby?"

Ashby rolled his eyes. "It will make for a good tale over a glass of your best red." He glanced again at Marc, who now clutched his stomach and rocked back and forth.

"What shall we do with him?" he asked.

"Indeed!"

The men turned and caught sight of brilliant scarlet robes headed in their direction.

Ashby's gaze met those of a rotund man dressed from head to foot in red. The man cocked his head and studied him a moment before throwing out his arms in greeting to Garrett. Then Ashby realized who he must be. It was confirmed when Garrett greeted the cleric.

"Good day, Cardinal Corot. We may need your help in settling a sticky situation."

CHAPTER TWENTY-EIGHT

THE TWO OLD friends greet each other. Marielle and Ashby went to help those who remained in the catacombs. She held the trap door steady while he gave Madeleine a hand up. Her cheeks were flushed.

She bobbed a quick curtsy to him. "My thanks, Father Ashby," she whispered mischievously and winked at him before stepping from the confessional.

Garrett called out to her and she crossed the church toward him and Cardinal Corot. Marielle watched as Garrett beamed with pride as Madeleine approached, then she turned back to their task. Within minutes, Ashby had lifted her family to safety. Two priests appeared and escorted her frail parents and siblings to warmer quarters where they would be fed and given clean clothes. They still looked dazed from their experience. She hoped rest and a good meal would set them all on the road to recovery.

Ashby took her arm. "We can do no more for them at the moment. Come, let us speak with the cardinal."

Marielle nodded and they approached the cleric. As her eyes met his, she caught a glimpse of the priest and young man he had once been. She fell to her knees and took his hand, kissing his ring.

"Rise up, child. You never showed me such respect before," the man of God said, his crinkling blue eyes buried in folds of excess flesh. He lifted her by the elbow and smiled at her.

"I doubt I was ever in this much trouble before, Father Julien. I mean, Your Grace."

The cardinal shook his head. "It's good to once again hear that name. Especially from your lips."

He turned to those gathered around him. "You should have seen this imp at age seven. Smart as a whip and more curious than a cat investigating a bowl of unattended fresh cream."

Marielle felt her face flush as he smiled fondly at her. "She was greedy for knowledge and could ask questions until the stars rose and fell in the sky."

"She is still full of lively intelligence, Your Grace," Ashby responded.

Cardinal Corot eyed her speculatively. "And

beauty, too. You are no longer a scrawny girl, Marielle. You have become an enchanting woman."

She smiled wistfully. "One who still has a propensity for getting into difficulties, Your Grace. I am sure you are here because you received word from Lord Montayne."

Corot frowned. "The missive reached me but two days ago, my child. I was away from court, having gone to Rome on the king's business, else I would have come straightway to your aid. Lord Montayne wrote of this troublesome brother-in-law and what hideous things he has done to your family."

The cardinal pursed his lips. "The king is most displeased with this Marc de la Tresse. After I have made my royal report, you can be certain action will be taken." He took Marielle's hand in his. The gesture comforted her. How many times had Father Julien sought her out, lonely child that she was, and soothed her wounded pride or frayed nerves? The years might have passed but the friendship they once shared remained.

"As for your family," he added, "they may want to rest for a day or two after undergoing such a terrible ordeal. I have more than enough men with me who will escort them to their homes when they so desire."

Tears sprang to Marielle's eyes and flowed down her cheeks. "Oh, thank you, Your Grace."

She took his hand and kissed it fervently.

The old cardinal blushed. "Enough." He turned to Garrett. "I still owe you a great deal, Lord Montayne. I would hope you and your wife and friend join Marielle and me for supper. I am eager to hear of England, as my half-brother, the Earl of Lambert, lives there. We've remained close all the years, despite the distance between us."

MARC DE LA Tresse tired of their inane conversation. His body ached in more places than he could count. Fitz Waryn had broken his nose and several ribs. The swelling in his eye limited his vision. Even his head throbbed as if he'd drunk too many bottles of wine.

And yet despite it all, anger seared through his veins, more powerful than any pain.

What would they do to him? Turn him over to Brideau, who had lured him from the protective walls of Monteville with a false message and smashed his entourage to pieces? Or would they hand him directly to the king? Either way, his life would be over before he had begun to enjoy the spoils won by his brother's death. His enemy would more than likely seize Monteville, probably with the king's own knights aiding him. He'd been foolish. Gambled too much too soon. Made foes of the wrong men in the space of a few weeks. A lifetime of mistakes now caught up with him.

But it wasn't too late. Wouldn't it give him the greatest pleasure to become the stuff of legend? He pictured himself burning the vines and the castle itself, then dying with Marielle in his arms. Peasants far and wide would spread the tale of their great love.

Should they leap from the highest parapet, hand in hand—or take poison together? Should he stab her in the heart then himself, their hands entwined as their blood ran hot, melting into one?

He fantasized of the romantic legends that would spring to the lips of Frenchmen everywhere. Yes, if he must die, so be it—but it would be on his own terms.

Whatever he did, Marielle must be a part of it. He'd longed to possess her for too many years. Acted rashly so he could lay the world at her feet, only to have her flee his presence. When he died, he must take Marielle with him.

He imagined the look on Ashby fitz Waryn's face at losing his beloved. That alone proved worth the risk. He slipped the small dirk from his boot. It was the only weapon left to him.

Silently, he moved to a crouching position as those gathered were speaking with each other. He was over to one side of their circle. If only he could move to that pillar, he could seize Marielle . . .

THE TENSION IN his body slowly leaked away. Ashby was grateful for the cardinal's presence and found himself drawn to the jovial cleric. He was happy knowing this man had been of some comfort to Marielle during her wretched childhood at the convent. Ashby knew he couldn't change her past but he would certainly change her future.

He had decided that land be damned! He would make this woman his own. He'd been blind to the fact that love is the greatest gift of all. They needed only each other to face the world. Be it a single bedchamber Garrett granted them at Stanbury or a little cottage in the countryside or even under the stars themselves, he vowed he would always have her by his side. He had found a woman of courage and honor, one of beauty and intelligence. He refused to be a fool and let Marielle slip through his fingers again.

A sudden blur caught his attention. In that moment, Ashby cursed his carelessness. Marc de la Tresse had recovered and clutched a blade. He lurched at Marielle, grabbing for her with his free hand, but only connected with her arm. Marielle shrieked and pushed him away with such force that Marc crashed into Cardinal Corot. Both men fell to the floor.

Marc swung his hand with the knife around and lay it against the cleric's throat before he scrambled to his knees. Ashby saw the wild look in his eyes as Marc scowled from one person to the next and back again. He feared Marc had toppled over into madness.

"Don't come near me," the disgraced comte warned, "or I will plunge the dagger into his throat."

Corot lay unblinking, flat on his back, his face a mask. Ashby wondered if the cardinal really was that calm, certain he would go to God if death awaited him around the corner, or if fright caused him to go numb.

"Release him, Marc." All eyes turned to Marielle. "It's me you want. Not Father Julien."

Ashby gripped her arm tightly to prevent her from taking another step.

Marielle turned to him, tears swimming in her eyes. "I must go to him," she said softly. "I'll not have that madman place another death at my doorstep. Jean-Paul is burden enough to bear."

Her lips trembled as she tried to smile and failed. In that moment, Ashby saw his future, a bleak one without her, and knew he must act.

"To your feet, you tub of lard," Marc ordered the cardinal. "You may accompany Marielle and me from this place and marry us."

He dragged the cleric to a sitting position, the knife pricking his throat. Corot gave a small cry of astonishment as blood trickled from the wound. Marc yanked him to his feet and winced, pain evident on his face at lifting the heavy clergyman.

Corot's girth almost dwarfed the younger

man. Ashby knew it was now or never. As Marielle took her first steps toward Marc, Ashby saw Marc's gaze was focused on her. With a swiftness he'd never known he possessed, Ashby lunged at Marc, coming from the side that Corot blocked with his huge frame and the eye that was swollen shut, thus limiting Marc's vision.

He thrust a hand out and upward, knocking the blade from Marc's grasp. The movement threw both the cardinal and the comte off-balance and they toppled to the floor. Ashby pitched forward and rolled, landing next to the dirk. He scooped it up and tossed it to Garrett before landing a solid blow to Marc de la Tresse's jaw. A few quick, punishing blows followed and Marc fell back to the floor again. He curled into a tight ball and began weeping as a babe.

"Mercy," he cried out, his sobs the only noise in the still church. "Have mercy." Fat tears rolled down his cheeks.

Ashby felt nothing, much less the pity Marc de la Tresse sought. This man murdered in cold blood, cheated others, and put Marielle and her family through hell. If they weren't in a house of God, Ashby's actions would have gone farther.

Much farther.

This time, he stood directly over Marc, not taking his eyes from the sniveling comte, as he called out, "Cardinal, are you all right?"

In response, Corot came to stand beside him.

He placed a trembling hand on Ashby's shoulder.

"You saved me from death."

Ashby smiled grimly. "It's merely a small cut on your throat, Your Grace. I think you would have survived that."

Corot cleared his throat. "No, my son. If I would have left this church with that lunatic, I doubt I would have seen tomorrow's sunrise."

His gaze connected with the cardinal's and Ashby saw gratitude etched on the cleric's chubby face. "It was my pleasure." He bowed. "Ashby fitz Waryn. At your service, Your Grace."

"And this will be mine." Garrett stepped up and placed a booted foot atop Marc's heaving chest. "I will see to this blubbering coward."

Ashby nodded his thanks to Garrett and faced Corot. He saw the cardinal pull a gold ring encrusted with rubies from his finger. He pushed it into Ashby's hand and closed it into a fist, his hands wrapped around his rescuer's.

"I must reward you, my son. Both you and Lord Montayne have come to my aid. What is it about you Englishmen?"

Those gathered laughed heartily. Marielle moved beside Ashby, needing to be near him. He slid an arm around her waist as he opened his hand. The ring in his palm glistened. He frowned and reached his hand back to Corot.

"I cannot accept this, Your Grace. It's much too valuable."

The man of the cloth cocked a head and studied him briefly. "So is my life, young man. King Jean would be sorely distressed to lose me, his favorite confidant. If you will not accept this token of my appreciation, what can I give you?"

Marielle swallowed. She knew, more than anything, that Ashby wanted land of his own. They would never have a future together without it. He had made that abundantly clear in the past.

"Land," a strong voice called out.

Corot turned to Madeleine. "What did you say, my lady?"

Madeleine flashed a brilliant smile. "Land, Your Grace. Ashby has none of his own. It would help him start a new life with his wife."

The cardinal looked at Ashby. "You are married?"

Marielle watched a beautiful smile break out on her beloved's face. "I will be soon, Your Grace." He looked down at Marielle, love shining in his eyes. Ashby turned back to the cardinal. "That is, if you would be willing to perform the ceremony once Advent has come to an end."

"Ah," said Corot, his eyes disappearing into slits as he beamed at the couple. "Being a cardinal has its advantages. That is easy to arrange. I can issue a special license so you can forego the usual formalities."

Marielle's heart began beating fast. Ashby's arm tightened around her waist.

"As to land? That is a simple matter. Would you and Marielle be happier in England or France?"

Ashby looked down at her. "It's up to you, sweetheart. I can be happy anywhere. As long as I am with you."

Marielle didn't hesitate. "England, Father Julien." She had nothing but poor memories of her homeland. England's beauty beckoned her with a fresh start.

"That settles the matter. I will arrange it with the Earl of Lambert. He manages a property of mine, left to me by my father. I'd hoped to retire there one day back in my Father Julien days." He shrugged. "Being a cardinal now, I will never have a chance to go back. I would see the estate put into your hands. It's the least I can do."

"But King Edward—"

"England's king is a reasonable man," pointed out the cardinal. "I will speak to both my half-brother and the bishop in London. The pope if necessary—but you will gain a home for yourself and your bride. Your king will be no problem, Ashby fitz Waryn. Lay that fear to rest."

"Then you shall have my undying gratitude, Your Grace." Ashby slipped to his knees and took the cleric's hand, sliding the ruby ring back onto it. He kissed the signet ring on the cardinal's other hand and rose again to his feet.

"How long does it take to arrange a special

license, Your Grace?"

"I will call my scribe. You can be married within the hour if you choose."

"But what of Advent?" Marielle asked. "I thought no marriage could occur during it."

Corot chuckled. "I am a cardinal, my child. We write the rules of the Church—and can make certain exceptions when we see fit." He smiled broadly. "I believe this would be one of those occasions."

Ashby turned to Marielle. "So, my love? Will you marry me by day's end?"

She thought about her first wedding, being perfectly coifed and groomed, and then looked down at her filthy gown. She knew she looked a mess but the love in her heart was too strong to delay the ceremony even by an hour.

"I have waited a lifetime for you, Ashby fitz Waryn. I need not wait a minute further."

The warmth in his smile rained sunshine down upon her as his lips touched hers. Marielle gave herself over to the kiss, no longer aware of their surroundings or companions.

"I love you," Ashby murmured against her mouth as he pulled her into his arms for a searing kiss.

Marielle reveled in the flush of love. They would soon make their promises to one another. Those promises would turn their tomorrows into days of bliss and hope.

And love. Most of all, there would be love.

CHAPTER TWENTY-NINE

MARIELLE THANKED THE servant as he poured the last of the hot water into the porcelain basin.

"If you need anything else, let me know."

Cardinal Corot had set his scribe to work and told Marielle and Ashby to make themselves presentable for their wedding. A priest had led Garrett and Ashby off in one direction while a servant had brought her and Madeleine to this small chamber. They were to be reunited once the scribe had completed his work.

She bathed her face and then hands in the water, already feeling refreshed by it. Her gown was worse for the wear after all she had gone through but it wouldn't matter.

She was going to marry the love of her life minutes from now.

"Let me rebraid your hair," Madeleine offered, loosening it and combing her fingers through Marielle's hair since they had no comb. "Too many strands have escaped."

Her friend sectioned off pieces and braided Marielle's locks again.

"There," Madeleine said. "I do believe Ashby will find you to be a most beautiful bride."

"I almost cannot believe my good fortune," she said. "Who would have thought things could work out so well? I will have the best husband in the world. He will have the land he has always desired. And we will live in sunshine. No dark cloud called Marc de la Tresse will ever hover over us again."

Madeleine embraced her. "You are my dearest friend and the sister of my heart, as Ashby is my brother. I have always believed in miracles, Marielle. Most of all, I believe in love. You and Ashby have found each other and love will sustain you."

A knock sounded at the door and Madeleine answered it. She stepped aside and allowed Cardinal Corot to enter.

"Might I have a few minutes alone with the bride?" he asked, his eyes twinkling.

"Certainly, Your Grace," Madeleine said and exited the room, closing the door behind her.

The cardinal came and took Marielle's hands in his. "How are you, old friend?" he asked.

"I am the happiest I have ever been in my

entire life," she confided. "Ashby is such a good man. I love him so very much."

"You were the brightest light at the convent, Marielle," he told her. "I always knew you were destined for great things. True, you suffered much at the hands of the sisters there. I tried my best to get them to see you for the sweet child you were."

Tears brimmed in her eyes. "I looked forward to your visits more than I could ever say, Your Grace."

He chuckled. "I would rather you address me as Father Julien, Marielle. I miss him. That was a much simpler time in my life. I tried to do good everywhere I went and didn't have to worry or be caught up in the politics of the Church."

"You always had a kind word for me, Father. I remember how you would lead me away from the others and I was able to have you all to myself for a few minutes during each of your visits. You let me prattle on about things that must have seemed so unimportant to you."

"You were a child of God, Marielle. Remember how the Christ said to his disciples to let the children come to Him and do not hinder them. Children are the purest of all of God's creatures. You were honest and open and the sweetest of them all. How I hated when I rose in the ranks and could no longer come and visit with you. Sharing conversations with you all those years ago are some of my fondest memories."

He squeezed her hands and finally released them. "And here you are now, ready to be wed to a good man." He chuckled. "Even if he is an Englishman."

Marielle almost burst with joy, thinking of how soon she would become Ashby's wife. "Ashby is the best man I have known, next to you, Father Julien."

"Well, if he is anything like his friend, Lord Montayne, then I know you will be in excellent hands. The earl saved my life."

"And Ashby has saved mine," she said fervently. "I love him with all my heart."

"It is good to know that you have made a love match, my child. I hope you will be blessed with an abundance children." He paused. "Might we sit for a moment?"

"Of course," she said.

They took seats and the cardinal said, "I have a final thing I wish to speak to you about. Arielle."

A quick rush of pain rippled through her at the mention of her long-lost twin.

Father Julien took Marielle's hands again. "You told me about her death once you learned to trust me."

She nodded. "I never spoke to anyone about it but you. The sisters all knew Arielle's death was the reason I had been sent to them. That I had caused it."

"But you weren't to blame," he said softly.

"I was, Father. I dared Arielle to climb that tree. She was always terrified of heights but she did so to please me." Her voice broke. "If only she had waited for me to return. I brought my brother. He could have helped her down. She didn't need to die."

"Oh, Marielle. Haven't you realized after all this time that your twin's death was an accident? You didn't cause it. You didn't force her or deliberately push her. These things happen."

"But she did it for me. She always tried to please me. I was so selfish."

"You were a small child. Yet you have carried this heavy burden of guilt around all your life." He looked into her eyes with compassion. "You haven't asked for it but I will give it to you all the same."

"What?"

"Absolution. I want you to be free of the guilt. I have the power to exonerate you from it and I freely exercise it now, Marielle. I want you to be able to go and live your life with your husband with no worries. It was Arielle's time to go home to Heaven. God called her there because He was ready for her to be with Him. He forgives you. I forgive you.

"And you must forgive yourself."

Wrenching sobs erupted from her. Marielle

buried her face in Father Julien's chest. The cardinal spoke softly to her, soothing her, rubbing her back up and down until she calmed.

Looking up at him, she said, "It's just that I have been given all these years that were taken from her."

"Arielle has watched over you this entire time, my child. She watches over you now, Marielle. Go to your husband and live your life to the fullest, knowing you have Arielle's approval and her forgiveness. Can you do so?"

Marielle had always felt responsible for her twin's death. During the lonely years at the convent, she had grown to believe that everything bad that happened to her was her punishment for her role in her sister's death. She continued to feel this after her marriage to Jean-Paul, believing she didn't deserve any happiness because she had been responsible for Arielle's life being cut short.

Forgiveness now was being offered to her. Though she had never officially confessed to this sin, Father Julien had absolved her.

Suddenly, a lightness filled her. It was as if the spirit of Arielle filled her, showering her with grace and mercy.

"I feel as if she is inside me, Father," Marielle said through tears.

"She is. She has always been a part of you," the priest assured her. "She will be with you until the end and greet you at Heaven's gates."

"Thank you," she said, hugging him tightly. "For releasing me from my shame. I have blamed myself every day for Arielle's loss and have regretted my actions." She smiled. "You are helping me to make a fresh start, Father Julien."

"I am happy to have done so, Marielle. Shall we go now and send you off into a new life?"

They rose and retreated to the chapel. Madeleine and Garrett stood together and would serve as their witnesses.

Ashby awaited her, pacing nervously, and when he caught sight of Marielle, a brilliant smile appeared on his handsome face. It took extreme willpower not to break away from Father Julien and run to him.

They reached Ashby and Garrett and Madeleine stepped toward them, standing on either side of them. Father Julien consulted with his scribe and then nodded.

"All is in order," he shared. "Are you ready to begin the journey of your new lives together?"

Ashby entwined his fingers with hers. "We are," he answered for the both of them.

As they faced one another and spoke their vows, Marielle felt the presence of Arielle within her and knew her twin gave her blessing to this union. A peace descended upon her. She promised herself to live life to the fullest and show Ashby every day how very much she loved him.

EPILOGUE

Newbury Manor, Sussex—3 months later

ASHBY AWOKE, SAVORING the feel of his wife in his arms. As he did every morning, he offered up a swift prayer of gratitude to the Virgin Mary, thanking Her for bring Marielle into his life.

Cardinal Corot had actually accompanied them back to London in order to smooth the way for gifting his estate to Ashby and Marielle. While Lord and Lady Montayne and their children had returned to Stanbury, the cleric had taken the newlyweds to the English court, where he was received by the king and queen. Edward graciously allowed the cardinal to gift his large tract of land to Ashby and the official documents were drawn up giving him complete ownership of the manor house and surrounding acreage.

After a short visit to see the Earl of Lambert, the cardinal's half-brother, the trio went on to Newbury, where Ashby and Marielle were introduced to their tenants and household staff. He could never thank Father Julien enough for the magnanimous gesture. It gave him and Marielle a home and the income from their tenants would be ample to live on and was only fifteen miles to the southwest of Stanbury.

Ashby hadn't bothered to write his older brothers of the changes in his circumstances. They'd lost touch many years earlier. He did, however, want to send word to Faylinn, his younger sister. They had always stayed in touch, with Ashby sending short messages to her several times a year. Faylinn, on the other hand, wrote pages to him every month. He'd almost finish composing his missive to her and would finish it this morning and send it to her at Mallowbourne in Somerset. She would be surprised to receive such a lengthy letter from him, detailing his good fortune. In it, he'd asked her to come and visit them at Newbury, so he could introduce Faylinn to Marielle. He hoped his sister would make the journey someday. She'd never had children and sounded lonely in her letters to him.

Marielle stirred and he kissed her awake, making love to her. He didn't know if he could ever get enough of this woman—but it wouldn't be from lack of trying.

Afterward, they lay together, their limbs entwined, Marielle stroking his arm lightly.

"I have something to tell you," she said softly.

He kissed her hair. "That you love me madly?" he teased.

"You know I do. But I also love another."

Her words slammed into him, bringing fear. He couldn't lose her. He wouldn't. "Who is it?" he demanded angrily. "I'll have his name."

She chuckled. "I don't know it."

Now he was thoroughly confused.

"You don't know it either," she continued, a smile playing about her lips. "We haven't talked about names before."

It dawned on him what she meant.

"You're with child?" he asked eagerly.

Marielle nodded and he showered her face with kisses, moving down to her bare belly and kissing it soundly.

Looking up at her, he said, "I understand what you mean. I've never met this babe—and yet I already love it fiercely."

"Do you have any names you're partial to?" she asked.

"Not really," he said and considered it a moment, an idea coming to him. "If you carry a boy, we can decide on his name when we see him. But if it's a girl, I think we should name her Arielle."

Marielle burst into tears, burying her face against his chest. He drew her close, angry at himself that he'd upset her. Through her sobs, though, she began nodding.

Finally, she lifted her tearstained face to him. "Yes. It's perfect."

Ashby kissed away her tears. As he did, he said, "Our child is a promise of what our tomorrows will bring. Days lived together. In love."

With that, he pressed a fervent kiss against her belly again, eager for their child to come into the world.

About the Author

Award-winning and international bestselling author Alexa Aston's historical romances use history as a backdrop to place her characters in extraordinary circumstances, where their intense desire for one another grows into the treasured gift of love.

She is the author of Medieval and Regency romance, including *The Knights of Honor*, *The King's Cousins*, *The St Clairs*, and *The de Wolfes of Esterley Castle*.

A native Texan, Alexa lives with her husband in a Dallas suburb, where she eats her fair share of dark chocolate and plots out stories while she walks every morning. She enjoys reading, Netflix binge-watching, and can't get enough of *Survivor*, *The Crown*, or *Game of Thrones*.